The Middle T

Joseph Smith Fletcher

Chapter 1 THE SCRAP OF GREY PAPER

As a rule, Spargo left the *Watchman* office at two o'clock. The paper had then gone to press. There was nothing for him, recently promoted to a sub-editorship, to do after he had passed the column for which he was responsible; as a matter of fact he could have gone home before the machines began their clatter. But he generally hung about, trifling, until two o'clock came. On this occasion, the morning of the 22nd of June, 1912, he stopped longer than usual, chatting with Hacket, who had charge of the foreign news, and who began telling him about a telegram which had just come through from Durazzo. What Hacket had to tell was interesting: Spargo lingered to hear all about it, and to discuss it. Altogether it was well beyond half-past two when he went out of the office, unconsciously puffing away from him as he reached the threshold the last breath of the atmosphere in which he had spent his midnight. In Fleet Street the air was fresh, almost to sweetness, and the first grey of the coming dawn was breaking faintly around the high silence of St. Paul's.

Spargo lived in Bloomsbury, on the west side of Russell Square. Every night and every morning he walked to and from the *Watchman* office by the same route—Southampton Row, Kingsway, the Strand, Fleet Street. He came to know several faces, especially amongst the police; he formed the habit of exchanging greetings with various officers whom he encountered at regular points as he went slowly homewards, smoking his pipe. And on this morning, as he drew near to Middle Temple Lane, he saw a policeman whom he knew, one Driscoll, standing at the entrance, looking about him. Further away another policeman appeared, sauntering. Driscoll raised an arm and signalled; then, turning, he saw Spargo. He moved a step or two towards him. Spargo saw news in his face.

"What is it?" asked Spargo.

Driscoll jerked a thumb over his shoulder, towards the partly open door of the lane. Within, Spargo saw a man hastily donning a waistcoat and jacket.

"He says," answered Driscoll, "him, there—the porter—that there's a man lying in one of them entries down the lane, and he thinks he's dead. Likewise, he thinks he's murdered."

Spargo echoed the word.

"But what makes him think that?" he asked, peeping with curiosity beyond Driscoll's burly form. "Why?"

"He says there's blood about him," answered Driscoll. He turned and glanced at the oncoming constable, and then turned again to Spargo. "You're a newspaper man, sir?" he suggested.

"I am," replied Spargo.

"You'd better walk down with us," said Driscoll, with a grin. "There'll be something to write pieces in the paper about. At least, there may be." Spargo made no answer. He continued to look down the lane, wondering what secret it held, until the other policeman came up. At the same moment the porter, now fully clothed, came out.

"Come on!" he said shortly. "I'll show you."

Driscoll murmured a word or two to the newly-arrived constable, and then turned to the porter.

"How came you to find him, then?" he asked

The porter jerked his head at the door which they were leaving.

"I heard that door slam," he replied, irritably, as if the fact which he mentioned caused him offence. "I know I did! So I got up to look around. Then—well, I saw that!"

He raised a hand, pointing down the lane. The three men followed his outstretched finger. And Spargo then saw a man's foot, booted, grey-socked, protruding from an entry on the left hand.

"Sticking out there, just as you see it now," said the porter. "I ain't touched it. And so—"

He paused and made a grimace as if at the memory of some unpleasant thing. Driscoll nodded comprehendingly.

"And so you went along and looked?" he suggested. "Just so—just to see who it belonged to, as it might be."

"Just to see—what there was to see," agreed the porter. "Then I saw there was blood. And then—well, I made up the lane to tell one of you chaps."

"Best thing you could have done," said Driscoll. "Well, now then—"

The little procession came to a halt at the entry. The entry was a cold and formal thing of itself; not a nice place to lie dead in, having glazed white tiles for its walls and concrete for its flooring; something about its appearance in that grey morning air suggested to Spargo the idea of a mortuary. And that the man whose foot projected over the step was dead he had no doubt: the limpness of his pose certified to it.

For a moment none of the four men moved or spoke. The two policemen unconsciously stuck their thumbs in their belts and made play with their fingers; the porter rubbed his chin thoughtfully—Spargo remembered afterwards the rasping sound of this action; he himself put his hands in his pockets and began to jingle his money and his keys. Each man had his own thoughts as he contemplated the piece of human wreckage which lay before him.

"You'll notice," suddenly observed Driscoll, speaking in a hushed voice, "You'll notice that he's lying there in a queer way— same as if—as if he'd been put there. Sort of propped up against that wall, at first, and had slid down, like."

Spargo was taking in all the details with a professional eye. He saw at his feet the body of an elderly man; the face was turned away from him, crushed in against the glaze of the wall, but he judged the man to be elderly because of grey hair and whitening whisker; it was clothed in a good, well-made suit of grey check cloth—tweed—and the boots were good: so, too, was the linen cuff which projected from the sleeve that hung so limply. One leg was half doubled under the body; the other was stretched straight out across the threshold; the trunk was twisted to the wall. Over the white glaze of the tiles against which it and the shoulder towards which it had sunk were crushed there were gouts and stains of blood. And Driscoll, taking a hand out of his belt, pointed a finger at them.

"Seems to me," he said, slowly, "seems to me as how he's been struck down from behind as he came out of here. That blood's from his nose—gushed out as he fell. What do you say, Jim?" The other policeman coughed.

"Better get the inspector here," he said. "And the doctor and the ambulance. Dead—ain't he?"

Driscoll bent down and put a thumb on the hand which lay on the pavement.

"As ever they make 'em," he remarked laconically. "And stiff, too. Well, hurry up, Jim!"

Spargo waited until the inspector arrived; waited until the hand-ambulance came. More policemen came with it; they moved the body for transference to the mortuary, and Spargo then saw the dead man's face. He looked long and steadily at it while the police arranged the limbs, wondering all the time who it was that he gazed at, how he came to that end, what was the object of his murderer, and many other things. There was some professionalism in Spargo's curiosity, but there was also a natural dislike that a fellow-being should have been so unceremoniously smitten out of the world.

There was nothing very remarkable about the dead man's face. It was that of a man of apparently sixty to sixty-five years of age; plain, even homely of feature, clean-shaven, except for a fringe of white whisker, trimmed, after an old-fashioned pattern, between the ear and the point of the jaw. The only remarkable thing about it was that it was much lined and seamed; the wrinkles were many and deep around the corners of the lips and the angles of the eyes; this man, you would have said to yourself, has led a hard life and weathered storm, mental as well as physical.

Driscoll nudged Spargo with a turn of his elbow. He gave him a wink. "Better come down to the dead-house," he muttered confidentially.

"Why?" asked Spargo.

"They'll go through him," whispered Driscoll. "Search him, d'ye see? Then you'll get to know all about him, and so on. Help to write that piece in the paper, eh?"

Spargo hesitated. He had had a stiff night's work, and until his encounter with Driscoll he had cherished warm anticipation of the meal which would be laid out for him at his rooms, and of the bed into which he would subsequently tumble. Besides, a telephone message would send a man from the *Watchman* to the mortuary. This sort of thing was not in his line now, now —

"You'll be for getting one o' them big play-cards out with something about a mystery on it," suggested Driscoll. "You never know what lies at the bottom o' these affairs, no more you don't."

That last observation decided Spargo; moreover, the old instinct for getting news began to assert itself.

"All right," he said. "I'll go along with you."

And re-lighting his pipe he followed the little cortège through the streets, still deserted and quiet, and as he walked behind he reflected on the unobtrusive fashion in which murder could stalk about. Here was the work of murder, no doubt, and it was being quietly carried along a principal London thoroughfare, without fuss or noise, by officials to whom the dealing with it was all a matter of routine. Surely —

"My opinion," said a voice at Spargo's elbow, "my opinion is that it was done elsewhere. Not there! He was put there. That's what I say." Spargo turned and saw that the porter was at his side. He, too, was accompanying the body.

"Oh!" said Spargo. "You think —"

"I think he was struck down elsewhere and carried there," said the porter. "In somebody's chambers, maybe. I've known of some queer games in our bit of London! Well! — he never came in at my lodge last night — I'll stand to that. And who is he, I should like to know? From what I see of him, not the sort to be about our place."

"That's what we shall hear presently," said Spargo. "They're going to search him."

But Spargo was presently made aware that the searchers had found nothing. The police-surgeon said that the dead man had, without doubt, been struck down from behind by a terrible blow which had fractured the skull and caused death almost instantaneously. In Driscoll's opinion, the murder had been committed for the sake of plunder. For there was nothing whatever on the body. It was reasonable to suppose that a man who is well dressed would possess a watch and chain, and have money in his pockets, and possibly rings on his fingers. But there was nothing valuable to be found; in fact there was nothing at all to be found that could lead to identification — no letters, no papers, nothing. It was plain that whoever had struck the dead man down had subsequently stripped him of whatever was on him. The only clue to possible identity lay in the fact that a soft cap of grey cloth appeared to have been newly purchased at a fashionable shop in the West End.

Spargo went home; there seemed to be nothing to stop for. He ate his food and he went to bed, only to do poor things in the way of sleeping. He was not the sort to be impressed by horrors, but he recognized at last that the morning's event had destroyed his chance of rest; he accordingly rose, took a cold bath, drank a cup of coffee, and went out. He was not sure of any particular idea when he strolled away from Bloomsbury, but it did not surprise him when, half an hour later he found that he had walked down to the police station near which the unknown man's body lay in the mortuary. And there he met Driscoll, just going off duty. Driscoll grinned at sight of him.

"You're in luck," he said. "'Tisn't five minutes since they found a bit of grey writing paper crumpled up in the poor man's waistcoat pocket—it had slipped into a crack. Come in, and you'll see it."

Spargo went into the inspector's office. In another minute he found himself staring at the scrap of paper. There was nothing on it but an address, scrawled in pencil:—Ronald Breton, Barrister, King's Bench Walk, Temple, London.

Spargo looked up at the inspector with a quick jerk of his head. "I know this man," he said.

The inspector showed new interest.

"What, Mr. Breton?" he asked.

"Yes. I'm on the *Watchman*, you know, sub-editor. I took an article from him the other day — article on 'Ideal Sites for Campers-Out.' He came to the office about it. So this was in the dead man's pocket?"

"Found in a hole in his pocket, I understand: I wasn't present myself. It's not much, but it may afford some clue to identity."

Spargo picked up the scrap of grey paper and looked closely at it. It seemed to him to be the sort of paper that is found in hotels and in clubs; it had been torn roughly from the sheet.

"What," he asked meditatively, "what will you do about getting this man identified?"

The inspector shrugged his shoulders.

"Oh, usual thing, I suppose. There'll be publicity, you know. I suppose you'll be doing a special account yourself, for your paper, eh? Then there'll be the others. And we shall put out the usual notice. Somebody will come forward to identify — sure to. And — "

A man came into the office — a stolid-faced, quiet-mannered, soberly attired person, who might have been a respectable tradesman out for a stroll, and who gave the inspector a sidelong nod as he approached his desk, at the same time extending his hand towards the scrap of paper which Spargo had just laid down.

"I'll go along to King's Bench Walk and see Mr. Breton," he observed, looking at his watch. "It's just about ten — I daresay he'll be there now."

"I'm going there, too," remarked Spargo, but as if speaking to himself. "Yes, I'll go there."

The newcomer glanced at Spargo, and then at the inspector. The inspector nodded at Spargo.

"Journalist," he said, "Mr. Spargo of the *Watchman*. Mr. Spargo was there when the body was found. And he knows Mr. Breton." Then he nodded from Spargo to the stolid-faced person. "This is Detective-Sergeant Rathbury, from the Yard," he said to Spargo. "He's come to take charge of this case."

"Oh?" said Spargo blankly. "I see — what," he went on, with sudden abruptness, "what shall you do about Breton?"

"Get him to come and look at the body," replied Rathbury. "He may know the man and he mayn't. Anyway, his name and address are here, aren't they?"

"Come along," said Spargo. "I'll walk there with you."

Spargo remained in a species of brown study all the way along Tudor Street; his companion also maintained silence in a fashion which showed that he was by nature and custom a man of few words. It was not until the two were climbing the old balustrated staircase of the house in King's Bench Walk in which Ronald Breton's chambers were somewhere situate that Spargo spoke.

"Do you think that old chap was killed for what he may have had on him?" he asked, suddenly turning on the detective.

"I should like to know what he had on him before I answered that question, Mr. Spargo," replied Rathbury, with a smile.

"Yes," said Spargo, dreamily. "I suppose so. He might have had — nothing on him, eh?"

The detective laughed, and pointed to a board on which names were printed.

"We don't know anything yet, sir," he observed, "except that Mr. Breton is on the fourth floor. By which I conclude that it isn't long since he was eating his dinner."

"Oh, he's young — he's quite young," said Spargo. "I should say he's about four-and-twenty. I've met him only — "

At that moment the unmistakable sounds of girlish laughter came down the staircase. Two girls seemed to be laughing — presently masculine laughter mingled with the lighter feminine.

"Seems to be studying law in very pleasant fashion up here, anyway," said Rathbury. "Mr. Breton's chambers, too. And the door's open."

The outer oak door of Ronald Breton's chambers stood thrown wide; the inner one was well ajar; through the opening thus made Spargo and the detective obtained a full view of the interior of Mr. Ronald Breton's rooms. There, against a background of law books, bundles of papers tied up with pink tape, and black-framed pictures of famous legal notabilities, they saw a pretty, vivacious-eyed girl, who, perched on a chair, wigged and gowned, and flourishing a mass of crisp paper, was haranguing an imaginary judge and jury, to the amusement of a young man who had his back to the door, and of another girl who leant confidentially against his shoulder.

"I put it to you, gentlemen of the jury—I put it to you with confidence, feeling that you must be, must necessarily be, some, perhaps brothers, perhaps husbands, and fathers, can you, on your consciences do my client the great wrong, the irreparable injury, the—the—"

"Think of some more adjectives!" exclaimed the young man. "Hot and strong 'uns—pile 'em up. That's what they like—they—Hullo!"

This exclamation arose from the fact that at this point of the proceedings the detective rapped at the inner door, and then put his head round its edge. Whereupon the young lady who was orating from the chair, jumped hastily down; the other young lady withdrew from the young man's protecting arm; there was a feminine giggle and a feminine swishing of skirts, and a hasty bolt into an inner room, and Mr. Ronald Breton came forward, blushing a little, to greet the interrupter.

"Come in, come in!" he exclaimed hastily. "I—"

Then he paused, catching sight of Spargo, and held out his hand with a look of surprise.

"Oh—Mr. Spargo?" he said. "How do you do?—we—I—we were just having a lark—I'm off to court in a few minutes. What can I do for you, Mr. Spargo?"

He had backed to the inner door as he spoke, and he now closed it and turned again to the two men, looking from one to the other. The detective, on his part, was looking at the young barrister. He saw a tall, slimly-built youth, of handsome features and engaging presence, perfectly groomed, and immaculately garbed, and having upon him a general air of well-to-do-ness, and he formed the impression from these matters that Mr. Breton was one of those fortunate young men who may take up a profession but are certainly not dependent upon it. He turned and glanced at the journalist.

"How do you do?" said Spargo slowly. "I—the fact is, I came here with Mr. Rathbury. He—wants to see you. Detective-Sergeant Rathbury—of New Scotland Yard."

Spargo pronounced this formal introduction as if he were repeating a lesson. But he was watching the young barrister's face. And Breton turned to the detective with a look of surprise.

"Oh!" he said. "You wish—"

Rathbury had been fumbling in his pocket for the scrap of grey paper, which he had carefully bestowed in a much-worn memorandum-book. "I wished to ask a question, Mr. Breton," he said. "This morning, about a quarter to three, a man—elderly man—was found dead in Middle Temple Lane, and there seems little doubt that he was murdered. Mr. Spargo here—he was present when the body was found."

"Soon after," corrected Spargo. "A few minutes after."

"When this body was examined at the mortuary," continued Rathbury, in his matter-of-fact, business-like tones, "nothing was found that could lead to identification. The man appears to have been robbed. There was nothing whatever on him—but this bit of torn paper, which was found in a hole in the lining of his waistcoat pocket. It's got your name and address on it, Mr. Breton. See?"

Ronald Breton took the scrap of paper and looked at it with knitted brows.

"By Jove!" he muttered. "So it has; that's queer. What's he like, this man?"

Rathbury glanced at a clock which stood on the mantelpiece.

"Will you step round and take a look at him, Mr. Breton?" he said. "It's close by."

"Well—I—the fact is, I've got a case on, in Mr. Justice Borrow's court," Breton answered, also glancing at his clock. "But it won't be called until after eleven. Will—"

"Plenty of time, sir," said Rathbury; "it won't take you ten minutes to go round and back again—a look will do. You don't recognize this handwriting, I suppose?"

Breton still held the scrap of paper in his fingers. He looked at it again, intently.

"No!" he answered. "I don't. I don't know it at all—I can't think, of course, who this man could be, to have my name and address. I thought he might have been some country solicitor, wanting my professional services, you know," he went on, with a shy smile at Spargo; "but, three—three o'clock in the morning, eh?"

"The doctor," observed Rathbury, "the doctor thinks he had been dead about two and a half hours."

Breton turned to the inner door.

"I'll—I'll just tell these ladies I'm going out for a quarter of an hour," he said. "They're going over to the court with me—I got my first brief yesterday," he went on with a boyish laugh, glancing right and left at his visitors. "It's nothing much—small case—but I promised my fiancée and her sister that they should be present, you know. A moment."

He disappeared into the next room and came back a moment later in all the glory of a new silk hat. Spargo, a young man who was never very particular about his dress, began to contrast his own attire with the butterfly appearance of this youngster; he had been quick to notice that the two girls who had whisked into the inner room had been similarly garbed in fine raiment, more characteristic of Mayfair than of Fleet Street. Already he felt a strange curiosity about Breton, and about the young ladies whom he heard talking behind the inner door.

"Well, come on," said Breton. "Let's go straight there."

The mortuary to which Rathbury led the way was cold, drab, repellent to the general gay sense of the summer morning. Spargo shivered involuntarily as he entered it and took a first glance around. But the young barrister showed no sign of feeling or concern; he looked quickly about him and stepped alertly to the side of the dead man, from whose face the detective was turning back a cloth. He looked steadily and earnestly at the fixed features. Then he drew back, shaking his head.

"No!" he said with decision. "Don't know him — don't know him from Adam. Never set eyes on him in my life, that I know of."

Rathbury replaced the cloth.

"I didn't suppose you would," he remarked. "Well, I expect we must go on the usual lines. Somebody'll identify him."

"You say he was murdered?" said Breton. "Is that — certain?"

Rathbury jerked his thumb at the corpse.

"The back of his skull is smashed in," he said laconically. "The doctor says he must have been struck down from behind — and a fearful blow, too. I'm much obliged to you, Mr. Breton."

"Oh, all right!" said Breton. "Well, you know where to find me if you want me. I shall be curious about this. Good-bye — good-bye, Mr. Spargo."

The young barrister hurried away, and Rathbury turned to the journalist.

"I didn't expect anything from that," he remarked. "However, it was a thing to be done. You are going to write about this for your paper?"

Spargo nodded.

"Well," continued Rathbury, "I've sent a man to Fiskie's, the hatter's, where that cap came from, you know. We may get a bit of information from that quarter — it's possible. If you like to meet me here at twelve o'clock I'll tell you anything I've heard. Just now I'm going to get some breakfast."

"I'll meet you here," said Spargo, "at twelve o'clock."

He watched Rathbury go away round one corner; he himself suddenly set off round another. He went to the *Watchman* office, wrote a few lines, which he enclosed in an envelope for the day-editor, and went out again. Somehow or other, his feet led him up Fleet Street, and before he quite realized what he was doing he found himself turning into the Law Courts.

Chapter 3 THE CLUE OF THE CAP

Having no clear conception of what had led him to these scenes of litigation, Spargo went wandering aimlessly about in the great hall and the adjacent corridors until an official, who took him to be lost, asked him if there was any particular part of the building he wanted. For a moment Spargo stared at the man as if he did not comprehend his question. Then his mental powers reasserted themselves.

"Isn't Mr. Justice Borrow sitting in one of the courts this morning?" he suddenly asked.

"Number seven," replied the official. "What's your case — when's it down?"

"I haven't got a case," said Spargo. "I'm a pressman — reporter, you know."

The official stuck out a finger.

"Round the corner — first to your right — second on the left," he said automatically. "You'll find plenty of room — nothing much doing there this morning."

He turned away, and Spargo recommenced his apparently aimless perambulation of the dreary, depressing corridors.

"Upon my honour!" he muttered. "Upon my honour, I really don't know what I've come up here for. I've no business here."

Just then he turned a corner and came face to face with Ronald Breton. The young barrister was now in his wig and gown and carried a bundle of papers tied up with pink tape; he was escorting two young ladies, who were laughing and chattering as they tripped along at his side. And Spargo, glancing at them meditatively, instinctively told himself which of them it was that he and Rathbury had overheard as she made her burlesque speech: it was not the elder one, who walked by Ronald Breton with something of an air of proprietorship, but the younger, the girl with the laughing eyes and the vivacious smile, and it suddenly dawned upon him that somewhere, deep within him, there had been a notion, a hope of seeing this girl again — why, he could not then think.

Spargo, thus coming face to face with these three, mechanically lifted his hat. Breton stopped, half inquisitive. His eyes seemed to ask a question.

"Yes," said Spargo. "I—the fact is, I remembered that you said you were coming up here, and I came after you. I want—when you've time—to have a talk, to ask you a few questions. About—this affair of the dead man, you know."

Breton nodded. He tapped Spargo on the arm.

"Look here," he said. "When this case of mine is over, I can give you as much time as you like. Can you wait a bit? Yes? Well, I say, do me a favour. I was taking these ladies round to the gallery — round there, and up the stairs—and I'm a bit pressed for time—I've a solicitor waiting for me. You take them—there's a good fellow; then, when the case is over, bring them down here, and you and I will talk. Here—I'll introduce you all—no ceremony. Miss Aylmore—Miss Jessie Aylmore. Mr. Spargo—of the *Watchman*. Now, I'm off!" Breton turned on the instant; his gown whisked round a corner, and Spargo found himself staring at two smiling girls. He saw then that both were pretty and attractive, and that one seemed to be the elder by some three or four years.

"That is very cool of Ronald," observed the elder young lady. "Perhaps his scheme doesn't fit in with yours, Mr. Spargo? Pray don't—"

"Oh, it's all right!" said Spargo, feeling himself uncommonly stupid. "I've nothing to do. But—where did Mr. Breton say you wished to be taken?"

"Into the gallery of number seven court," said the younger girl promptly. "Round this corner—I think I know the way."

Spargo, still marvelling at the rapidity with which affairs were moving that morning, bestirred himself to act as cicerone, and presently led the two young ladies to the very front of one of those public galleries from which idlers and specially-interested spectators may see and hear the proceedings which obtain in the badly-ventilated, ill-lighted tanks wherein justice is dispensed at the Law Courts. There was no one else in that gallery; the attendant in the corridor outside seemed to be vastly amazed that any one should wish to enter it, and he presently opened the door, beckoned to Spargo, and came half-way down the stairs to meet him.

"Nothing much going on here this morning," he whispered behind a raised hand. "But there's a nice breach case in number five—get you three good seats there if you like."

Spargo declined this tempting offer, and went back to his charges. He had decided by that time that Miss Aylmore was about twenty-three, and her sister about eighteen; he also thought that young Breton was a lucky dog to be in possession of such a charming future wife and an equally charming sister-in-law. And he dropped into a seat at Miss Jessie Aylmore's side, and looked around him as if he were much awed by his surroundings.

"I suppose one can talk until the judge enters?" he whispered. "Is this really Mr. Breton's first case?"

"His very first—all on his own responsibility, any way," replied Spargo's companion, smiling. "And he's very nervous—and so's my sister. Aren't you, now, Evelyn?"

Evelyn Aylmore looked at Spargo, and smiled quietly.

"I suppose one's always nervous about first appearances," she said. "However, I think Ronald's got plenty of confidence, and, as he says, it's not much of a case: it isn't even a jury case. I'm afraid you'll find it dull, Mr. Spargo—it's only something about a promissory note."

"Oh, I'm all right, thank you," replied Spargo, unconsciously falling back on a favourite formula. "I always like to hear lawyers—they manage to say such a lot about—about—"

"About nothing," said Jessie Aylmore. "But there—so do gentlemen who write for the papers, don't they?"

Spargo was about to admit that there was a good deal to be said on that point when Miss Aylmore suddenly drew her sister's attention to a man who had just entered the well of the court.

"Look, Jessie!" she observed. "There's Mr. Elphick!"

Spargo looked down at the person indicated: an elderly, large-faced, smooth-shaven man, a little inclined to stoutness, who, wigged and gowned, was slowly making his way to a corner seat just outside that charmed inner sanctum wherein only King's Counsel are permitted to sit. He dropped into this in a fashion which showed that he was one of those men who loved personal comfort; he bestowed his plump person at the most convenient angle and fitting a monocle in his right eye, glanced around him. There were a few of his professional brethren in his vicinity; there were half a dozen solicitors and their clerks in conversation with one or other of them; there were court officials. But the gentleman of the monocle swept all these with an indifferent look and cast his eyes upward until he caught sight of the two girls. Thereupon he made a most gracious bow in their direction; his broad face beamed in a genial smile, and he waved a white hand.

"Do you know Mr. Elphick, Mr. Spargo?" enquired the younger Miss Aylmore.

"I rather think I've seen him, somewhere about the Temple," answered Spargo. "In fact, I'm sure I have."

"His chambers are in Paper Buildings," said Jessie. "Sometimes he gives tea-parties in them. He is Ronald's guardian, and preceptor, and mentor, and all that, and I suppose he's dropped into this court to hear how his pupil goes on."

"Here is Ronald," whispered Miss Aylmore.

"And here," said her sister, "is his lordship, looking very cross. Now, Mr. Spargo, you're in for it."

Spargo, to tell the truth, paid little attention to what went on beneath him. The case which young Breton presently opened was a commercial one, involving certain rights and properties in a promissory note; it seemed to the journalist that Breton dealt with it very well, showing himself master of the financial details, and speaking with readiness and assurance. He was much more interested in his companions, and especially in the younger one, and he was meditating on how he could improve his further acquaintance when he awoke to the fact that the defence, realizing that it stood no chance, had agreed to withdraw, and that Mr. Justice Borrow was already giving judgment in Ronald Breton's favour.

In another minute he was walking out of the gallery in rear of the two sisters.

"Very good—very good, indeed," he said, absent-mindedly. "I thought he put his facts very clearly and concisely."

Downstairs, in the corridor, Ronald Breton was talking to Mr. Elphick. He pointed a finger at Spargo as the latter came up with the girls: Spargo gathered that Breton was speaking of the murder and of his, Spargo's, connection with it. And directly they approached, he spoke.

"This is Mr. Spargo, sub-editor of the *Watchman*." Breton said. "Mr. Elphick—Mr. Spargo. I was just telling Mr. Elphick, Spargo, that you saw this poor man soon after he was found."

Spargo, glancing at Mr. Elphick, saw that he was deeply interested. The elderly barrister took him—literally—by the button-hole.

"My dear sir!" he said. "You—saw this poor fellow? Lying dead—in the third entry down Middle Temple Lane! The third entry, eh?"

"Yes," replied Spargo, simply. "I saw him. It was the third entry."

"Singular!" said Mr. Elphick, musingly. "I know a man who lives in that house. In fact, I visited him last night, and did not leave until nearly midnight. And this unfortunate man had Mr. Ronald Breton's name and address in his pocket?"

Spargo nodded. He looked at Breton, and pulled out his watch. Just then he had no idea of playing the part of informant to Mr. Elphick.

"Yes, that's so," he answered shortly. Then, looking at Breton significantly, he added, "If you can give me those few minutes, now—?"

"Yes—yes!" responded Ronald Breton, nodding. "I understand. Evelyn—I'll leave you and Jessie to Mr. Elphick; I must go."

Mr. Elphick seized Spargo once more.

"My dear sir!" he said, eagerly. "Do you—do you think I could possibly see—the body?"

"It's at the mortuary," answered Spargo. "I don't know what their regulations are."

Then he escaped with Breton. They had crossed Fleet Street and were in the quieter shades of the Temple before Spargo spoke.

"About what I wanted to say to you," he said at last. "It was—this. I—well, I've always wanted, as a journalist, to have a real big murder case. I think this is one. I want to go right into it—thoroughly, first and last. And—I think you can help me."

"How do you know that it is a murder case?" asked Breton quietly.

"It's a murder case," answered Spargo, stolidly. "I feel it. Instinct, perhaps. I'm going to ferret out the truth. And it seems to me—"

He paused and gave his companion a sharp glance.

"It seems to me," he presently continued, "that the clue lies in that scrap of paper. That paper and that man are connecting links between you and—somebody else."

"Possibly," agreed Breton. "You want to find the somebody else?"

"I want you to help me to find the somebody else," answered Spargo. "I believe this is a big, very big affair: I want to do it. I don't believe in police methods—much. By the by, I'm just going to meet Rathbury. He may have heard of something. Would you like to come?"

Breton ran into his chambers in King's Bench Walk, left his gown and wig, and walked round with Spargo to the police office. Rathbury came out as they were stepping in.

"Oh!" he said. "Ah!—I've got what may be helpful, Mr. Spargo. I told you I'd sent a man to Fiskie's, the hatter! Well, he's just returned. The cap which the dead man was wearing was bought at Fiskie's yesterday afternoon, and it was sent to Mr. Marbury, Room 20, at the Anglo-Orient Hotel."

"Where is that?" asked Spargo.

"Waterloo district," answered Rathbury. "A small house, I believe. Well, I'm going there. Are you coming?"

"Yes," replied Spargo. "Of course. And Mr. Breton wants to come, too."

"If I'm not in the way," said Breton.

Rathbury laughed.

"Well, we may find out something about this scrap of paper," he observed. And he waved a signal to the nearest taxi-cab driver.

The house at which Spargo and his companions presently drew up was an old-fashioned place in the immediate vicinity of Waterloo Railway Station — a plain-fronted, four-square erection, essentially mid-Victorian in appearance, and suggestive, somehow, of the very early days of railway travelling. Anything more in contrast with the modern ideas of a hotel it would have been difficult to find in London, and Ronald Breton said so as he and the others crossed the pavement.

"And yet a good many people used to favour this place on their way to and from Southampton in the old days," remarked Rathbury. "And I daresay that old travellers, coming back from the East after a good many years' absence, still rush in here. You see, it's close to the station, and travellers have a knack of walking into the nearest place when they've a few thousand miles of steamboat and railway train behind them. Look there, now!" They had crossed the threshold as the detective spoke, and as they entered a square, heavily-furnished hall, he made a sidelong motion of his head towards a bar on the left, wherein stood or lounged a number of men who from their general appearance, their slouched hats, and their bronzed faces appeared to be Colonials, or at any rate to have spent a good part of their time beneath Oriental skies. There was a murmur of tongues that had a Colonial accent in it; an aroma of tobacco that suggested Sumatra and Trichinopoly, and Rathbury wagged his head sagely. "Lay you anything the dead man was a Colonial, Mr. Spargo," he remarked. "Well, now, I suppose that's the landlord and landlady."

There was an office facing them, at the rear of the hall, and a man and woman were regarding them from a box window which opened above a ledge on which lay a register book. They were middle-aged folk: the man, a fleshy, round-faced, somewhat pompous-looking individual, who might at some time have been a butler; the woman a tall, spare-figured, thin-featured, sharp-eyed person, who examined the newcomers with an enquiring gaze. Rathbury went up to them with easy confidence.

"You the landlord of this house, sir?" he asked. "Mr. Walters? Just so — and Mrs. Walters, I presume?"

The landlord made a stiff bow and looked sharply at his questioner.

"What can I do for you, sir?" he enquired.

"A little matter of business, Mr. Walters," replied Rathbury, pulling out a card. "You'll see there who I am—Detective-Sergeant Rathbury, of the Yard. This is Mr. Frank Spargo, a newspaper man; this is Mr. Ronald Breton, a barrister."

The landlady, hearing their names and description, pointed to a side door, and signed Rathbury and his companions to pass through. Obeying her pointed finger, they found themselves in a small private parlour. Walters closed the two doors which led into it and looked at his principal visitor.

"What is it, Mr. Rathbury?" he enquired. "Anything wrong?"

"We want a bit of information," answered Rathbury, almost with indifference.

"Did anybody of the name of Marbury put up here yesterday—elderly man, grey hair, fresh complexion?"

Mrs. Walters started, glancing at her husband.

"There!" she exclaimed. "I knew some enquiry would be made. Yes—a Mr. Marbury took a room here yesterday morning, just after the noon train got in from Southampton. Number 20 he took. But—he didn't use it last night. He went out—very late—and he never came back."

Rathbury nodded. Answering a sign from the landlord, he took a chair and, sitting down, looked at Mrs. Walters.

"What made you think some enquiry would be made, ma'am?" he asked. "Had you noticed anything?"

Mrs. Walters seemed a little confused by this direct question. Her husband gave vent to a species of growl.

"Nothing to notice," he muttered. "Her way of speaking—that's all."

"Well—why I said that was this," said the landlady. "He happened to tell us, did Mr. Marbury, that he hadn't been in London for over twenty years, and couldn't remember anything about it, him, he said, never having known much about London at any time. And, of course, when he went out so late and never came back, why, naturally, I thought something had happened to him, and that there'd be enquiries made."

"Just so—just so!" said Rathbury. "So you would, ma'am—so you would. Well, something has happened to him. He's dead. What's more, there's strong reason to think he was murdered."

Mr. and Mrs. Walters received this announcement with proper surprise and horror, and the landlord suggested a little refreshment to his visitors. Spargo and Breton declined, on the ground that they had work to do during the afternoon; Rathbury accepted it, evidently as a matter of course.

"My respects," he said, lifting his glass. "Well, now, perhaps you'll just tell me what you know of this man? I may as well tell you, Mr. and Mrs. Walters, that he was found dead in Middle Temple Lane this morning, at a quarter to three; that there wasn't anything on him but his clothes and a scrap of paper which bore this gentleman's name and address; that this gentleman knows nothing whatever of him, and that I traced him here because he bought a cap at a West End hatter's yesterday, and had it sent to your hotel."

"Yes," said Mrs. Walters quickly, "that's so. And he went out in that cap last night. Well—we don't know much about him. As I said, he came in here about a quarter past twelve yesterday morning, and booked Number 20. He had a porter with him that brought a trunk and a bag—they're in 20 now, of course. He told me that he had stayed at this house over twenty years ago, on his way to Australia—that, of course, was long before we took it. And he signed his name in the book as John Marbury."

"We'll look at that, if you please," said Rathbury.

Walters fetched in the register and turned the leaf to the previous day's entries. They all bent over the dead man's writing.

"'John Marbury, Coolumbidgee, New South Wales,'" said Rathbury. "Ah—now I was wondering if that writing would be the same as that on the scrap of paper, Mr. Breton. But, you see, it isn't—it's quite different."

"Quite different," said Breton. He, too, was regarding the handwriting with great interest. And Rathbury noticed his keen inspection of it, and asked another question.

"Ever seen that writing before?" he suggested.

"Never," answered Breton. "And yet—there's something very familiar about it."

"Then the probability is that you have seen it before," remarked Rathbury. "Well—now we'll hear a little more about Marbury's doings here. Just tell me all you know, Mr. and Mrs. Walters."

"My wife knows most," said Walters. "I scarcely saw the man—I don't remember speaking with him."

"No," said Mrs. Walters. "You didn't—you weren't much in his way. Well," she continued, "I showed him up to his room. He talked a bit—said he'd just landed at Southampton from Melbourne."

"Did he mention his ship?" asked Rathbury. "But if he didn't, it doesn't matter, for we can find out."

"I believe the name's on his things," answered the landlady. "There are some labels of that sort. Well, he asked for a chop to be cooked for him at once, as he was going out. He had his chop, and he went out at exactly one o'clock, saying to me that he expected he'd get lost, as he didn't know London well at any time, and shouldn't know it at all now. He went outside there—I saw him—looked about him and walked off towards Blackfriars way. During the afternoon the cap you spoke of came for him—from Fiskie's. So, of course, I judged he'd been Piccadilly way. But he himself never came in until ten o'clock. And then he brought a gentleman with him."

"Aye?" said Rathbury. "A gentleman, now? Did you see him?"

"Just," replied the landlady. "They went straight up to 20, and I just caught a mere glimpse of the gentleman as they turned up the stairs. A tall, well-built gentleman, with a grey beard, very well dressed as far as I could see, with a top hat and a white silk muffler round his throat, and carrying an umbrella."

"And they went to Marbury's room?" said Rathbury. "What then?"

"Well, then, Mr. Marbury rang for some whiskey and soda," continued Mrs. Walters. "He was particular to have a decanter of whiskey: that, and a syphon of soda were taken up there. I heard nothing more until nearly midnight; then the hall-porter told me that the gentleman in 20 had gone out, and had asked him if there was a night-porter—as, of course, there is. He went out at half-past eleven."

"And the other gentleman?" asked Rathbury.

"The other gentleman," answered the landlady, "went out with him. The hall-porter said they turned towards the station. And that was the last anybody in this house saw of Mr. Marbury. He certainly never came back."

"That," observed Rathbury with a quiet smile, "that is quite certain, ma'am? Well—I suppose we'd better see this Number 20 room, and have a look at what he left there."

"Everything," said Mrs. Walters, "is just as he left it. Nothing's been touched."

It seemed to two of the visitors that there was little to touch. On the dressing-table lay a few ordinary articles of toilet—none of them of any quality or value: the dead man had evidently been satisfied with the plain necessities of life. An overcoat hung from a peg: Rathbury, without ceremony, went through its pockets; just as unceremoniously he proceeded to examine trunk and bag, and finding both unlocked, he laid out on the bed every article they contained and examined each separately and carefully. And he found nothing whereby he could gather any clue to the dead owner's identity.

"There you are!" he said, making an end of his task. "You see, it's just the same with these things as with the clothes he had on him. There are no papers—there's nothing to tell who he was, what he was after, where he'd come from—though that we may find out in other ways. But it's not often that a man travels without some clue to his identity. Beyond the fact that some of this linen was, you see, bought in Melbourne, we know nothing of him. Yet he must have had papers and money on him. Did you see anything of his money, now, ma'am?" he asked, suddenly turning to Mrs. Walters. "Did he pull out his purse in your presence, now?"

"Yes," answered the landlady, with promptitude. "He came into the bar for a drink after he'd been up to his room. He pulled out a handful of gold when he paid for it—a whole handful. There must have been some thirty to forty sovereigns and half-sovereigns."

"And he hadn't a penny piece on him—when found," muttered Rathbury.

"I noticed another thing, too," remarked the landlady. "He was wearing a very fine gold watch and chain, and had a splendid ring on his left hand—little finger—gold, with a big diamond in it."

"Yes," said the detective, thoughtfully, "I noticed that he'd worn a ring, and that it had been a bit tight for him. Well—now there's only one thing to ask about. Did your chambermaid notice if he left any torn paper around—tore any letters up, or anything like that?"

But the chambermaid, produced, had not noticed anything of the sort; on the contrary, the gentleman of Number 20 had left his room very tidy indeed. So Rathbury intimated that he had no more to ask, and nothing further to say, just then, and he bade the landlord and landlady of the Anglo-Orient Hotel good morning, and went away, followed by the two young men.

"What next?" asked Spargo, as they gained the street.

"The next thing," answered Rathbury, "is to find the man with whom Marbury left this hotel last night."

"And how's that to be done?" asked Spargo.

"At present," replied Rathbury, "I don't know."

And with a careless nod, he walked off, apparently desirous of being alone.

The barrister and the journalist, left thus unceremoniously on a crowded pavement, looked at each other. Breton laughed.

"We don't seem to have gained much information," he remarked. "I'm about as wise as ever."

"No—wiser," said Spargo. "At any rate, I am. I know now that this dead man called himself John Marbury; that he came from Australia; that he only landed at Southampton yesterday morning, and that he was in the company last night of a man whom we have had described to us—a tall, grey-bearded, well-dressed man, presumably a gentleman."

Breton shrugged his shoulders.

"I should say that description would fit a hundred thousand men in London," he remarked.

"Exactly—so it would," answered Spargo. "But we know that it was one of the hundred thousand, or half-million, if you like. The thing is to find that one—the one."

"And you think you can do it?"

"I think I'm going to have a big try at it."

Breton shrugged his shoulders again.

"What?—by going up to every man who answers the description, and saying 'Sir, are you the man who accompanied John Marbury to the Aglo——"

Spargo suddenly interrupted him.

"Look here!" he said. "Didn't you say that you knew a man who lives in that block in the entry of which Marbury was found?"

"No, I didn't," answered Breton. "It was Mr. Elphick who said that. All the same, I do know that man—he's Mr. Cardlestone, another barrister. He and Mr. Elphick are friends—they're both enthusiastic philatelists—stamp collectors, you know—and I dare say Mr. Elphick was round there last night examining something new Cardlestone's got hold of. Why?"

"I'd like to go round there and make some enquiries," replied Spargo. "If you'd be kind enough to——"

"Oh, I'll go with you!" responded Breton, with alacrity. "I'm just as keen about this business as you are, Spargo! I want to know who this man Marbury is, and how he came to have my name and address on him. Now, if I had been a well-known man in my profession, you know, why — "

"Yes," said Spargo, as they got into a cab, "yes, that would have explained a lot. It seems to me that we'll get at the murderer through that scrap of paper a lot quicker than through Rathbury's line. Yes, that's what I think."

Breton looked at his companion with interest.

"But — you don't know what Rathbury's line is," he remarked.

"Yes, I do," said Spargo. "Rathbury's gone off to discover who the man is with whom Marbury left the Anglo-Orient Hotel last night. That's his line." "And you want — — ?"

"I want to find out the full significance of that bit of paper, and who wrote it," answered Spargo. "I want to know why that old man was coming to you when he was murdered."

Breton started.

"By Jove!" he exclaimed. "I — I never thought of that. You — you really think he was coming to me when he was struck down?"

"Certain. Hadn't he got an address in the Temple? Wasn't he in the Temple? Of course, he was trying to find you."

"But — the late hour?"

"No matter. How else can you explain his presence in the Temple? I think he was asking his way. That's why I want to make some enquiries in this block."

It appeared to Spargo that a considerable number of people, chiefly of the office-boy variety, were desirous of making enquiries about the dead man. Being luncheon-hour, that bit of Middle Temple Lane where the body was found, was thick with the inquisitive and the sensation-seeker, for the news of the murder had spread, and though there was nothing to see but the bare stones on which the body had lain, there were more open mouths and staring eyes around the entry than Spargo had seen for many a day. And the nuisance had become so great that the occupants of the adjacent chambers had sent for a policeman to move the curious away, and when Spargo and his companion presented themselves at the entry this policeman was being lectured as to his duties by a little weazen-faced gentleman, in very snuffy and old-fashioned garments, and an ancient silk hat, who was obviously greatly exercised by the unwonted commotion.

"Drive them all out into the street!" exclaimed this personage. "Drive them all away, constable—into Fleet Street or upon the Embankment—anywhere, so long as you rid this place of them. This is a disgrace, and an inconvenience, a nuisance, a— —"

"That's old Cardlestone," whispered Breton. "He's always irascible, and I don't suppose we'll get anything out of him. Mr. Cardlestone," he continued, making his way up to the old gentleman who was now retreating up the stone steps, brandishing an umbrella as ancient as himself. "I was just coming to see you, sir. This is Mr. Spargo, a journalist, who is much interested in this murder. He— —"

"I know nothing about the murder, my dear sir!" exclaimed Mr. Cardlestone. "And I never talk to journalists—a pack of busybodies, sir, saving your presence. I am not aware that any murder has been committed, and I object to my doorway being filled by a pack of office boys and street loungers. Murder indeed! I suppose the man fell down these steps and broke his neck—drunk, most likely."

He opened his outer door as he spoke, and Breton, with a reassuring smile and a nod at Spargo, followed him into his chambers on the first landing, motioning the journalist to keep at their heels.

"Mr. Elphick tells me that he was with you until a late hour last evening, Mr. Cardlestone," he said. "Of course, neither of you heard anything suspicious?"

"What should we hear that was suspicious in the Temple, sir?" demanded Mr. Cardlestone, angrily. "I hope the Temple is free from that sort of thing, young Mr. Breton. Your respected guardian and myself had a quiet evening on our usual peaceful pursuits, and when he went away all was as quiet as the grave, sir. What may have gone on in the chambers above and around me I know not! Fortunately, our walls are thick, sir—substantial. I say, sir, the man probably fell down and broke his neck. What he was doing here, I do not presume to say."

"Well, it's guess, you know, Mr. Cardlestone," remarked Breton, again winking at Spargo. "But all that was found on this man was a scrap of paper on which my name and address were written. That's practically all that was known of him, except that he'd just arrived from Australia."

Mr. Cardlestone suddenly turned on the young barrister with a sharp, acute glance.

"Eh?" he exclaimed. "What's this? You say this man had your name and address on him, young Breton!—yours? And that he came from—Australia?"

"That's so," answered Breton. "That's all that's known."

Mr. Cardlestone put aside his umbrella, produced a bandanna handkerchief of strong colours, and blew his nose in a reflective fashion.

"That's a mysterious thing," he observed. "Um—does Elphick know all that?"

Breton looked at Spargo as if he was asking him for an explanation of Mr. Cardlestone's altered manner. And Spargo took up the conversation.

"No," he said. "All that Mr. Elphick knows is that Mr. Ronald Breton's name and address were on the scrap of paper found on the body. Mr. Elphick"—here Spargo paused and looked at Breton— "Mr. Elphick," he presently continued, slowly transferring his glance to the old barrister, "spoke of going to view the body."

"Ah!" exclaimed Mr. Cardlestone, eagerly. "It can be seen? Then I'll go and see it. Where is it?"

Breton started.

"But—my dear sir!" he said. "Why?"

Mr. Cardlestone picked up his umbrella again.

"I feel a proper curiosity about a mystery which occurs at my very door," he said. "Also, I have known more than one man who went to Australia. This might—I say might, young gentlemen—might be a man I had once known. Show me where this body is."

Breton looked helplessly at Spargo: it was plain that he did not understand the turn that things were taking. But Spargo was quick to seize an opportunity. In another minute he was conducting Mr. Cardlestone through the ins and outs of the Temple towards Blackfriars. And as they turned into Tudor Street they encountered Mr. Elphick.

"I am going to the mortuary," he remarked. "So, I suppose, are you, Cardlestone? Has anything more been discovered, young man?"

Spargo tried a chance shot—at what he did not know. "The man's name was Marbury," he said. "He was from Australia."

He was keeping a keen eye on Mr. Elphick, but he failed to see that Mr. Elphick showed any of the surprise which Mr. Cardlestone had exhibited. Rather, he seemed indifferent.

"Oh?" he said—"Marbury? And from Australia. Well—I should like to see the body."

Spargo and Breton had to wait outside the mortuary while the two elder gentlemen went in. There was nothing to be learnt from either when they reappeared.

"We don't know the man," said Mr. Elphick, calmly. "As Mr. Cardlestone, I understand, has said to you already—we have known men who went to Australia, and as this man was evidently wandering about the Temple, we thought it might have been one of them, come back. But—we don't recognize him."

"Couldn't recognize him," said Mr. Cardlestone. "No!"

They went away together arm in arm, and Breton looked at Spargo.

"As if anybody on earth ever fancied they'd recognize him!" he said. "Well—what are you going to do now, Spargo? I must go."

Spargo, who had been digging his walking-stick into a crack in the pavement, came out of a fit of abstraction.

"I?" he said. "Oh—I'm going to the office." And he turned abruptly away, and walking straight off to the editorial rooms at the *Watchman*, made for one in which sat the official guardian of the editor. "Try to get me a few minutes with the chief," he said.

The private secretary looked up.

"Really important?" he asked.

"Big!" answered Spargo. "Fix it."

Once closeted with the great man, whose idiosyncrasies he knew pretty well by that time, Spargo lost no time.

"You've heard about this murder in Middle Temple Lane?" he suggested.

"The mere facts," replied the editor, tersely.

"I was there when the body was found," continued Spargo, and gave a brief résumé of his doings. "I'm certain this is a most unusual affair," he went on. "It's as full of mystery as—as it could be. I want to give my attention to it. I want to specialize on it. I can make such a story of it as we haven't had for some time—ages. Let me have it. And to start with, let me have two columns for tomorrow morning. I'll make it—big!"

The editor looked across his desk at Spargo's eager face.

"Your other work?" he said.

"Well in hand," replied Spargo. "I'm ahead a whole week—both articles and reviews. I can tackle both."

The editor put his finger tips together.

"Have you got some idea about this, young man?" he asked.

"I've got a great idea," answered Spargo. He faced the great man squarely, and stared at him until he had brought a smile to the editorial face. "That's why I want to do it," he added. "And—it's not mere boasting nor over-confidence—I know I shall do it better than anybody else."

The editor considered matters for a brief moment.

"You mean to find out who killed this man?" he said at last.

Spargo nodded his head—twice.

"I'll find that out," he said doggedly.

The editor picked up a pencil, and bent to his desk.

"All right," he said. "Go ahead. You shall have your two columns."

Spargo went quietly away to his own nook and corner. He got hold of a block of paper and began to write. He was going to show how to do things.

Ronald Breton walked into the *Watchman* office and into Spargo's room next morning holding a copy of the current issue in his hand. He waved it at Spargo with an enthusiasm which was almost boyish.

"I say!" he exclaimed. "That's the way to do it, Spargo! I congratulate you. Yes, that's the way — certain!"

Spargo, idly turning over a pile of exchanges, yawned.

"What way?" he asked indifferently.

"The way you've written this thing up," said Breton. "It's a hundred thousand times better than the usual cut-and-dried account of a murder. It's — it's like a — a romance!"

"Merely a new method of giving news," said Spargo. He picked up a copy of the *Watchman*, and glanced at his two columns, which had somehow managed to make themselves into three, viewing the displayed lettering, the photograph of the dead man, the line drawing of the entry in Middle Temple Lane, and the facsimile of the scrap of grey paper, with a critical eye. "Yes — merely a new method," he continued. "The question is — will it achieve its object?"

"What's the object?" asked Breton.

Spargo fished out a box of cigarettes from an untidy drawer, pushed it over to his visitor, helped himself, and tilting back his chair, put his feet on his desk.

"The object?" he said, drily. "Oh, well, the object is the ultimate detection of the murderer."

"You're after that?"

"I'm after that — just that."

"And not — not simply out to make effective news?"

"I'm out to find the murderer of John Marbury," said Spargo deliberately slow in his speech. "And I'll find him."

"Well, there doesn't seem to be much in the way of clues, so far," remarked Breton. "I see — nothing. Do you?"

Spargo sent a spiral of scented smoke into the air.

"I want to know an awful lot," he said. "I'm hungering for news. I want to know who John Marbury is. I want to know what he did with himself between the time when he walked out of the Anglo-Orient Hotel, alive and well, and the time when he was found in Middle Temple Lane, with his skull beaten in and dead. I want to know where he got that scrap of paper. Above everything, Breton, I want to know what he'd got to do with you!"

He gave the young barrister a keen look, and Breton nodded.

"Yes," he said. "I confess that's a corker. But I think — —"

"Well?" said Spargo.

"I think he may have been a man who had some legal business in hand, or in prospect, and had been recommended to — me," said Breton.

Spargo smiled — a little sardonically.

"That's good!" he said. "You had your very first brief — yesterday. Come — your fame isn't blown abroad through all the heights yet, my friend! Besides — don't intending clients approach — isn't it strict etiquette for them to approach? — barristers through solicitors?"

"Quite right — in both your remarks," replied Breton, good-humouredly. "Of course, I'm not known a bit, but all the same I've known several cases where a barrister has been approached in the first instance and asked to recommend a solicitor. Somebody who wanted to do me a good turn may have given this man my address."

"Possible," said Spargo. "But he wouldn't have come to consult you at midnight. Breton! — the more I think of it, the more I'm certain there's a tremendous mystery in this affair! That's why I got the chief to let me write it up as I have done — here. I'm hoping that this photograph — though to be sure, it's of a dead face — and this facsimile of the scrap of paper will lead to somebody coming forward who can — —"

Just then one of the uniformed youths who hang about the marble pillared vestibule of the *Watchman* office came into the room with the unmistakable look and air of one who carries news of moment.

"I dare lay a sovereign to a cent that I know what this is," muttered Spargo in an aside. "Well?" he said to the boy. "What is it?"

The messenger came up to the desk.

"Mr. Spargo," he said, "there's a man downstairs who says that he wants to see somebody about that murder case that's in the paper this morning, sir. Mr. Barrett said I was to come to you."

"Who is the man?" asked Spargo.

"Won't say, sir," replied the boy. "I gave him a form to fill up, but he said he wouldn't write anything—said all he wanted was to see the man who wrote the piece in the paper."

"Bring him here," commanded Spargo. He turned to Breton when the boy had gone, and he smiled. "I knew we should have somebody here sooner or later," he said. "That's why I hurried over my breakfast and came down at ten o'clock. Now then, what will you bet on the chances of this chap's information proving valuable?"

"Nothing," replied Breton. "He's probably some crank or faddist who's got some theory that he wants to ventilate."

The man who was presently ushered in by the messenger seemed from preliminary and outward appearance to justify Breton's prognostication. He was obviously a countryman, a tall, loosely-built, middle-aged man, yellow of hair, blue of eye, who was wearing his Sunday-best array of pearl-grey trousers and black coat, and sported a necktie in which were several distinct colours. Oppressed with the splendour and grandeur of the *Watchman* building, he had removed his hard billycock hat as he followed the boy, and he ducked his bared head at the two young men as he stepped on to the thick pile of the carpet which made luxurious footing in Spargo's room. His blue eyes, opened to their widest, looked round him in astonishment at the sumptuousness of modern newspaper-office accommodation.

"How do you do, sir?" said Spargo, pointing a finger to one of the easy-chairs for which the *Watchman* office is famous. "I understand that you wish to see me?"

The caller ducked his yellow head again, sat down on the edge of the chair, put his hat on the floor, picked it up again, and endeavoured to hang it on his knee, and looked at Spargo innocently and shyly.

"What I want to see, sir," he observed in a rustic accent, "is the gentleman as wrote that piece in your newspaper about this here murder in Middle Temple Lane."

"You see him," said Spargo. "I am that man."

The caller smiled — generously.

"Indeed, sir?" he said. "A very nice bit of reading, I'm sure. And what might your name be, now, sir? I can always talk free-er to a man when I know what his name is."

"So can I," answered Spargo. "My name is Spargo — Frank Spargo. What's yours?"

"Name of Webster, sir — William Webster. I farm at One Ash Farm, at Gosberton, in Oakshire. Me and my wife," continued Mr. Webster, again smiling and distributing his smile between both his hearers, "is at present in London on a holiday. And very pleasant we find it — weather and all."

"That's right," said Spargo. "And — you wanted to see me about this murder, Mr. Webster?"

"I did, sir. Me, I believe, knowing, as I think, something that'll do for you to put in your paper. You see, Mr. Spargo, it come about in this fashion — happen you'll be for me to tell it in my own way."

"That," answered Spargo, "is precisely what I desire."

"Well, to be sure, I couldn't tell it in no other," declared Mr. Webster. "You see, sir, I read your paper this morning while I was waiting for my breakfast — they take their breakfasts so late in them hotels — and when I'd read it, and looked at the pictures, I says to my wife 'As soon as I've had my breakfast,' I says, 'I'm going to where they print this newspaper to tell 'em something.' 'Aye?' she says, 'Why, what have you to tell, I should like to know?' just like that, Mr. Spargo."

"Mrs. Webster," said Spargo, "is a lady of businesslike principles. And what have you to tell?"

Mr. Webster looked into the crown of his hat, looked out of it, and smiled knowingly.

"Well, sir," he continued, "Last night, my wife, she went out to a part they call Clapham, to take her tea and supper with an old friend of hers as lives there, and as they wanted to have a bit of woman-talk, like, I didn't go. So thinks I to myself, I'll go and see this here House of Commons. There was a neighbour of mine as had told me that all you'd got to do was to tell the policeman at the door that you wanted to see your own Member of Parliament. So when I got there I told 'em that I wanted to see our M.P., Mr. Stonewood — you'll have heard tell of him, no doubt; he knows me very well — and they passed me, and I wrote out a ticket for him, and they told me to sit down while they found him. So I sat down in a grand sort of hall where there were a rare lot of people going and coming, and some fine pictures and images to look at, and for a time I looked at them, and then I began to take a bit of notice of the folk near at hand, waiting, you know, like myself. And as sure as I'm a christened man, sir, the gentleman whose picture you've got in your paper — him as was murdered — was sitting next to me! I knew that picture as soon as I saw it this morning."

Spargo, who had been making unmeaning scribbles on a block of paper, suddenly looked at his visitor.

"What time was that?" he asked.

"It was between a quarter and half-past nine, sir," answered Mr. Webster. "It might ha' been twenty past — it might ha' been twenty-five past."

"Go on, if you please," said Spargo.

"Well, sir, me and this here dead gentleman talked a bit. About what a long time it took to get a member to attend to you, and such-like. I made mention of the fact that I hadn't been in there before. 'Neither have I!' he says, 'I came in out of curiosity,' he says, and then he laughed, sir — queer-like. And it was just after that that what I'm going to tell you about happened."

"Tell," commanded Spargo.

"Well, sir, there was a gentleman came along, down this grand hall that we were sitting in — a tall, handsome gentleman, with a grey beard. He'd no hat on, and he was carrying a lot of paper and documents in his hand, so I thought he was happen one of the members. And all of a sudden this here man at my side, he jumps up with a sort of start and an exclamation, and— —"

Spargo lifted his hand. He looked keenly at his visitor.

"Now, you're absolutely sure about what you heard him exclaim?" he asked. "Quite sure about it? Because I see you are going to tell us what he did exclaim."

"I'll tell you naught but what I'm certain of, sir," replied Webster. "What he said as he jumped up was 'Good God!' he says, sharp-like—and then he said a name, and I didn't right catch it, but it sounded like Danesworth, or Painesworth, or something of that sort—one of them there, or very like 'em, at any rate. And then he rushed up to this here gentleman, and laid his hand on his arm—sudden-like."

"And—the gentleman?" asked Spargo, quietly.

"Well, he seemed taken aback, sir. He jumped. Then he stared at the man. Then they shook hands. And then, after they'd spoken a few words together-like, they walked off, talking. And, of course, I never saw no more of 'em. But when I saw your paper this morning, sir, and that picture in it, I said to myself 'That's the man I sat next to in that there hall at the House of Commons!' Oh, there's no doubt of it, sir!"

"And supposing you saw a photograph of the tall gentleman with the grey beard?" suggested Spargo. "Could you recognize him from that?"

"Make no doubt of it, sir," answered Mr. Webster. "I observed him particular."

Spargo rose, and going over to a cabinet, took from it a thick volume, the leaves of which he turned over for several minutes.

"Come here, if you please, Mr. Webster," he said.

The farmer went across the room.

"There is a full set of photographs of members of the present House of Commons here," said Spargo. "Now, pick out the one you saw. Take your time—and be sure."

He left his caller turning over the album and went back to Breton.

"There!" he whispered. "Getting nearer—a bit nearer—eh?"

"To what?" asked Breton. "I don't see—"

A sudden exclamation from the farmer interrupted Breton's remark.

"This is him, sir!" answered Mr. Webster. "That's the gentleman—know him anywhere!"

The two young men crossed the room. The farmer was pointing a stubby finger to a photograph, beneath which was written *Stephen Aylmore, Esq., M.P. for Brookminster.*

Spargo, keenly observant and watchful, felt, rather than saw, Breton start; he himself preserved an imperturbable equanimity. He gave a mere glance at the photograph to which Mr. Webster was pointing.

"Oh!" he said. "That he?"

"That's the gentleman, sir," replied Webster. "Done to the life, that is. No difficulty in recognizing of that, Mr. Spargo."

"You're absolutely sure?" demanded Spargo. "There are a lot of men in the House of Commons, you know, who wear beards, and many of the beards are grey."

But Webster wagged his head.

"That's him, sir!" he repeated. "I'm as sure of that as I am that my name's William Webster. That's the man I saw talking to him whose picture you've got in your paper. Can't say no more, sir."

"Very good," said Spargo. "I'm much obliged to you. I'll see Mr. Aylmore. Leave me your address in London, Mr. Webster. How long do you remain in town?"

"My address is the Beachcroft Hotel, Bloomsbury, sir, and I shall be there for another week," answered the farmer. "Hope I've been of some use, Mr. Spargo. As I says to my wife——"

Spargo cut his visitor short in polite fashion and bowed him out. He turned to Breton, who still stood staring at the album of portraits.

"There!—what did I tell you?" he said. "Didn't I say I should get some news? There it is."

Breton nodded his head. He seemed thoughtful.

"Yes," he agreed. "Yes, I say, Spargo!"

"Well?"

"Mr. Aylmore is my prospective father-in-law, you know."

"Quite aware of it. Didn't you introduce me to his daughters—only yesterday?"

"But—how did you know they were his daughters?"

Spargo laughed as he sat down to his desk.

"Instinct—intuition," he answered. "However, never mind that, just now. Well—I've found something out. Marbury—if that is the dead man's real name, and anyway, it's all we know him by—was in the company of Mr. Aylmore that night. Good!"

"What are you going to do about it?" asked Breton.

"Do? See Mr. Aylmore, of course."

He was turning over the leaves of a telephone address-book; one hand had already picked up the mouthpiece of the instrument on his desk.

"Look here," said Breton. "I know where Mr. Aylmore is always to be found at twelve o'clock. At the A. and P.—the Atlantic and Pacific Club, you know, in St. James's. If you like, I'll go with you."

Spargo glanced at the clock and laid down the telephone.

"All right," he said. "Eleven o'clock, now. I've something to do. I'll meet you outside the A. and P. at exactly noon."

"I'll be there," agreed Breton. He made for the door, and with his hand on it, turned. "What do you expect from—from what we've just heard?" he asked.

Spargo shrugged his shoulders.

"Wait—until we hear what Mr. Aylmore has to say," he answered. "I suppose this man Marbury was some old acquaintance."

Breton closed the door and went away: left alone, Spargo began to mutter to himself.

"Good God!" he says. "Dainsworth—Painsworth—something of that sort—one of the two. Excellent—that our farmer friend should have so much observation. Ah!—and why should Mr. Stephen Aylmore be recognized as Dainsworth or Painsworth or something of that sort. Now, who is Mr. Stephen Aylmore—beyond being what I know him to be?"

Spargo's fingers went instinctively to one of a number of books of reference which stood on his desk: they turned with practised swiftness to a page over which his eye ran just as swiftly. He read aloud:

"AYLMORE, STEPHEN, M.P. for Brookminster since 1910. Residences: 23, St. Osythe Court, Kensington: Buena Vista, Great Marlow. Member Atlantic and Pacific and City Venturers' Clubs. Interested in South American enterprise."

"Um!" muttered Spargo, putting the book away. "That's not very illuminating. However, we've got one move finished. Now we'll make another."

Going over to the album of photographs, Spargo deftly removed that of Mr. Aylmore, put it in an envelope and the envelope in his pocket and, leaving the office, hailed a taxi-cab, and ordered its driver to take him to the Anglo-Orient Hotel. This was the something-to-do of which he had spoken to Breton: Spargo wanted to do it alone.

Mrs. Walters was in her low-windowed office when Spargo entered the hall; she recognized him at once and motioned him into her parlour.

"I remember you," said Mrs., Walters; "you came with the detective—Mr. Rathbury."

"Have you seen him, since?" asked Spargo.

"Not since," replied Mrs. Walters. "No—and I was wondering if he'd be coming round, because——" She paused there and looked at Spargo with particular enquiry—"You're a friend of his, aren't you?" she asked. "I suppose you know as much as he does—about this?"

"He and I," replied Spargo, with easy confidence, "are working this case together. You can tell me anything you'd tell him."

The landlady rummaged in her pocket and produced an old purse, from an inner compartment of which she brought out a small object wrapped in tissue paper.

"Well," she said, unwrapping the paper, "we found this in Number 20 this morning—it was lying under the dressing-table. The girl that found it brought it to me, and I thought it was a bit of glass, but Walters, he says as how he shouldn't be surprised if it's a diamond. And since we found it, the waiter who took the whisky up to 20, after Mr. Marbury came in with the other gentleman, has told me that when he went into the room the two gentlemen were looking at a paper full of things like this. So there?"

Spargo fingered the shining bit of stone.

"That's a diamond—right enough," he said. "Put it away, Mrs. Walters—I shall see Rathbury presently, and I'll tell him about it. Now, that other gentleman! You told us you saw him. Could you recognize him—I mean, a photograph of him? Is this the man?"

Spargo knew from the expression of Mrs. Walters' face that she had no more doubt than Webster had.

"Oh, yes!" she said. "That's the gentleman who came in with Mr. Marbury — I should have known him in a thousand. Anybody would recognize him from that — perhaps you'd let our hall-porter and the waiter I mentioned just now look at it?"

"I'll see them separately and see if they've ever seen a man who resembles this," replied Spargo.

The two men recognized the photograph at once, without any prompting, and Spargo, after a word or two with the landlady, rode off to the Atlantic and Pacific Club, and found Ronald Breton awaiting him on the steps. He made no reference to his recent doings, and together they went into the house and asked for Mr. Aylmore.

Spargo looked with more than uncommon interest at the man who presently came to them in the visitors' room. He was already familiar with Mr. Aylmore's photograph, but he never remembered seeing him in real life; the Member for Brookminster was one of that rapidly diminishing body of legislators whose members are disposed to work quietly and unobtrusively, doing yeoman service on committees, obeying every behest of the party whips, without forcing themselves into the limelight or seizing every opportunity to air their opinions. Now that Spargo met him in the flesh he proved to be pretty much what the journalist had expected — a rather cold-mannered, self-contained man, who looked as if he had been brought up in a school of rigid repression, and taught not to waste words. He showed no more than the merest of languid interests in Spargo when Breton introduced him, and his face was quite expressionless when Spargo brought to an end his brief explanation — purposely shortened — of his object in calling upon him.

"Yes," he said indifferently. "Yes, it is quite true that I met Marbury and spent a little time with him on the evening your informant spoke of. I met him, as he told you, in the lobby of the House. I was much surprised to meet him. I had not seen him for — I really don't know how many years."

He paused and looked at Spargo as if he was wondering what he ought or not to say to a newspaper man. Spargo remained silent, waiting. And presently Mr. Aylmore went on.

"I read your account in the *Watchman* this morning," he said. "I was wondering, when you called just now, if I would communicate with you or with the police. The fact is—I suppose you want this for your paper, eh?" he continued after a sudden breaking off.

"I shall not print anything that you wish me not to print," answered Spargo. "If you care to give me any information——"

"Oh, well!" said Mr. Aylmore. "I don't mind. The fact is, I knew next to nothing. Marbury was a man with whom I had some—well, business relations, of a sort, a great many years ago. It must be twenty years—perhaps more—since I lost sight of him. When he came up to me in the lobby the other night, I had to make an effort of memory to recall him. He wished me, having once met me, to give him some advice, and as there was little doing in the House that night, and as he had once been—almost a friend—I walked to his hotel with him, chatting. He told me that he had only landed from Australia that morning, and what he wanted my advice about, principally, was—diamonds. Australian diamonds."

"I was unaware," remarked Spargo, "that diamonds were ever found in Australia."

Mr. Aylmore smiled—a little cynically.

"Perhaps so," he said. "But diamonds have been found in Australia from time to time, ever since Australia was known to Europeans, and in the opinion of experts, they will eventually be found there in quantity. Anyhow, Marbury had got hold of some Australian diamonds, and he showed them to me at his hotel—a number of them. We examined them in his room."

"What did he do with them—afterwards?" asked Spargo. "He put them in his waistcoat pocket—in a very small wash-leather bag, from which he had taken them. There were, in all, sixteen or twenty stones—not more, and they were all small. I advised him to see some expert—I mentioned Streeter's to him. Now, I can tell you how he got hold of Mr. Breton's address."

The two young men pricked up their ears. Spargo unconsciously tightened his hold on the pencil with which he was making notes.

"He got it from me," continued Mr. Aylmore. "The handwriting on the scrap of paper is mine, hurriedly scrawled. He wanted legal advice. As I knew very little about lawyers, I told him that if he called on Mr. Breton, Mr. Breton would be able to tell him of a first-class, sharp solicitor. I wrote down Mr. Breton's address for him, on a scrap of paper which he tore off a letter that he took from his pocket. By the by, I observe that when his body was found there was nothing on it in the shape of papers or money. I am quite sure that when I left him he had a lot of gold on him, those diamonds, and a breast-pocket full of letters."

"Where did you leave him, sir?" asked Spargo. "You left the hotel together, I believe?"

"Yes. We strolled along when we left it. Having once met, we had much to talk of, and it was a fine night. We walked across Waterloo Bridge and very shortly afterwards he left me. And that is really all I know. My own impression— —" He paused for a moment and Spargo waited silently.

"My own impression—though I confess it may seem to have no very solid grounds—is that Marbury was decoyed to where he was found, and was robbed and murdered by some person who knew he had valuables on him. There is the fact that he was robbed, at any rate."

"I've had a notion," said Breton, diffidently. "Mayn't be worth much, but I've had it, all the same. Some fellow-passenger of Marbury's may have tracked him all day—Middle Temple Lane's pretty lonely at night, you know."

No one made any comment upon this suggestion, and on Spargo looking at Mr. Aylmore, the Member of Parliament rose and glanced at the door.

"Well, that's all I can tell you, Mr. Spargo," he said. "You see, it's not much, after all. Of course, there'll be an inquest on Marbury, and I shall have to re-tell it. But you're welcome to print what I've told you."

Spargo left Breton with his future father-in-law and went away towards New Scotland Yard. He and Rathbury had promised to share news—now he had some to communicate.

Chapter 8 THE MAN FROM THE SAFE DEPOSIT

Spargo found Rathbury sitting alone in a small, somewhat dismal apartment which was chiefly remarkable for the business-like paucity of its furnishings and its indefinable air of secrecy. There was a plain writing-table and a hard chair or two; a map of London, much discoloured, on the wall; a few faded photographs of eminent bands in the world of crime, and a similar number of well-thumbed books of reference. The detective himself, when Spargo was shown in to him, was seated at the table, chewing an unlighted cigar, and engaged in the apparently aimless task of drawing hieroglyphics on scraps of paper. He looked up as the journalist entered, and held out his hand.

"Well, I congratulate you on what you stuck in the *Watchman* this morning," he said. "Made extra good reading, I thought. They did right to let you tackle that job. Going straight through with it now, I suppose, Mr. Spargo?"

Spargo dropped into the chair nearest to Rathbury's right hand. He lighted a cigarette, and having blown out a whiff of smoke, nodded his head in a fashion which indicated that the detective might consider his question answered in the affirmative.

"Look here," he said. "We settled yesterday, didn't we, that you and I are to consider ourselves partners, as it were, in this job? That's all right," he continued, as Rathbury nodded very quietly. "Very well—have you made any further progress?"

Rathbury put his thumbs in the armholes of his waistcoat and, leaning back in his chair, shook his head.

"Frankly, I haven't," he replied. "Of course, there's a lot being done in the usual official-routine way. We've men out making various enquiries. We're enquiring about Marbury's voyage to England. All that we know up to now is that he was certainly a passenger on a liner which landed at Southampton in accordance with what he told those people at the Anglo-Orient, that he left the ship in the usual way and was understood to take the train to town—as he did. That's all. There's nothing in that. We've cabled to Melbourne for any news of him from there. But I expect little from that."

"All right," said Spargo. "And — what are you doing — you, yourself? Because, if we're to share facts, I must know what my partner's after. Just now, you seemed to be — drawing."

Rathbury laughed.

"Well, to tell you the truth," he said, "when I want to work things out, I come into this room — it's quiet, as you see — and I scribble anything on paper while I think. I was figuring on my next step, and — "

"Do you see it?" asked Spargo, quickly.

"Well — I want to find the man who went with Marbury to that hotel," replied Rathbury. "It seems to me — "

Spargo wagged his finger at his fellow-contriver.

"I've found him," he said. "That's what I wrote that article for — to find him. I knew it would find him. I've never had any training in your sort of work, but I knew that article would get him. And it has got him."

Rathbury accorded the journalist a look of admiration.

"Good!" he said. "And — who is he?"

"I'll tell you the story," answered Spargo, "and in a summary. This morning a man named Webster, a farmer, a visitor to London, came to me at the office, and said that being at the House of Commons last night he witnessed a meeting between Marbury and a man who was evidently a Member of Parliament, and saw them go away together. I showed him an album of photographs of the present members, and he immediately recognized the portrait of one of them as the man in question. I thereupon took the portrait to the Anglo-Orient Hotel — Mrs. Walters also at once recognized it as that of the man who came to the hotel with Marbury, stopped with him a while in his room, and left with him. The man is Mr. Stephen Aylmore, the member for Brookminster."

Rathbury expressed his feelings in a sharp whistle.

"I know him!" he said. "Of course — I remember Mrs. Walters's description now. But his is a familiar type — tall, grey-bearded, well-dressed. Um! — well, we'll have to see Mr. Aylmore at once."

"I've seen him," said Spargo. "Naturally! For you see, Mrs. Walters gave me a bit more evidence. This morning they found a loose diamond on the floor of Number 20, and after it was found the waiter who took the drinks up to Marbury and his guest that night remembered that when he entered the room the two gentlemen were looking at a paper full of similar objects. So then I went on to see Mr. Aylmore. You know young Breton, the barrister? — you met him with me, you remember?"

"The young fellow whose name and address were found on Marbury," replied Rathbury. "I remember."

"Breton is engaged to Aylmore's daughter," continued Spargo. "Breton took me to Aylmore's club. And Aylmore gives a plain, straightforward account of the matter which he's granted me leave to print. It clears up a lot of things. Aylmore knew Marbury over twenty years ago. He lost sight of him. They met accidentally in the lobby of the House on the evening preceding the murder. Marbury told him that he wanted his advice about those rare things, Australian diamonds. He went back with him to his hotel and spent a while with him; then they walked out together as far as Waterloo Bridge, where Aylmore left him and went home. Further, the scrap of grey paper is accounted for. Marbury wanted the address of a smart solicitor; Aylmore didn't know of one but told Marbury that if he called on young Breton, he'd know, and would put him in the way to find one. Marbury wrote Breton's address down. That's Aylmore's story. But it's got an important addition. Aylmore says that when he left Marbury, Marbury had on him a quantity of those diamonds in a wash-leather bag, a lot of gold, and a breast-pocket full of letters and papers. Now — there was nothing on him when he was found dead in Middle Temple Lane."

Spargo stopped and lighted a fresh cigarette.

"That's all I know," he said. "What do you make of it?"

Rathbury leaned back in his chair in his apparently favourite attitude and stared hard at the dusty ceiling above him.

"Don't know," he said. "It brings things up to a point, certainly. Aylmore and Marbury parted at Waterloo Bridge—very late. Waterloo Bridge is pretty well next door to the Temple. But—how did Marbury get into the Temple, unobserved? We've made every enquiry, and we can't trace him in any way as regards that movement. There's a clue for his going there in the scrap of paper bearing Breton's address, but even a Colonial would know that no business was done in the Temple at midnight, eh?"

"Well," said Spargo, "I've thought of one or two things. He may have been one of those men who like to wander around at night. He may have seen—he would see—plenty of lights in the Temple at that hour; he may have slipped in unobserved—it's possible, it's quite possible. I once had a moonlight saunter in the Temple myself after midnight, and had no difficulty about walking in and out, either. But—if Marbury was murdered for the sake of what he had on him—how did he meet with his murderer or murderers in there? Criminals don't hang about Middle Temple Lane."

The detective shook his head. He picked up his pencil and began making more hieroglyphics.

"What's your theory, Mr. Spargo?" he asked suddenly. "I suppose you've got one."

"Have you?" asked Spargo, bluntly.

"Well," returned Rathbury, hesitatingly, "I hadn't, up to now. But now—now, after what you've told me, I think I can make one. It seems to me that after Marbury left Aylmore he probably mooned about by himself, that he was decoyed into the Temple, and was there murdered and robbed. There are a lot of queer ins and outs, nooks and corners in that old spot, Mr. Spargo, and the murderer, if he knew his ground well, could easily hide himself until he could get away in the morning. He might be a man who had access to chambers or offices—think how easy it would be for such a man, having once killed and robbed his victim, to lie hid for hours afterwards? For aught we know, the man who murdered Marbury may have been within twenty feet of you when you first saw his dead body that morning. Eh?"

Before Spargo could reply to this suggestion an official entered the room and whispered a few words in the detective's ear.

"Show him in at once," said Rathbury. He turned to Spargo as the man quitted the room and smiled significantly. "Here's somebody wants to tell something about the Marbury case," he remarked. "Let's hope it'll be news worth hearing."

Spargo smiled in his queer fashion.

"It strikes me that you've only got to interest an inquisitive public in order to get news," he said. "The principal thing is to investigate it when you've got it. Who's this, now?"

The official had returned with a dapper-looking gentleman in a frock-coat and silk hat, bearing upon him the unmistakable stamp of the city man, who inspected Rathbury with deliberation and Spargo with a glance, and being seated turned to the detective as undoubtedly the person he desired to converse with.

"I understand that you are the officer in charge of the Marbury murder case," he observed. "I believe I can give you some valuable information in respect to that. I read the account of the affair in the *Watchman* newspaper this morning, and saw the portrait of the murdered man there, and I was at first inclined to go to the *Watchman* office with my information, but I finally decided to approach the police instead of the Press, regarding the police as being more—more responsible."

"Much obliged to you, sir," said Rathbury, with a glance at Spargo. "Whom have I the pleasure of — — "

"My name," replied the visitor, drawing out and laying down a card, "is Myerst—Mr. E.P. Myerst, Secretary of the London and Universal Safe Deposit Company. I may, I suppose, speak with confidence," continued Mr. Myerst, with a side-glance at Spargo. "My information is—confidential."

Rathbury inclined his head and put his fingers together.

"You may speak with every confidence, Mr. Myerst," he answered. "If what you have to tell has any real bearing on the Marbury case, it will probably have to be repeated in public, you know, sir. But at present it will be treated as private."

"It has a very real bearing on the case, I should say," replied Mr. Myerst. "Yes, I should decidedly say so. The fact is that on June 21st at about—to be precise—three o'clock in the afternoon, a stranger, who gave the name of John Marbury, and his present address as the Anglo-Orient Hotel, Waterloo, called at our establishment, and asked if he could rent a small safe. He explained to me that he desired to deposit in such a safe a small leather box—which, by the by, was of remarkably ancient appearance—that he had brought with him. I showed him a safe such as he wanted, informed him of the rent, and of the rules of the place, and he engaged the safe, paid the rent for one year in advance, and deposited his leather box—an affair of about a foot square—there and then. After that, having exchanged a remark or two about the altered conditions of London, which, I understood him to say, he had not seen for a great many years, he took his key and his departure. I think there can be no doubt about this being the Mr. Marbury who was found murdered."

"None at all, I should say, Mr. Myerst," said Rathbury. "And I'm much obliged to you for coming here. Now you might tell me a little more, sir. Did Marbury tell you anything about the contents of the box?"

"No. He merely remarked that he wished the greatest care to be taken of it," replied the secretary.

"Didn't give you any hint as to what was in it?" asked Rathbury.

"None. But he was very particular to assure himself that it could not be burnt, nor burgled, nor otherwise molested," replied Mr. Myerst. "He appeared to be greatly relieved when he found that it was impossible for anyone but himself to take his property from his safe."

"Ah!" said Rathbury, winking at Spargo. "So he would, no doubt. And Marbury himself, sir, now? How did he strike you?"

Mr. Myerst gravely considered this question.

"Mr. Marbury struck me," he answered at last, "as a man who had probably seen strange places. And before leaving he made, what I will term, a remarkable remark. About—in fact, about his leather box."

"His leather box?" said Rathbury. "And what was it, sir?"

"This," replied the secretary. "'That box,' he said, 'is safe now. But it's been safer. It's been buried—and deep-down, too—for many and many a year!'"

"Buried — and deep-down, too — for many and many a year," repeated Mr. Myerst, eyeing his companions with keen glances. "I consider that, gentlemen, a very remarkable remark — very remarkable!"

Rathbury stuck his thumbs in the armholes of his waistcoat again and began swaying backwards and forwards in his chair. He looked at Spargo. And with his knowledge of men, he knew that all Spargo's journalistic instincts had been aroused, and that he was keen as mustard to be off on a new scent.

"Remarkable — remarkable, Mr. Myerst!" he assented. "What do you say, Mr. Spargo?"

Spargo turned slowly, and for the first time since Myerst had entered made a careful inspection of him. The inspection lasted several seconds; then Spargo spoke.

"And what did you say to that?" he asked quietly.

Myerst looked from his questioner to Rathbury. And Rathbury thought it time to enlighten the caller.

"I may as well tell you, Mr. Myerst," he said smilingly, "that this is Mr. Spargo, of the *Watchman*. Mr. Spargo wrote the article about the Marbury case of which you spoke when you came in. Mr. Spargo, you'll gather, is deeply interested in this matter — and he and I, in our different capacities, are working together. So — you understand?" Myerst regarded Spargo in a new light. And while he was so looking at him. Spargo repeated the question he had just put.

"I said — What did you say to that?"

Myerst hesitated.

"Well — er — I don't think I said anything," he replied. "Nothing that one might call material, you know."

"Didn't ask him what he meant?" suggested Spargo.

"Oh, no — not at all," replied Myerst.

Spargo got up abruptly from his chair.

"Then you missed one of the finest opportunities I ever heard of!" he said, half-sneeringly. "You might have heard such a story — "

He paused, as if it were not worth while to continue, and turned to Rathbury, who was regarding him with amusement.

"Look here, Rathbury," he said. "Is it possible to get that box opened?"

"It'll have to be opened," answered Rathbury, rising. "It's got to be opened. It probably contains the clue we want. I'm going to ask Mr. Myerst here to go with me just now to take the first steps about having it opened. I shall have to get an order. We may get the matter through today, but at any rate we'll have it done tomorrow morning."

"Can you arrange for me to be present when that comes off?" asked Spargo. "You can—certain? That's all right, Rathbury. Now I'm off, and you'll ring me up or come round if you hear anything, and I'll do the same by you."

And without further word, Spargo went quickly away, and just as quickly returned to the *Watchman* office. There the assistant who had been told off to wait upon his orders during this new crusade met him with a business card.

"This gentleman came in to see you about an hour ago, Mr. Spargo," he said. "He thinks he can tell you something about the Marbury affair, and he said that as he couldn't wait, perhaps you'd step round to his place when you came in."

Spargo took the card and read:

MR. JAMES CRIEDIR, DEALER IN PHILATELIC RARITIES, 2,021, STRAND.

Spargo put the card in his waistcoat pocket and went out again, wondering why Mr. James Criedir could not, would not, or did not call himself a dealer in rare postage stamps, and so use plain English. He went up Fleet Street and soon found the shop indicated on the card, and his first glance at its exterior showed that whatever business might have been done by Mr. Criedir in the past at that establishment there was to be none done there in the future by him, for there were newly-printed bills in the window announcing that the place was to let. And inside he found a short, portly, elderly man who was superintending the packing-up and removal of the last of his stock. He turned a bright, enquiring eye on the journalist.

"Mr. Criedir?" said Spargo.

"The same, sir," answered the philatelist. "You are—?"

"Mr. Spargo, of the *Watchman*. You called on me."

Mr. Criedir opened the door of a tiny apartment at the rear of the very little shop and motioned his caller to enter. He followed him in and carefully closed the door.

"Glad to see you, Mr. Spargo," he said genially. "Take a seat, sir—I'm all in confusion here—giving up business, you see. Yes, I called on you. I think, having read the *Watchman* account of that Marbury affair, and having seen the murdered man's photograph in your columns, that I can give you a bit of information."

"Material?" asked Spargo, tersely.

Mr. Criedir cocked one of his bright eyes at his visitor. He coughed drily.

"That's for you to decide—when you've heard it," he said. "I should say, considering everything, that it was material. Well, it's this—I kept open until yesterday—everything as usual, you know—stock in the window and so on—so that anybody who was passing would naturally have thought that the business was going on, though as a matter of fact, I'm retiring—retired," added Mr. Criedir with a laugh, "last night. Now—but won't you take down what I've got to tell you?"

"I am taking it down," answered Spargo. "Every word. In my head."

Mr. Criedir laughed and rubbed his hands.

"Oh!" he said. "Ah, well, in my young days journalists used to pull out pencil and notebook at the first opportunity. But you modern young men—"

"Just so," agreed Spargo. "This information, now?"

"Well," said Mr. Criedir, "we'll go on then. Yesterday afternoon the man described as Marbury came into my shop. He—"

"What time—exact time?" asked Spargo.

"Two—to the very minute by St. Clement Danes clock," answered Mr. Criedir. "I'd swear twenty affidavits on that point. He was precisely as you've described him—dress, everything—I tell you I knew his photo as soon as I saw it. He was carrying a little box—"

"What sort of box?" said Spargo.

"A queer, old-fashioned, much-worn leather box — a very miniature trunk, in fact," replied Mr. Criedir. "About a foot square; the sort of thing you never see nowadays. It was very much worn; it attracted me for that very reason. He set it on the counter and looked at me. 'You're a dealer in stamps — rare stamps?' he said. 'I am,' I replied. 'I've something here I'd like to show you,' he said, unlocking the box. 'It's — '"

"Stop a bit," said Spargo. "Where did he take the key from with which he unlocked the box?"

"It was one of several which he carried on a split ring, and he took the bunch out of his left-hand trousers pocket," replied Mr. Criedir. "Oh, I keep my eyes open, young gentleman! Well — he opened his box. It seemed to me to be full of papers — at any rate there were a lot of legal-looking documents on the top, tied up with red tape. To show you how I notice things I saw that the papers were stained with age, and that the red tape was faded to a mere washed-out pink."

"Good — good!" murmured Spargo. "Excellent! Proceed, sir,"

"He put his hand under the topmost papers and drew out an envelope," continued Mr. Criedir. "From the envelope he produced an exceedingly rare, exceedingly valuable set of Colonial stamps — the very-first ever issued. 'I've just come from Australia,' he said. 'I promised a young friend of mine out there to sell these stamps for him in London, and as I was passing this way I caught sight of your shop. Will you buy 'em, and how much will you give for 'em?'"

"Prompt," muttered Spargo.

"He seemed to me the sort of man who doesn't waste words," agreed Mr. Criedir. "Well, there was no doubt about the stamps, nor about their great value. But I had to explain to him that I was retiring from business that very day, and did not wish to enter into even a single deal, and that, therefore, I couldn't do anything. 'No matter,' he says, 'I daresay there are lots of men in your line of trade—perhaps you can recommend me to a good firm?' 'I could recommend you to a dozen extra-good firms,' I answered. 'But I can do better for you. I'll give you the name and address of a private buyer who, I haven't the least doubt, will be very glad to buy that set from you and will give you a big price.' 'Write it down,' he says, 'and thank you for your trouble.' So I gave him a bit of advice as to the price he ought to get, and I wrote the name and address of the man I referred to on the back of one of my cards."

"Whose name and address?" asked Spargo.

"Mr. Nicholas Cardlestone, 2, Pilcox Buildings, Middle Temple Lane," replied Mr. Criedir. "Mr. Cardlestone is one of the most enthusiastic and accomplished philatelists in Europe. And I knew he didn't possess that set of stamps."

"I know Mr. Cardlestone," remarked Spargo. "It was at the foot of his stairs that Marbury was found murdered."

"Just so," said Mr. Criedir. "Which makes me think that he was going to see Mr. Cardlestone when he was set upon, murdered, and robbed."

Spargo looked fixedly at the retired stamp-dealer.

"What, going to see an elderly gentleman in his rooms in the Temple, to offer to sell him philatelic rarities at—past midnight?" he said. "I think—not much!"

"All right," replied Mr. Criedir. "You think and argue on modern lines—which are, of course, highly superior. But—how do you account for my having given Marbury Mr. Cardlestone's address and for his having been found dead—murdered—at the foot of Cardlestone's stairs a few hours later?"

"I don't account for it," said Spargo. "I'm trying to."

Mr. Criedir made no comment on this. He looked his visitor up and down for a moment; gathered some idea of his capabilities, and suddenly offered him a cigarette. Spargo accepted it with a laconic word of thanks, and smoked half-way through it before he spoke again.

"Yes," he said. "I'm trying to account. And I shall account. And I'm much obliged to you, Mr. Criedir, for what you've told me. Now, then, may I ask you a question or two?"

"A thousand!" responded Mr. Criedir with great geniality.

"Very well. Did Marbury say he'd call on Cardlestone?"

"He did. Said he'd call as soon as he could — that day."

"Have you told Cardlestone what you've just told me?"

"I have. But not until an hour ago — on my way back from your office, in fact. I met him in Fleet Street and told him."

"Had he received a call from Marbury?"

"No! Never heard of or seen the man. At least, never heard of him until he heard of the murder. He told me he and his friend, Mr. Elphick, another philatelist, went to see the body, wondering if they could recognize it as any man they'd ever known, but they couldn't."

"I know they did," said Spargo. "I saw 'em at the mortuary. Um! Well — one more question. When Marbury left you, did he put those stamps in his box again, as before?"

"No," replied Mr. Criedir. "He put them in his right-hand breast pocket, and he locked up his old box, and went off swinging it in his left hand."

Spargo went away down Fleet Street, seeing nobody. He muttered to himself, and he was still muttering when he got into his room at the office. And what he muttered was the same thing, repeated over and over again:

"Six hours — six hours — six hours! Those six hours!"

Next morning the *Watchman* came out with four leaded columns of up-to-date news about the Marbury Case, and right across the top of the four ran a heavy double line of great capitals, black and staring: —

WHO SAW JOHN MARBURY BETWEEN 3.15 P.M. AND 9.15 P.M. ON THE DAY PRECEDING HIS MURDER?

Whether Spargo was sanguine enough to expect that his staring headline would bring him information of the sort he wanted was a secret which he kept to himself. That a good many thousands of human beings must have set eyes on John Marbury between the hours which Spargo set forth in that headline was certain; the problem was — What particular owner or owners of a pair or of many pairs of those eyes would remember him? Why should they remember him? Walters and his wife had reason to remember him; Criedir had reason to remember him; so had Myerst; so had William Webster. But between a quarter past three, when he left the London and Universal Safe Deposit, and a quarter past nine, when he sat down by Webster's side in the lobby of the House of Commons, nobody seemed to have any recollection of him except Mr. Fiskie, the hatter, and he only remembered him faintly, and because Marbury had bought a fashionable cloth cap at his shop. At any rate, by noon of that day, nobody had come forward with any recollection of him. He must have gone West from seeing Myerst, because he bought his cap at Fiskie's; he must eventually have gone South-West, because he turned up at Westminster. But where else did he go? What did he do? To whom did he speak? No answer came to these questions.

"That shows," observed young Mr. Ronald Breton, lazing an hour away in Spargo's room at the *Watchman* at that particular hour which is neither noon nor afternoon, wherein even busy men do nothing, "that shows how a chap can go about London as if he were merely an ant that had strayed into another ant-heap than his own. Nobody notices."

"You'd better go and read up a little elementary entomology, Breton," said Spargo. "I don't know much about it myself, but I've a pretty good idea that when an ant walks into the highways and byways of a colony to which he doesn't belong he doesn't survive his intrusion by many seconds."

"Well, you know what I mean," said Breton. "London's an ant-heap, isn't it? One human ant more or less doesn't count. This man Marbury must have gone about a pretty tidy lot during those six hours. He'd ride on a 'bus—almost certain. He'd get into a taxi-cab—I think that's much more certain, because it would be a novelty to him. He'd want some tea—anyway, he'd be sure to want a drink, and he'd turn in somewhere to get one or the other. He'd buy things in shops—these Colonials always do. He'd go somewhere to get his dinner. He'd—but what's the use of enumeration in this case?"

"A mere piling up of platitudes," answered Spargo.

"What I mean is," continued Breton, "that piles of people must have seen him, and yet it's now hours and hours since your paper came out this morning, and nobody's come forward to tell anything. And when you come to think of it, why should they? Who'd remember an ordinary man in a grey tweed suit?"

"'An ordinary man in a grey tweed suit,'" repeated Spargo. "Good line. You haven't any copyright in it, remember. It would make a good cross-heading."

Breton laughed. "You're a queer chap, Spargo," he said. "Seriously, do you think you're getting any nearer anything?"

"I'm getting nearer something with everything that's done," Spargo answered. "You can't start on a business like this without evolving something out of it, you know."

"Well," said Breton, "to me there's not so much mystery in it. Mr. Aylmore's explained the reason why my address was found on the body; Criedir, the stamp-man, has explained—"

Spargo suddenly looked up.

"What?" he said sharply.

"Why, the reason of Marbury's being found where he was found," replied Breton. "Of course, I see it all! Marbury was mooning around Fleet Street; he slipped into Middle Temple Lane, late as it was, just to see where old Cardlestone hangs out, and he was set upon and done for. The thing's plain to me. The only thing now is to find who did it."

"Yes, that's it," agreed Spargo. "That's it." He turned over the leaves of the diary which lay on his desk. "By the by," he said, looking up with some interest, "the adjourned inquest is at eleven o'clock tomorrow morning. Are you going?"

"I shall certainly go," answered Breton. "What's more, I'm going to take Miss Aylmore and her sister. As the gruesome details were over at the first sitting, and as there'll he nothing but this new evidence tomorrow, and as they've never been in a coroner's court— —"

"Mr. Aylmore'll be the principal witness tomorrow," interrupted Spargo. "I suppose he'll be able to tell a lot more than he told — me."

Breton shrugged his shoulders.

"I don't see that there's much more to tell," he said. "But," he added, with a sly laugh, "I suppose you want some more good copy, eh?"

Spargo glanced at his watch, rose, and picked up his hat. "I'll tell you what I want," he said. "I want to know who John Marbury was. That would make good copy. Who he was — twenty — twenty-five — forty years ago. Eh?"

"And you think Mr. Aylmore can tell?" asked Breton.

"Mr. Aylmore," answered Spargo as they walked towards the door, "is the only person I have met so far who has admitted that he knew John Marbury in the — past. But he didn't tell me — much. Perhaps he'll tell the coroner and his jury — more. Now, I'm off Breton — I've an appointment."

And leaving Breton to find his own way out, Spargo hurried away, jumped into a taxi-cab and speeded to the London and Universal Safe Deposit. At the corner of its building he found Rathbury awaiting him.

"Well?" said Spargo, as he sprang out: "How is it?"

"It's all right," answered Rathbury. "You can be present: I got the necessary permission. As there are no relations known, there'll only be one or two officials and you, and the Safe Deposit people, and myself. Come on — it's about time."

"It sounds," observed Spargo, "like an exhumation."

Rathbury laughed. "Well, we're certainly going to dig up a dead man's secrets," he said. "At least, we may be going to do so. In my opinion, Mr. Spargo, we'll find some clue in this leather box."

Spargo made no answer. They entered the office, to be shown into a room where were already assembled Mr. Myerst, a gentleman who turned out to be the chairman of the company, and the officials of whom Rathbury had spoken. And in another moment Spargo heard the chairman explaining that the company possessed duplicate keys to all safes, and that the proper authorization having been received from the proper authorities, those present would now proceed to the safe recently tenanted by the late Mr. John Marbury, and take from it the property which he himself had deposited there, a small leather box, which they would afterwards bring to that room and cause to be opened in each other's presence.

It seemed to Spargo that there was an unending unlocking of bolts and bars before he and his fellow-processionists came to the safe so recently rented by the late Mr. John Marbury, now undoubtedly deceased. And at first sight of it, he saw that it was so small an affair that it seemed ludicrous to imagine that it could contain anything of any importance. In fact, it looked to be no more than a plain wooden locker, one amongst many in a small strong room: it reminded Spargo irresistibly of the locker in which, in his school days, he had kept his personal belongings and the jam tarts, sausage rolls, and hardbake smuggled in from the tuck-shop. Marbury's name had been newly painted upon it; the paint was scarcely dry. But when the wooden door — the front door, as it were, of this temple of mystery, had been solemnly opened by the chairman, a formidable door of steel was revealed, and expectation still leapt in the bosoms of the beholders.

"The duplicate key, Mr. Myerst, if you please," commanded the chairman, "the duplicate key!"

Myerst, who was fully as solemn as his principal, produced a curious-looking key: the chairman lifted his hand as if he were about to christen a battleship: the steel door swung slowly back. And there, in a two-foot square cavity, lay the leather box.

It struck Spargo as they filed back to the secretary's room that the procession became more funereal-like than ever. First walked the chairman, abreast with the high official, who had brought the necessary authorization from the all-powerful quarter; then came Myerst carrying the box: followed two other gentlemen, both legal lights, charged with watching official and police interests; Rathbury and Spargo brought up the rear. He whispered something of his notions to the detective; Rathbury nodded a comprehensive understanding.

"Let's hope we're going to see — something!" he said.

In the secretary's room a man waited who touched his forelock respectfully as the heads of the procession entered. Myerst set the box on the table: the man made a musical jingle of keys: the other members of the procession gathered round.

"As we naturally possess no key to this box," announced the chairman in grave tones, "it becomes our duty to employ professional assistance in opening it. Jobson!"

He waved a hand, and the man of the keys stepped forward with alacrity. He examined the lock of the box with a knowing eye; it was easy to see that he was anxious to fall upon it. While he considered matters, Spargo looked at the box. It was pretty much what it had been described to him as being; a small, square box of old cow-hide, very strongly made, much worn and tarnished, fitted with a handle projecting from the lid, and having the appearance of having been hidden away somewhere for many a long day.

There was a click, a spring: Jobson stepped back.

"That's it, if you please, sir," he said.

The chairman motioned to the high official.

"If you would be good enough to open the box, sir," he said. "Our duty is now concluded."

As the high official laid his hand on the lid the other men gathered round with craning necks and expectant eyes. The lid was lifted: somebody sighed deeply. And Spargo pushed his own head and eyes nearer.

The box was empty!

Empty, as anything that can be empty is empty! thought Spargo: there was literally nothing in it. They were all staring into the interior of a plain, time-worn little receptacle, lined out with old-fashioned chintz stuff, such as our Mid-Victorian fore-fathers were familiar with, and containing—nothing.

"God bless my soul!" exclaimed the chairman. "This is—dear me!—why, there is nothing in the box!"

"That," remarked the high official, drily, "appears to be obvious."

The chairman looked at the secretary.

"I understood the box was valuable, Mr. Myerst," he said, with the half-injured air of a man who considers himself to have been robbed of an exceptionally fine treat. "Valuable!"

Myerst coughed.

"I can only repeat what I have already said, Sir Benjamin," he answered. "The—er late Mr. Marbury spoke of the deposit as being of great value to him; he never permitted it out of his hand until he placed it in the safe. He appeared to regard it as of the greatest value."

"But we understand from the evidence of Mr. Criedir, given to the *Watchman* newspaper, that it was full of papers and—and other articles," said the chairman. "Criedir saw papers in it about an hour before it was brought here."

Myerst spread out his hands.

"I can only repeat what I have said, Sir Benjamin," he answered. "I know nothing more."

"But why should a man deposit an empty box?" began the chairman. "I—"

The high official interposed.

"That the box is empty is certain," he observed. "Did you ever handle it yourself, Mr. Myerst?"

Myerst smiled in a superior fashion.

"I have already observed, sir, that from the time the deceased entered this room until the moment he placed the box in the safe which he rented, the box was never out of his hands," he replied.

Then there was silence. At last the high official turned to the chairman.

"Very well," he said. "We've made the enquiry. Rathbury, take the box away with you and lock it up at the Yard."

So Spargo went out with Rathbury and the box; and saw excellent, if mystifying, material for the article which had already become the daily feature of his paper.

Chapter 11 MR. AYLMORE IS QUESTIONED

It seemed to Spargo as he sat listening to the proceedings at the adjourned inquest next day that the whole story of what was now world-famous as the Middle Temple Murder Case was being reiterated before him for the thousandth time. There was not a detail of the story with which he had not become familiar to fulness. The first proceeding before the coroner had been of a merely formal nature; these were thorough and exhaustive; the representative of the Crown and twelve good men and true of the City of London were there to hear and to find out and to arrive at a conclusion as to how the man known as John Marbury came by his death. And although he knew all about it, Spargo found himself tabulating the evidence in a professional manner, and noting how each successive witness contributed, as it were, a chapter to the story. The story itself ran quite easily, naturally, consecutively — you could make it in sections. And Spargo, sitting merely to listen, made them:

1. The Temple porter and Constable Driscoll proved the finding of the body.

2. The police surgeon testified as to the cause of death — the man had been struck down from behind by a blow, a terrible blow — from some heavy instrument, and had died immediately.

3. The police and the mortuary officials proved that when the body was examined nothing was found in the clothing but the now famous scrap of grey paper.

4. Rathbury proved that by means of the dead man's new fashionable cloth cap, bought at Fiskie's well-known shop in the West-End, he traced Marbury to the Anglo-Orient Hotel in the Waterloo District.

5. Mr. and Mrs. Walters gave evidence of the arrival of Marbury at the Anglo-Orient Hotel, and of his doings while he was in and about there.

6. The purser of the ss. *Wambarino* proved that Marbury sailed from Melbourne to Southampton on that ship, excited no remark, behaved himself like any other well-regulated passenger, and left the *Wambarino* at Southampton early in the morning of what was to be the last day of his life in just the ordinary manner.

7. Mr. Criedir gave evidence of his rencontre with Marbury in the matter of the stamps.

8. Mr. Myerst told of Marbury's visit to the Safe Deposit, and further proved that the box which he placed there proved, on official examination, to be empty.

9. William Webster re-told the story of his encounter with Marbury in one of the vestibules of the House of Commons, and of his witnessing the meeting between him and the gentleman whom he (Webster) now knew to be Mr. Aylmore, a Member of Parliament.

All this led up to the appearance of Mr. Aylmore, M.P., in the witness-box. And Spargo knew and felt that it was that appearance for which the crowded court was waiting. Thanks to his own vivid and realistic specials in the *Watchman*, everybody there had already become well and thoroughly acquainted with the mass of evidence represented by the nine witnesses who had been in the box before Mr. Aylmore entered it. They were familiar, too, with the facts which Mr. Aylmore had permitted Spargo to print after the interview at the club, which Ronald Breton arranged. Why, then, the extraordinary interest which the Member of Parliament's appearance aroused? For everybody was extraordinarily interested; from the Coroner downwards to the last man who had managed to squeeze himself into the last available inch of the public gallery, all who were there wanted to hear and see the man who met Marbury under such dramatic circumstances, and who went to his hotel with him, hobnobbed with him, gave him advice, walked out of the hotel with him for a stroll from which Marbury never returned. Spargo knew well why the interest was so keen — everybody knew that Aylmore was the only man who could tell the court anything really pertinent about Marbury; who he was, what he was after; what his life had been.

He looked round the court as the Member of Parliament entered the witness-box — a tall, handsome, perfectly-groomed man, whose beard was only slightly tinged with grey, whose figure was as erect as a well-drilled soldier's, who carried about him an air of conscious power. Aylmore's two daughters sat at a little distance away, opposite Spargo, with Ronald Breton in attendance upon them; Spargo had encountered their glance as they entered the court, and they had given him a friendly nod and smile. He had watched them from time to time; it was plain to him that they regarded the whole affair as a novel sort of entertainment; they might have been idlers in some Eastern bazaar, listening to the unfolding of many tales from the professional tale-tellers. Now, as their father entered the box, Spargo looked at them again; he saw nothing more than a little heightening of colour in their cheeks, a little brightening of their eyes.

"All that they feel," he thought, "is a bit of extra excitement at the idea that their father is mixed up in this delightful mystery. Um! Well — now how much is he mixed up?"

And he turned to the witness-box and from that moment never took his eyes off the man who now stood in it. For Spargo had ideas about the witness which he was anxious to develop.

The folk who expected something immediately sensational in Mr. Aylmore's evidence were disappointed. Aylmore, having been sworn, and asked a question or two by the Coroner, requested permission to tell, in his own way, what he knew of the dead man and of this sad affair; and having received that permission, he went on in a calm, unimpassioned manner to repeat precisely what he had told Spargo. It sounded a very plain, ordinary story. He had known Marbury many years ago. He had lost sight of him for — oh, quite twenty years. He had met him accidentally in one of the vestibules of the House of Commons on the evening preceding the murder. Marbury had asked his advice. Having no particular duty, and willing to do an old acquaintance a good turn, he had gone back to the Anglo-Orient Hotel with Marbury, had remained awhile with him in his room, examining his Australian diamonds, and had afterwards gone out with him. He had given him the advice he wanted; they had strolled across Waterloo Bridge; shortly afterwards they had parted. That was all he knew.

The court, the public, Spargo, everybody there, knew all this already. It had been in print, under a big headline, in the *Watchman*. Aylmore had now told it again; having told it, he seemed to consider that his next step was to leave the box and the court, and after a perfunctory question or two from the Coroner and the foreman of the jury he made a motion as if to step down. But Spargo, who had been aware since the beginning of the enquiry of the presence of a certain eminent counsel who represented the Treasury, cocked his eye in that gentleman's direction, and was not surprised to see him rise in his well-known, apparently indifferent fashion, fix his monocle in his right eye, and glance at the tall figure in the witness-box.

"The fun is going to begin," muttered Spargo.

The Treasury representative looked from Aylmore to the Coroner and made a jerky bow; from the Coroner to Aylmore and straightened himself. He looked like a man who is going to ask indifferent questions about the state of the weather, or how Smith's wife was last time you heard of her, or if stocks are likely to rise or fall. But Spargo had heard this man before, and he knew many signs of his in voice and manner and glance.

"I want to ask you a few questions, Mr. Aylmore, about your acquaintanceship with the dead man. It was an acquaintanceship of some time ago?" began the suave, seemingly careless voice.

"A considerable time ago," answered Aylmore.

"How long—roughly speaking?"

"I should say from twenty to twenty-two or three years."

"Never saw him during that time until you met accidentally in the way you have described to us?"

"Never."

"Ever heard from him?"

"No."

"Ever heard of him?"

"No."

"But when you met, you knew each other at once?"

"Well—almost at once."

"Almost at once. Then, I take it, you were very well known to each other twenty or twenty-two years ago?"

"We were—yes, well known to each other."

"Close friends?"

"I said we were acquaintances."

"Acquaintances. What was his name when you knew him at that time?"

"His name? It was — Marbury."

"Marbury — the same name. Where did you know him?"

"I — oh, here in London."

"What was he?"

"Do you mean — what was his occupation?"

"What was his occupation?"

"I believe he was concerned in financial matters."

"Concerned in financial matters. Had you dealings with him?"

"Well, yes — on occasions."

"What was his business address in London?"

"I can't remember that."

"What was his private address?"

"That I never knew."

"Where did you transact your business with him?"

"Well, we met, now and then."

"Where? What place, office, resort?"

"I can't remember particular places. Sometimes — in the City."

"In the City. Where in the City? Mansion House, or Lombard Street, or St. Paul's Churchyard, or the Old Bailey, or where?"

"I have recollections of meeting him outside the Stock Exchange."

"Oh! Was he a member of that institution?"

"Not that I know of."

"Were you?"

"Certainly not!"

"What were the dealings that you had with him?"

"Financial dealings — small ones."

"How long did your acquaintanceship with him last — what period did it extend over?"

"I should say about six months to nine months."

"No more?"

"Certainly no more."

"It was quite a slight acquaintanceship, then?"

"Oh, quite!"

"And yet, after losing sight of this merely slight acquaintance for over twenty years, you, on meeting him, take great interest in him?"

"Well, I was willing to do him a good turn, I was interested in what he told me the other evening."

"I see. Now you will not object to my asking you a personal question or two. You are a public man, and the facts about the lives of public men are more or less public property. You are represented in this work of popular reference as coming to this country in 1902, from Argentina, where you made a considerable fortune. You have told us, however, that you were in London, acquainted with Marbury, about the years, say 1890 to 1892. Did you then leave England soon after knowing Marbury?"

"I did. I left England in 1891 or 1892—I am not sure which."

"We are wanting to be very sure about this matter, Mr. Aylmore. We want to solve the important question—who is, who was John Marbury, and how did he come by his death? You seem to be the only available person who knows anything about him. What was your business before you left England?"

"I was interested in financial affairs."

"Like Marbury. Where did you carry on your business?"

"In London, of course."

"At what address?"

For some moments Aylmore had been growing more and more restive. His brow had flushed; his moustache had begun to twitch. And now he squared his shoulders and faced his questioner defiantly.

"I resent these questions about my private affairs!" he snapped out.

"Possibly. But I must put them. I repeat my last question."

"And I refuse to answer it."

"Then I ask you another. Where did you live in London at the time you are telling us of, when you knew John Marbury?"

"I refuse to answer that question also!"

The Treasury Counsel sat down and looked at the Coroner.

The voice of the Coroner, bland, suave, deprecating, broke the silence. He was addressing the witness.

"I am sure, Mr. Aylmore," he said, "there is no wish to trouble you with unnecessary questions. But we are here to get at the truth of this matter of John Marbury's death, and as you are the only witness we have had who knew him personally —"

Aylmore turned impatiently to the Coroner.

"I have every wish to respect your authority, sir!" he exclaimed. "And I have told you all that I know of Marbury and of what happened when I met him the other evening. But I resent being questioned on my private affairs of twenty years ago — I very much resent it! Any question that is really pertinent I will answer, but I will not answer questions that seem to me wholly foreign to the scope of this enquiry."

The Treasury Counsel rose again. His manner had become of the quietest, and Spargo again became keenly attentive.

"Perhaps I can put a question or two to Mr. Aylmore which will not yield him offence," he remarked drily. He turned once more to the witness, regarding him as if with interest. "Can you tell us of any person now living who knew Marbury in London at the time under discussion — twenty to twenty-two or three years ago?" he asked.

Aylmore shook his head angrily.

"No, I can't," he replied.

"And yet you and he must have had several business acquaintances at that time who knew you both!"

"Possibly — at that time. But when I returned to England my business and my life lay in different directions to those of that time. I don't know of anybody who knew Marbury then — anybody."

The Counsel turned to a clerk who sat behind him, whispered to him; Spargo saw the clerk make a sidelong motion of his head towards the door of the court. The Counsel looked again at the witness.

"One more question. You told the court a little time since that you parted with Marbury on the evening preceding his death at the end of Waterloo Bridge—at, I think you said, a quarter to twelve."

"About that time."

"And at that place?"

"Yes."

"That is all I want to ask you, Mr. Aylmore—just now," said the Counsel. He turned to the Coroner. "I am going to ask you, sir, at this point to call a witness who has volunteered certain evidence to the police authorities this morning. That evidence is of a very important nature, and I think that this is the stage at which it ought to be given to you and the jury. If you would be pleased to direct that David Lyell be called—"

Spargo turned instinctively to the door, having seen the clerk who had sat behind the Treasury Counsel make his way there. There came into view, ushered by the clerk, a smart-looking, alert, self-confident young man, evidently a Scotsman, who, on the name of David Lyell being called, stepped jauntily and readily into the place which the member of Parliament just vacated. He took the oath—Scotch fashion—with the same readiness and turned easily to the Treasury Counsel. And Spargo, glancing quickly round, saw that the court was breathless with anticipation, and that its anticipation was that the new witness was going to tell something which related to the evidence just given by Aylmore.

"Your name is David Lyell?"

"That is my name, sir."

"And you reside at 23, Cumbrae Side, Kilmarnock, Scotland?"

"I do."

"What are you, Mr. Lyell?"

"Traveller, sir, for the firm of Messrs. Stevenson, Robertson & Soutar, distillers, of Kilmarnock."

"Your duties take you, I think, over to Paris occasionally?"

"They do—once every six weeks I go to Paris."

"On the evening of June 21st last were you in London on your way to Paris?"

"I was."

"I believe you stayed at De Keyser's Hotel, at the Blackfriars end of the Embankment?"

"I did — it's handy for the continental trains."

"About half-past eleven, or a little later, that evening, did you go along the Embankment, on the Temple Gardens side, for a walk?"

"I did, sir. I'm a bad sleeper, and it's a habit of mine to take a walk of half an hour or so last thing before I go to bed."

"How far did you walk?"

"As far as Waterloo Bridge."

"Always on the Temple side?"

"Just so, sir — straight along on that side."

"Very good. When you got close to Waterloo Bridge, did you meet anybody you knew?"

"Yes."

"Mr. Aylmore, the Member of Parliament."

Spargo could not avoid a glance at the two sisters. The elder's head was averted; the younger was staring at the witness steadily. And Breton was nervously tapping his fingers on the crown of his shining silk hat.

"Mr. Aylmore, the Member of Parliament," repeated the Counsel's suave, clear tones. "Oh! And how did you come to recognize Mr. Aylmore, Member of Parliament?"

"Well, sir, in this way. At home, I'm the secretary of our Liberal Ward Club, and last year we had a demonstration, and it fell to me to arrange with the principal speakers. I got Mr. Aylmore to come and speak, and naturally I met him several times, in London and in Scotland."

"So that you knew him quite well?"

"Oh yes, sir."

"Do you see him now, Mr. Lyell?"

Lyell smiled and half turned in the box.

"Why, of course!" he answered. "There is Mr. Aylmore."

"There is Mr. Aylmore. Very good. Now we go on. You met Mr. Aylmore close to Waterloo Bridge? How close?"

"Well, sir, to be exact, Mr. Aylmore came down the steps from the bridge on to the Embankment."

"Alone?"

"No."

"Who was with him?"

"A man, sir."

"Did you know the man?"

"No. But seeing who he was with. I took a good look at him. I haven't forgotten his face."

"You haven't forgotten his face. Mr. Lyell—has anything recalled that face to you within this last day or two?"

"Yes, sir, indeed!"

"What?"

"The picture of the man they say was murdered—John Marbury."

"You're sure of that?"

"I'm as certain, sir, as that my name's what it is."

"It is your belief that Mr. Aylmore, when you met him, was accompanied by the man who, according to the photographs, was John Marbury?"

"It is, sir!"

"Very well. Now, having seen Mr. Aylmore and his companion, what did you do?"

"Oh, I just turned and walked after them."

"You walked after them? They were going eastward, then?"

"They were walking by the way I'd come."

"You followed them eastward?"

"I did—I was going back to the hotel, you see."

"What were they doing?"

"Talking uncommonly earnestly, sir."

"How far did you follow them?"

"I followed them until they came to the Embankment lodge of Middle Temple Lane, sir."

"And then?"

"Why, sir, they turned in there, and I went straight on to De Keyser's, and to my bed."

There was a deeper silence in court at that moment than at any other period of the long day, and it grew still deeper when the quiet, keen voice put the next question.

"You swear on your oath that you saw Mr. Aylmore take his companion into the Temple by the Embankment entrance of Middle Temple Lane on the occasion in question?"

"I do! I could swear no other, sir."

"Can you tell us, as near as possible, what time that would be?"

"Yes. It was, to a minute or so, about five minutes past twelve."

The Treasury Counsel nodded to the Coroner, and the Coroner, after a whispered conference with the foreman of the jury, looked at the witness.

"You have only just given this information to the police, I understand?" he said.

"Yes, sir. I have been in Paris, and in Amiens, and I only returned by this morning's boat. As soon as I had read all the news in the papers — the English papers — and seen the dead man's photographs I determined to tell the police what I knew, and I went to New Scotland Yard as soon as I got to London this morning."

Nobody else wanted to ask Mr. David Lyell any questions, and he stepped down. And Mr. Aylmore suddenly came forward again, seeking the Coroner's attention.

"May I be allowed to make an explanation, sir?" he began. "I — "

But the Treasury Counsel was on his feet, this time stern and implacable. "I would point out, sir, that you have had Mr. Aylmore in the box, and that he was not then at all ready to give explanations, or even to answer questions," he said. "And before you allow him to make any explanation now, I ask you to hear another witness whom I wish to interpose at this stage. That witness is — — "

Mr. Aylmore turned almost angrily to the Coroner.

"After the evidence of the last witness, I think I have a right to be heard at once!" he said with emphasis. "As matters stand at present, it looks as if I had trifled, sir, with you and the jury, whereas if I am allowed to make an explanation — "

"I must respectfully ask that before Mr. Aylmore is allowed to make any explanation, the witness I have referred to is heard," said the Treasury Counsel sternly. "There are weighty reasons."

"I am afraid you must wait a little, Mr. Aylmore, if you wish to give an explanation," said the Coroner. He turned to the Counsel. "Who is this other witness?" he asked.

Aylmore stepped back. And Spargo noticed that the younger of his two daughters was staring at him with an anxious expression. There was no distrust of her father in her face; she was anxious. She, too, slowly turned to the next witness. This man was the porter of the Embankment lodge of Middle Temple Lane. The Treasury Counsel put a straight question to him at once.

"You see that gentleman," he said, pointing to Aylmore. "Do you know him as an inmate of the Temple?"

The man stared at Aylmore, evidently confused.

"Why, certainly, sir!" he answered. "Quite well, sir."

"Very good. And now—what name do you know him by?"

The man grew evidently more bewildered.

"Name, sir. Why, Mr. Anderson, sir!" he replied. "Mr. Anderson!"

A distinct, uncontrollable murmur of surprise ran round the packed court as this man in the witness-box gave this answer. It signified many things — that there were people present who had expected some such dramatic development; that there were others present who had not; that the answer itself was only a prelude to further developments. And Spargo, looking narrowly about him, saw that the answer had aroused different feelings in Aylmore's two daughters. The elder one had dropped her face until it was quite hidden; the younger was sitting bolt upright, staring at her father in utter and genuine bewilderment. And for the first time, Aylmore made no response to her.

But the course of things was going steadily forward. There was no stopping the Treasury Counsel now; he was going to get at some truth in his own merciless fashion. He had exchanged one glance with the Coroner, had whispered a word to the solicitor who sat close by him, and now he turned again to the witness.

"So you know that gentleman — make sure now — as Mr. Anderson, an inmate of the Temple?"

"Yes, sir."

"You don't know him by any other name?"

"No, sir, I don't."

"How long have you known him by that name?"

"I should say two or three years, sir."

"See him go in and out regularly?"

"No, sir — not regularly."

"How often, then?"

"Now and then, sir — perhaps once a week."

"Tell us what you know of Mr. Anderson's goings-in-and-out."

"Well, sir, I might see him two nights running; then I mightn't see him again for perhaps a week or two. Irregular, as you might say, sir."

"You say 'nights.' Do I understand that you never see Mr. Anderson except at night?"

"Yes, sir. I've never seen him except at night. Always about the same time, sir."

"What time?"

"Just about midnight, sir."

"Very well. Do you remember the midnight of June 21st-22nd?"

"I do, sir."

"Did you see Mr. Anderson enter then?"

"Yes, sir, just after twelve."

"Was he alone?"

"No, sir; there was another gentleman with him."

"Remember anything about that other gentleman?"

"Nothing, sir, except that I noticed as they walked through, that the other gentleman had grey clothes on."

"Had grey clothes on. You didn't see his face?"

"Not to remember it, sir. I don't remember anything but what I've told you, sir."

"That is that the other gentleman wore a grey suit. Where did Mr. Anderson and this gentleman in the grey suit go when they'd passed through?"

"Straight up the Lane, sir."

"Do you know where Mr. Anderson's rooms in the Temple are?"

"Not exactly, sir, but I understood in Fountain Court."

"Now, on that night in question, did Mr. Anderson leave again by your lodge?"

"No, sir."

"You heard of the discovery of the body of a dead man in Middle Temple Lane next morning?"

"I did, sir."

"Did you connect that man with the gentleman in the grey suit?"

"No, sir, I didn't. It never occurred to me. A lot of the gentlemen who live in the Temple bring friends in late of nights; I never gave the matter any particular thought."

"Never mentioned it to anybody until now, when you were sent for to come here?"

"No, sir, never, to anybody."

"And you have never known the gentleman standing there as anybody but Mr. Anderson?"

"No, sir, never heard any other name but Anderson."

The Coroner glanced at the Counsel.

"I think this may be a convenient opportunity for Mr. Aylmore to give the explanation he offered a few minutes ago," he said. "Do you suggest anything?"

"I suggest, sir, that if Mr. Aylmore desires to give any explanation he should return to the witness-box and submit himself to examination again on his oath," replied the Counsel. "The matter is in your hands."

The Coroner turned to Aylmore.

"Do you object to that?" he asked.

Aylmore stepped boldly forward and into the box.

"I object to nothing," he said in clear tones, "except to being asked to reply to questions about matters of the past which have not and cannot have anything to do with this case. Ask me what questions you like, arising out of the evidence of the last two witnesses, and I will answer them so far as I see myself justified in doing so. Ask me questions about matters of twenty years ago, and I shall answer them or not as I see fit. And I may as well say that I will take all the consequences of my silence or my speech."

The Treasury Counsel rose again.

"Very well, Mr. Aylmore," he said. "I will put certain questions to you. You heard the evidence of David Lyell?"

"I did."

"Was that quite true as regards yourself?"

"Quite true — absolutely true."

"And you heard that of the last witness. Was that also true!"

"Equally true."

"Then you admit that the evidence you gave this morning, before these witnesses came on the scene, was not true?"

"No, I do not! Most emphatically I do not. It was true."

"True? You told me, on oath, that you parted from John Marbury on Waterloo Bridge!"

"Pardon me, I said nothing of the sort. I said that from the Anglo-Orient Hotel we strolled across Waterloo Bridge, and that shortly afterwards we parted — I did not say where we parted. I see there is a shorthand writer here who is taking everything down — ask him if that is not exactly what I said?"

A reference to the stenographer proved Aylmore to be right, and the Treasury Counsel showed plain annoyance.

"Well, at any rate, you so phrased your answer that nine persons out of ten would have understood that you parted from Marbury in the open streets after crossing Waterloo Bridge," he said. "Now — ?"

Aylmore smiled.

"I am not responsible for the understanding of nine people out of ten any more than I am for your understanding," he said, with a sneer. "I said what I now repeat — Marbury and I walked across Waterloo Bridge, and shortly afterwards we parted. I told you the truth."

"Indeed! Perhaps you will continue to tell us the truth. Since you have admitted that the evidence of the last two witnesses is absolutely correct, perhaps you will tell us exactly where you and Marbury did part?"

"I will — willingly. We parted at the door of my chambers in Fountain Court."

"Then — to reiterate — it was you who took Marbury into the Temple that night?"

"It was certainly I who took Marbury into the Temple that night."

There was another murmur amongst the crowded benches. Here at any rate was fact — solid, substantial fact. And Spargo began to see a possible course of events which he had not anticipated.

"That is a candid admission, Mr. Aylmore. I suppose you see a certain danger to yourself in making it."

"I need not say whether I do or I do not. I have made it."

"Very good. Why did you not make it before?"

"For my own reasons. I told you as much as I considered necessary for the purpose of this enquiry. I have virtually altered nothing now. I asked to be allowed to make a statement, to give an explanation, as soon as Mr. Lyell had left this box: I was not allowed to do so. I am willing to make it now."

"Make it then."

"It is simply this," said Aylmore, turning to the Coroner. "I have found it convenient, during the past three years, to rent a simple set of chambers in the Temple, where I could occasionally — very occasionally, as a rule — go late at night. I also found it convenient, for my own reasons — with which, I think, no one has anything to do — to rent those chambers under the name of Mr. Anderson. It was to my chambers that Marbury accompanied me for a few moments on the midnight with which we are dealing. He was not in them more than five minutes at the very outside: I parted from him at my outer door, and I understood that he would leave the Temple by the way we had entered and would drive or walk straight back to his hotel. That is the whole truth. I wish to add that I ought perhaps to have told all this at first. I had reasons for not doing so. I told what I considered necessary, that I parted from Marbury, leaving him well and alive, soon after midnight."

"What reasons were or are they which prevented you from telling all this at first?" asked the Treasury Counsel.

"Reasons which are private to me."

"Will you tell them to the court?"

"No!"

"Then will you tell us why Marbury went with you to the chambers in Fountain Court which you tenant under the name of Anderson?"

"Yes. To fetch a document which I had in my keeping, and had kept for him for twenty years or more."

"A document of importance?"

"Of very great importance."

"He would have it on him when he was — as we believe he was — murdered and robbed?"

"He had it on him when he left me."

"Will you tell us what it was?"

"Certainly not!"

"In fact, you won't tell us any more than you choose to tell?"

"I have told you all I can tell of the events of that night."

"Then I am going to ask you a very pertinent question. Is it not a fact that you know a great deal more about John Marbury than you have told this court?"

"That I shall not answer."

"Is it not a fact that you could, if you would, tell this court more about John Marbury and your acquaintanceship with him twenty years ago?"

"I also decline to answer that."

The Treasury Counsel made a little movement of his shoulders and turned to the Coroner.

"I should suggest, sir, that you adjourn this enquiry," he said quietly.

"For a week," assented the Coroner, turning to the jury.

The crowd surged out of the court, chattering, murmuring, exclaiming— spectators, witnesses, jurymen, reporters, legal folk, police folk, all mixed up together. And Spargo, elbowing his own way out, and busily reckoning up the value of the new complexions put on everything by the day's work, suddenly felt a hand laid on his arm. Turning he found himself gazing at Jessie Aylmore.

Chapter 14 THE SILVER TICKET

With a sudden instinct of protection, Spargo quickly drew the girl aside from the struggling crowd, and within a moment had led her into a quiet by-street. He looked down at her as she stood recovering her breath.

"Yes?" he said quietly.

Jessie Aylmore looked up at him, smiling faintly.

"I want to speak to you," she said. "I must speak to you."

"Yes," said Spargo. "But—the others? Your sister?—Breton?"

"I left them on purpose to speak to you," she answered. "They knew I did. I am well accustomed to looking after myself."

Spargo moved down the by-street, motioning his companion to move with him.

"Tea," he said, "is what you want. I know a queer, old-fashioned place close by here where you can get the best China tea in London. Come and have some."

Jessie Aylmore smiled and followed her guide obediently. And Spargo said nothing, marching stolidly along with his thumbs in his waistcoat pockets, his fingers playing soundless tunes outside, until he had installed himself and his companion in a quiet nook in the old tea-house he had told her of, and had given an order for tea and hot tea-cakes to a waitress who evidently knew him. Then he turned to her.

"You want," he said, "to talk to me about your father."

"Yes," she answered. "I do."

"Why?" asked Spargo.

The girl gave him a searching look.

"Ronald Breton says you're the man who's written all those special articles in the *Watchman* about the Marbury case," she answered. "Are you?"

"I am," said Spargo.

"Then you're a man of great influence," she went on. "You can stir the public mind. Mr. Spargo—what are you going to write about my father and today's proceedings?"

Spargo signed to her to pour out the tea which had just arrived. He seized, without ceremony, upon a piece of the hot buttered tea-cake, and bit a great lump out of it.

"Frankly," he mumbled, speaking with his mouth full, "frankly, I don't know. I don't know—yet. But I'll tell you this—it's best to be candid—I shouldn't allow myself to be prejudiced or biassed in making up my conclusions by anything that you may say to me. Understand?"

Jessie Aylmore took a sudden liking to Spargo because of the unconventionality and brusqueness of his manners.

"I'm not wanting to prejudice or bias you," she said. "All I want is that you should be very sure before you say—anything."

"I'll be sure," said Spargo. "Don't bother. Is the tea all right?"

"Beautiful!" she answered, with a smile that made Spargo look at her again. "Delightful! Mr. Spargo, tell me!—what did you think about—about what has just happened?"

Spargo, regardless of the fact that his fingers were liberally ornamented with butter, lifted a hand and rubbed his always untidy hair. Then he ate more tea-cake and gulped more tea.

"Look here!" he said suddenly. "I'm no great hand at talking. I can write pretty decently when I've a good story to tell, but I don't talk an awful lot, because I never can express what I mean unless I've got a pen in my hand. Frankly, I find it hard to tell you what I think. When I write my article this evening, I'll get all these things marshalled in proper form, and I shall write clearly about 'em. But I'll tell you one thing I do think—I wish your father had made a clean breast of things to me at first, when he gave me that interview, or had told everything when he first went into that box."

"Why?" she asked.

"Because he's now set up an atmosphere of doubt and suspicion around himself. People'll think—Heaven knows what they'll think! They already know that he knows more about Marbury than he'll tell, that—"

"But does he?" she interrupted quickly. "Do you think he does?"

"Yes!" replied Spargo, with emphasis. "I do. A lot more! If he had only been explicit at first—however, he wasn't. Now it's done. As things stand—look here, does it strike you that your father is in a very serious position?"

"Serious?" she exclaimed.

"Dangerous! Here's the fact—he's admitted that he took Marbury to his rooms in the Temple that midnight. Well, next morning Marbury's found robbed and murdered in an entry, not fifty yards off!"

"Does anybody suppose that my father would murder him for the sake of robbing him of whatever he had on him?" she laughed scornfully. "My father is a very wealthy man, Mr. Spargo."

"May be," answered Spargo. "But millionaires have been known to murder men who held secrets."

"Secrets!" she exclaimed.

"Have some more tea," said Spargo, nodding at the teapot. "Look here—this way it is. The theory that people—some people—will build up (I won't say that it hasn't suggested itself to me) is this:—There's some mystery about the relationship, acquaintanceship, connection, call it what you like, of your father and Marbury twenty odd years ago. Must be. There's some mystery about your father's life, twenty odd years ago. Must be—or else he'd have answered those questions. Very well. 'Ha, ha!' says the general public. 'Now we have it!' 'Marbury,' says the general public, 'was a man who had a hold on Aylmore. He turned up. Aylmore trapped him into the Temple, killed him to preserve his own secret, and robbed him of all he had on him as a blind.' Eh?"

"You think—people will say that?" she exclaimed.

"Cock-sure! They're saying it. Heard half a dozen of 'em say it, in more or less elegant fashion as I came out of that court. Of course, they'll say it. Why, what else could they say?"

For a moment Jessie Aylmore sat looking silently into her tea-cup. Then she turned her eyes on Spargo, who immediately manifested a new interest in what remained of the tea-cakes.

"Is that what you're going to say in your article tonight?" she asked, quietly.

"No!" replied Spargo, promptly. "It isn't. I'm going to sit on the fence tonight. Besides, the case is *sub judice*. All I'm going to do is to tell, in my way, what took place at the inquest."

The girl impulsively put her hand across the table and laid it on Spargo's big fist.

"Is it what you think?" she asked in a low voice.

"Honour bright, no!" exclaimed Spargo. "It isn't—it isn't! I don't think it. I think there's a most extraordinary mystery at the bottom of Marbury's death, and I think your father knows an enormous lot about Marbury that he won't tell, but I'm certain sure that he neither killed Marbury nor knows anything whatever about his death. And as I'm out to clear this mystery up, and mean to do it, nothing'll make me more glad than to clear your father. I say, do have some more tea-cake? We'll have fresh ones—and fresh tea."

"No, thank you," she said smiling. "And thank you for what you've just said. I'm going now, Mr. Spargo. You've done me good."

"Oh, rot!" exclaimed Spargo. "Nothing—nothing! I've just told you what I'm thinking. You must go?… "

He saw her into a taxi-cab presently, and when she had gone stood vacantly staring after the cab until a hand clapped him smartly on the shoulder. Turning, he found Rathbury grinning at him.

"All right, Mr. Spargo, I saw you!" he said. "Well, it's a pleasant change to squire young ladies after being all day in that court. Look here, are you going to start your writing just now?"

"I'm not going to start my writing as you call it, until after I've dined at seven o'clock and given myself time to digest my modest dinner," answered Spargo. "What is it?"

"Come back with me and have another look at that blessed leather box," said Rathbury. "I've got it in my room, and I'd like to examine it for myself. Come on!"

"The thing's empty," said Spargo.

"There might be a false bottom in it," remarked Rathbury. "One never knows. Here, jump into this!"

He pushed Spargo into a passing taxi-cab, and following, bade the driver go straight to the Yard. Arrived there, he locked Spargo and himself into the drab-visaged room in which the journalist had seen him before.

"What d'ye think of today's doings, Spargo?" he asked, as he proceeded to unlock a cupboard.

"I think," said Spargo, "that some of you fellows must have had your ears set to tingling."

"That's so," assented Rathbury. "Of course, the next thing'll be to find out all about the Mr. Aylmore of twenty years since. When a man won't tell you where he lived twenty years ago, what he was exactly doing, what his precise relationship with another man was—why, then, you've just got to find out, eh? Oh, some of our fellows are at work on the life history of Stephen Aylmore, Esq., M.P., already—you bet! Well, now, Spargo, here's the famous box."

The detective brought the old leather case out of the cupboard in which he had been searching, and placed it on his desk. Spargo threw back the lid and looked inside, measuring the inner capacity against the exterior lines.

"No false bottom in that, Rathbury," he said. "There's just the outer leather case, and the inner lining, of this old bed-hanging stuff, and that's all. There's no room for any false bottom or anything of that sort, d'you see?"

Rathbury also sized up the box's capacity.

"Looks like it," he said disappointedly. "Well, what about the lid, then? I remember there was an old box like this in my grandmother's farmhouse, where I was reared—there was a pocket in the lid. Let's see if there's anything of the sort here?"

He threw the lid back and began to poke about the lining of it with the tips of his fingers, and presently he turned to his companion with a sharp exclamation.

"By George, Spargo!" he said. "I don't know about any pocket, but there's something under this lining. Feels like—here, you feel. There—and there."

Spargo put a finger on the places indicated.

"Yes, that's so," he agreed. "Feels like two cards—a large and a small one. And the small one's harder than the other. Better cut that lining out, Rathbury."

"That," remarked Rathbury, producing a pen-knife, "is just what I'm going to do. We'll cut along this seam."

He ripped the lining carefully open along the upper part of the lining of the lid, and looking into the pocket thus made, drew out two objects which he dropped on his blotting pad.

"A child's photograph," he said, glancing at one of them. "But what on earth is that?"

The object to which he pointed was a small, oblong piece of thin, much-worn silver, about the size of a railway ticket. On one side of it was what seemed to be a heraldic device or coat-of-arms, almost obliterated by rubbing; on the other, similarly worn down by friction, was the figure of a horse.

"That's a curious object," remarked Spargo, picking it up. "I never saw anything like that before. What can it be?"

"Don't know — I never saw anything of the sort either," said Rathbury. "Some old token, I should say. Now this photo. Ah — you see, the photographer's name and address have been torn away or broken off — there's nothing left but just two letters of what's apparently been the name of the town — see. Er — that's all there is. Portrait of a baby, eh?"

Spargo gave, what might have been called in anybody else but him, a casual glance at the baby's portrait. He picked up the silver ticket again and turned it over and over.

"Look here, Rathbury," he said. "Let me take this silver thing. I know where I can find out what it is. At least, I think I do."

"All right," agreed the detective, "but take the greatest care of it, and don't tell a soul that we found it in this box, you know. No connection with the Marbury case, Spargo, remember."

"Oh, all right," said Spargo. "Trust me."

He put the silver ticket in his pocket, and went back to the office, wondering about this singular find. And when he had written his article that evening, and seen a proof of it, Spargo went into Fleet Street intent on seeking peculiar information.

Chapter 15 MARKET MILCASTER

The haunt of well-informed men which Spargo had in view when he turned out of the *Watchman* office lay well hidden from ordinary sight and knowledge in one of those Fleet Street courts the like of which is not elsewhere in the world. Only certain folk knew of it. It was, of course, a club; otherwise it would not have been what it was. It is the simplest thing in life, in England, at any rate, to form a club of congenial spirits. You get so many of your choice friends and acquaintances to gather round you; you register yourselves under a name of your own choosing; you take a house and furnish it according to your means and your taste: you comply with the very easy letter of the law, and there you are. Keep within that easy letter, and you can do what you please on your own premises. It is much more agreeable to have a small paradise of your own of this description than to lounge about Fleet Street bars.

The particular club to which Spargo bent his steps was called the Octoneumenoi. Who evolved this extraordinary combination of Latin and Greek was a dark mystery: there it was, however, on a tiny brass plate you once reached the portals. The portals were gained by devious ways. You turned out of Fleet Street by an alley so narrow that it seemed as if you might suddenly find yourself squeezed between the ancient walls. Then you suddenly dived down another alley and found yourself in a small court, with high walls around you and a smell of printer's ink in your nose and a whirring of printing presses in your ears. You made another dive into a dark entry, much encumbered by bales of paper, crates of printing material, jars of printing ink; after falling over a few of these you struck an ancient flight of stairs and went up past various landings, always travelling in a state of gloom and fear. After a lot of twisting and turning you came to the very top of the house and found it heavily curtained off. You lifted a curtain and found yourself in a small entresol, somewhat artistically painted — the whole and sole work of an artistic member who came one day with a formidable array of lumber and paint-pots and worked his will on the ancient wood. Then you saw the brass plate and its fearful name, and beneath it the formal legal notice that this club was duly registered and so on, and if you were a member you went in, and if you weren't a member you tinkled an electric bell and asked to see a member — if you knew one.

Spargo was not a member, but he knew many members, and he tinkled the bell, and asked the boy who answered it for Mr. Starkey. Mr. Starkey, a young gentleman with the biceps of a prize-fighter and a head of curly hair that would have done credit to Antinous, came forth in due course and shook Spargo by the hand until his teeth rattled.

"Had we known you were coming," said Mr. Starkey, "we'd have had a brass band on the stairs."

"I want to come in," remarked Spargo.

"Sure!" said Mr. Starkey. "That's what you've come for."

"Well, stand out of the way, then, and let's get in," said Spargo. "Look here," he continued when they had penetrated into a small vestibule, "doesn't old Crowfoot turn in here about this time every night?"

"Every night as true as the clock, my son Spargo, Crowfoot puts his nose in at precisely eleven, having by that time finished that daily column wherein he informs a section of the populace as to the prospects of their spotting a winner tomorrow," answered Mr. Starkey. "It's five minutes to his hour now. Come in and drink till he comes. Want him?"

"A word with him," answered Spargo. "A mere word — or two."

He followed Starkey into a room which was so filled with smoke and sound that for a moment it was impossible to either see or hear. But the smoke was gradually making itself into a canopy, and beneath the canopy Spargo made out various groups of men of all ages, sitting around small tables, smoking and drinking, and all talking as if the great object of their lives was to get as many words as possible out of their mouths in the shortest possible time. In the further corner was a small bar; Starkey pulled Spargo up to it.

"Name it, my son," commanded Starkey. "Try the Octoneumenoi very extra special. Two of 'em, Dick. Come to beg to be a member, Spargo?"

"I'll think about being a member of this ante-room of the infernal regions when you start a ventilating fan and provide members with a route-map of the way from Fleet Street," answered Spargo, taking his glass. "Phew! — what an atmosphere!"

"We're considering a ventilating fan," said Starkey. "I'm on the house committee now, and I brought that very matter up at our last meeting. But Templeson, of the *Bulletin* — you know Templeson — he says what we want is a wine-cooler to stand under that sideboard — says no club is proper without a wine-cooler, and that he knows a chap — second-hand dealer, don't you know — what has a beauty to dispose of in old Sheffield plate. Now, if you were on our house committee, Spargo, old man, would you go in for the wine-cooler or the ventilating fan? You see — "

"There is Crowfoot," said Spargo. "Shout him over here, Starkey, before anybody else collars him."

Through the door by which Spargo had entered a few minutes previously came a man who stood for a moment blinking at the smoke and the lights. He was a tall, elderly man with a figure and bearing of a soldier; a big, sweeping moustache stood well out against a square-cut jaw and beneath a prominent nose; a pair of keen blue eyes looked out from beneath a tousled mass of crinkled hair. He wore neither hat nor cap; his attire was a carelessly put on Norfolk suit of brown tweed; he looked half-unkempt, half-groomed. But knotted at the collar of his flannel shirt were the colours of one of the most famous and exclusive cricket clubs in the world, and everybody knew that in his day their wearer had been a mighty figure in the public eye.

"Hi, Crowfoot!" shouted Starkey above the din and babel. "Crowfoot, Crowfoot! Come over here, there's a chap dying to see you!"

"Yes, that's the way to get him, isn't it?" said Spargo. "Here, I'll get him myself."

He went across the room and accosted the old sporting journalist.

"I want a quiet word with you," he said. "This place is like a pandemonium."

Crowfoot led the way into a side alcove and ordered a drink.

"Always is, this time," he said, yawning. "But it's companionable. What is it, Spargo?"

Spargo took a pull at the glass which he had carried with him. "I should say," he said, "that you know as much about sporting matters as any man writing about 'em?"

"Well, I think you might say it with truth," answered Crowfoot.

"And old sporting matters?" said Spargo.

"Yes, and old sporting matters," replied the other with a sudden flash of the eye. "Not that they greatly interest the modern generation, you know."

"Well, there's something that's interesting me greatly just now, anyway," said Spargo. "And I believe it's got to do with old sporting affairs. And I came to you for information about it, believing you to be the only man I know of that could tell anything."

"Yes—what is it?" asked Crowfoot.

Spargo drew out an envelope, and took from it the carefully-wrapped-up silver ticket. He took off the wrappings and laid the ticket on Crowfoot's outstretched palm.

"Can you tell me what that is?" he asked.

Another sudden flash came into the old sportsman's eyes—he eagerly turned the silver ticket over.

"God bless my soul!" he exclaimed. "Where did you get this?"

"Never mind, just now," replied Spargo. "You know what it is?"

"Certainly I know what it is! But—Gad! I've not seen one of these things for Lord knows how many years. It makes me feel something like a young 'un again!" said Crowfoot. "Quite a young 'un!"

"But what is it?" asked Spargo.

Crowfoot turned the ticket over, showing the side on which the heraldic device was almost worn away.

"It's one of the original silver stand tickets of the old racecourse at Market Milcaster," answered Crowfoot. "That's what it is. One of the old original silver stand tickets. There are the arms of Market Milcaster, you see, nearly worn away by much rubbing. There, on the obverse, is the figure of a running horse. Oh, yes, that's what it is! Bless me!—most interesting."

"Where's Market Milcaster?" enquired Spargo. "Don't know it."

"Market Milcaster," replied Crowfoot, still turning the silver ticket over and over, "is what the topographers call a decayed town in Elmshire. It has steadily decayed since the river that led to it got gradually silted up. There used to be a famous race-meeting there in June every year. It's nearly forty years since that meeting fell through. I went to it often when I was a lad—often!"

"And you say that's a ticket for the stand?" asked Spargo.

"This is one of fifty silver tickets, or passes, or whatever you like to call 'em, which were given by the race committee to fifty burgesses of the town," answered Crowfoot. "It was, I remember, considered a great privilege to possess a silver ticket. It admitted its possessor—for life, mind you!—to the stand, the paddocks, the ring, anywhere. It also gave him a place at the annual race-dinner. Where on earth did you get this, Spargo?"

Spargo took the ticket and carefully re-wrapped it, this time putting it in his purse.

"I'm awfully obliged to you, Crowfoot," he said, "The fact is, I can't tell you where I got it just now, but I'll promise you that I will tell you, and all about it, too, as soon as my tongue's free to do so."

"Some mystery, eh?" suggested Crowfoot.

"Considerable," answered Spargo. "Don't mention to anyone that I showed it to you. You shall know everything eventually."

"Oh, all right, my boy, all right!" said Crowfoot. "Odd how things turn up, isn't it? Now, I'll wager anything that there aren't half a dozen of these old things outside Market Milcaster itself. As I said, there were only fifty, and they were all in possession of burgesses. They were so much thought of that they were taken great care of. I've been in Market Milcaster myself since the races were given up, and I've seen these tickets carefully framed and hung over mantelpieces—oh, yes!"

Spargo caught at a notion.

"How do you get to Market Milcaster?" he asked.

"Paddington," replied Crowfoot. "It's a goodish way."

"I wonder," said Spargo, "if there's any old sporting man there who could remember—things. Anything about this ticket, for instance?"

"Old sporting man!" exclaimed Crowfoot. "Egad!—but no, he must be dead—anyhow, if he isn't dead, he must be a veritable patriarch. Old Ben Quarterpage, he was an auctioneer in the town, and a rare sportsman."

"I may go down there," said Spargo. "I'll see if he's alive."

"Then, if you do go down," suggested Crowfoot, "go to the old 'Yellow Dragon' in the High Street, a fine old place. Quarterpage's place of business and his private house were exactly opposite the 'Dragon.' But I'm afraid you'll find him dead—it's five and twenty years since I was in Market Milcaster, and he was an old bird then. Let's see, now. If Old Ben Quarterpage is alive, Spargo, he'll be ninety years of age!"

"Well, I've known men of ninety who were spry enough, even in my bit of experience," said Spargo. "I know one—now—my own grandfather. Well, the best of thanks, Crowfoot, and I'll tell you all about it some day."

"Have another drink?" suggested Crowfoot.

But Spargo excused himself. He was going back to the office, he said; he still had something to do. And he got himself away from the Octoneumenoi, in spite of Starkey, who wished to start a general debate on the wisest way of expending the club's ready money balance, and went back to the *Watchman*, and there he sought the presence of the editor, and in spite of the fact that it was the busiest hour of the night, saw him and remained closeted with him for the extraordinary space of ten minutes. And after that Spargo went home and fell into bed.

But next morning, bright and early, he was on the departure platform at Paddington, suit-case in hand, and ticket in pocket for Market Milcaster, and in the course of that afternoon he found himself in an old-fashioned bedroom looking out on Market Milcaster High Street. And there, right opposite him, he saw an ancient house, old brick, ivy-covered, with an office at its side, over the door of which was the name, *Benjamin Quarterpage*.

Spargo, changing his clothes, washing away the dust of his journey, in that old-fashioned lavender-scented bedroom, busied his mind in further speculations on his plan of campaign in Market Milcaster. He had no particularly clear plan. The one thing he was certain of was that in the old leather box which the man whom he knew as John Marbury had deposited with the London and Universal Safe Deposit Company, he and Rathbury had discovered one of the old silver tickets of Market Milcaster racecourse, and that he, Spargo, had come to Market Milcaster, with the full approval of his editor, in an endeavour to trace it. How was he going to set about this difficult task?

"The first thing," said Spargo to himself as he tied a new tie, "is to have a look round. That'll be no long job."

For he had already seen as he approached the town, and as he drove from the station to the "Yellow Dragon" Hotel, that Market Milcaster was a very small place. It chiefly consisted of one long, wide thoroughfare — the High Street — with smaller streets leading from it on either side. In the High Street seemed to be everything that the town could show — the ancient parish church, the town hall, the market cross, the principal houses and shops, the bridge, beneath which ran the river whereon ships had once come up to the town before its mouth, four miles away, became impassably silted up. It was a bright, clean, little town, but there were few signs of trade in it, and Spargo had been quick to notice that in the "Yellow Dragon," a big, rambling old hostelry, reminiscent of the old coaching days, there seemed to be little doing. He had eaten a bit of lunch in the coffee-room immediately on his arrival; the coffee-room was big enough to accommodate a hundred and fifty people, but beyond himself, an old gentleman and his daughter, evidently tourists, two young men talking golf, a man who looked like an artist, and an unmistakable honeymooning couple, there was no one in it. There was little traffic in the wide street beneath Spargo's windows; little passage of people to and fro on the sidewalks; here a countryman drove a lazy cow as lazily along; there a farmer in his light cart sat idly chatting with an aproned tradesman, who had come out of his shop to talk to him. Over everything lay the quiet of the sunlight of the summer afternoon, and through the open windows stole a faint, sweet scent of the new-mown hay lying in the meadows outside the old houses.

"A veritable Sleepy Hollow," mused Spargo. "Let's go down and see if there's anybody to talk to. Great Scott! — to think that I was in the poisonous atmosphere of the Octoneumenoi only sixteen hours ago!"

Spargo, after losing himself in various corridors and passages, finally landed in the wide, stone-paved hall of the old hotel, and with a sure instinct turned into the bar-parlour which he had noticed when he entered the place. This was a roomy, comfortable, bow-windowed apartment, looking out upon the High Street, and was furnished and ornamented with the usual appurtenances of country-town hotels. There were old chairs and tables and sideboards and cupboards, which had certainly been made a century before, and seemed likely to endure for a century or two longer; there were old prints of the road and the chase, and an old oil-painting or two of red-faced gentlemen in pink coats; there were foxes' masks on the wall, and a monster pike in a glass case on a side-table; there were ancient candlesticks on the mantelpiece and an antique snuff-box set between them. Also there was a small, old-fashioned bar in a corner of the room, and a new-fashioned young woman seated behind it, who was yawning over a piece of fancy needlework, and looked at Spargo when he entered as Andromeda may have looked at Perseus when he made arrival at her rock. And Spargo, treating himself to a suitable drink and choosing a cigar to accompany it, noted the look, and dropped into the nearest chair.

"This," he remarked, eyeing the damsel with enquiry, "appears to me to be a very quiet place."

"Quiet!" exclaimed the lady. "Quiet?"

"That," continued Spargo, "is precisely what I observed. Quiet. I see that you agree with me. You expressed your agreement with two shades of emphasis, the surprised and the scornful. We may conclude, thus far, that the place is undoubtedly quiet."

The damsel looked at Spargo as if she considered him in the light of a new specimen, and picking up her needlework she quitted the bar and coming out into the room took a chair near his own.

"It makes you thankful to see a funeral go by here," she remarked. "It's about all that one ever does see."

"Are there many?" asked Spargo. "Do the inhabitants die much of inanition?"

The damsel gave Spargo another critical inspection.

"Oh, you're joking!" she said. "It's well you can. Nothing ever happens here. This place is a back number."

"Even the back numbers make pleasant reading at times," murmured Spargo. "And the backwaters of life are refreshing. Nothing doing in this town, then?" he added in a louder voice.

"Nothing!" replied his companion. "It's fast asleep. I came here from Birmingham, and I didn't know what I was coming to. In Birmingham you see as many people in ten minutes as you see here in ten months."

"Ah!" said Spargo. "What you are suffering from is dulness. You must have an antidote."

"Dulness!" exclaimed the damsel. "That's the right word for Market Milcaster. There's just a few regular old customers drop in here of a morning, between eleven and one. A stray caller looks in — perhaps — during the afternoon. Then, at night, a lot of old fogies sit round that end of the room and talk about old times. Old times, indeed! — what they want in Market Milcaster is new times."

Spargo pricked up his ears.

"Well, but it's rather interesting to hear old fogies talk about old times," he said. "I love it!"

"Then you can get as much of it as ever you want here," remarked the barmaid. "Look in tonight any time after eight o'clock, and if you don't know more about the history of Market Milcaster by ten than you did when you sat down, you must be deaf. There are some old gentlemen drop in here every night, regular as clockwork, who seem to feel that they couldn't go to bed unless they've told each other stories about old days which I should think they've heard a thousand times already!"

"Very old men?" asked Spargo.

"Methuselahs," replied the lady. "There's old Mr. Quarterpage, across the way there, the auctioneer, though he doesn't do any business now — they say he's ninety, though I'm sure you wouldn't take him for more than seventy. And there's Mr. Lummis, further down the street — he's eighty-one. And Mr. Skene, and Mr. Kaye — they're regular patriarchs. I've sat here and listened to them till I believe I could write a history of Market Milcaster since the year One."

"I can conceive of that as a pleasant and profitable occupation," said Spargo.

He chatted a while longer in a fashion calculated to cheer the barmaid's spirits, after which he went out and strolled around the town until seven o'clock, the "Dragon's" hour for dinner. There were no more people in the big coffee-room than there had been at lunch and Spargo was glad, when his solitary meal was over, to escape to the bar-parlour, where he took his coffee in a corner near to that sacred part in which the old townsmen had been reported to him to sit.

"And mind you don't sit in one of their chairs," said the barmaid, warningly. "They all have their own special chairs and their special pipes there on that rack, and I suppose the ceiling would fall in if anybody touched pipe or chair. But you're all right there, and you'll hear all they've got to say."

To Spargo, who had never seen anything of the sort before, and who, twenty-four hours previously, would have believed the thing impossible, the proceedings of that evening in the bar-parlour of the "Yellow Dragon" at Market Milcaster were like a sudden transference to the eighteenth century. Precisely as the clock struck eight and a bell began to toll somewhere in the recesses of the High Street, an old gentleman walked in, and the barmaid, catching Spargo's eye, gave him a glance which showed that the play was about to begin.

"Good evening, Mr. Kaye," said the barmaid. "You're first tonight."

"Evening," said Mr. Kaye and took a seat, scowled around him, and became silent. He was a tall, lank old gentleman, clad in rusty black clothes, with a pointed collar sticking up on both sides of his fringe of grey whisker and a voluminous black neckcloth folded several times round his neck, and by the expression of his countenance was inclined to look on life severely. "Nobody been in yet?" asked Mr. Kaye. "No, but here's Mr. Lummis and Mr. Skene," replied the barmaid.

Two more old gentlemen entered the bar-parlour. Of these, one was a little, dapper-figured man, clad in clothes of an eminently sporting cut, and of very loud pattern; he sported a bright blue necktie, a flower in his lapel, and a tall white hat, which he wore at a rakish angle. The other was a big, portly, bearded man with a Falstaffian swagger and a rakish eye, who chaffed the barmaid as he entered, and gave her a good-humoured chuck under the chin as he passed her. These two also sank into chairs which seemed to have been specially designed to meet them, and the stout man slapped the arms of his as familiarly as he had greeted the barmaid. He looked at his two cronies.

"Well?" he said, "Here's three of us. And there's a symposium."

"Wait a bit, wait a bit," said the dapper little man. "Grandpa'll be here in a minute. We'll start fair."

The barmaid glanced out of the window.

"There's Mr. Quarterpage coming across the street now," she announced. "Shall I put the things on the table?"

"Aye, put them on, my dear, put them on!" commanded the fat man. "Have all in readiness."

The barmaid thereupon placed a round table before the sacred chairs, set out upon it a fine old punch-bowl and the various ingredients for making punch, a box of cigars, and an old leaden tobacco-box, and she had just completed this interesting prelude to the evening's discourse when the door opened again and in walked one of the most remarkable old men Spargo had ever seen. And by this time, knowing that this was the venerable Mr. Benjamin Quarterpage, of whom Crowfoot had told him, he took good stock of the newcomer as he took his place amongst his friends, who on their part received him with ebullitions of delight which were positively boyish.

Mr. Quarterpage was a youthful buck of ninety—a middle-sized, sturdily-built man, straight as a dart, still active of limb, clear-eyed, and strong of voice. His clean-shaven old countenance was ruddy as a sun-warmed pippin; his hair was still only silvered; his hand was steady as a rock. His clothes of buff-coloured whipcord were smart and jaunty, his neckerchief as gay as if he had been going to a fair. It seemed to Spargo that Mr. Quarterpage had a pretty long lease of life before him even at his age.

Spargo, in his corner, sat fascinated while the old gentlemen began their symposium. Another, making five, came in and joined them—the five had the end of the bar-parlour to themselves. Mr. Quarterpage made the punch with all due solemnity and ceremony; when it was ladled out each man lighted his pipe or took a cigar, and the tongues began to wag. Other folk came and went; the old gentlemen were oblivious of anything but their own talk. Now and then a young gentleman of the town dropped in to take his modest half-pint of bitter beer and to dally in the presence of the barmaid; such looked with awe at the patriarchs: as for the patriarchs themselves they were lost in the past.

Spargo began to understand what the damsel behind the bar meant when she said that she believed she could write a history of Market Milcaster since the year One. After discussing the weather, the local events of the day, and various personal matters, the old fellows got to reminiscences of the past, telling tale after tale, recalling incident upon incident of long years before. At last they turned to memories of racing days at Market Milcaster. And at that Spargo determined on a bold stroke. Now was the time to get some information. Taking the silver ticket from his purse, he laid it, the heraldic device uppermost, on the palm of his hand, and approaching the group with a polite bow, said quietly:

"Gentlemen, can any of you tell me anything about that?"

Chapter 17 MR. QUARTERPAGE HARKS BACK

If Spargo had upset the old gentlemen's bowl of punch — the second of the evening — or had dropped an infernal machine in their midst, he could scarcely have produced a more startling effect than that wrought upon them by his sudden production of the silver ticket. Their babble of conversation died out; one of them dropped his pipe; another took his cigar out of his mouth as if he had suddenly discovered that he was sucking a stick of poison; all lifted astonished faces to the interrupter, staring from him to the shining object exhibited in his outstretched palm, from it back to him. And at last Mr. Quarterpage, to whom Spargo had more particularly addressed himself, spoke, pointing with great *empressement* to the ticket.

"Young gentleman!" he said, in accents that seemed to Spargo to tremble a little, "young gentleman, where did you get that?"

"You know what it is, then?" asked Spargo, willing to dally a little with the matter. "You recognize it?"

"Know it! Recognize it!" exclaimed Mr. Quarterpage. "Yes, and so does every gentleman present. And it is just because I see you are a stranger to this town that I ask you where you got it. Not, I think, young gentleman, in this town."

"No," replied Spargo. "Certainly not in this town. How should I get it in this town if I'm a stranger?"

"Quite true, quite true!" murmured Mr. Quarterpage. "I cannot conceive how any person in the town who is in possession of one of those — what shall we call them — heirlooms? — yes, heirlooms of antiquity, could possibly be base enough to part with it. Therefore, I ask again — Where did you get that, young gentleman?"

"Before I tell you that," answered Spargo, who, in answer to a silent sign from the fat man had drawn a chair amongst them, "perhaps you will tell me exactly what this is? I see it to be a bit of old, polished, much worn silver, having on the obverse the arms or heraldic bearings of somebody or something; on the reverse the figure of a running horse. But — what is it?"

The five old men all glanced at each other and made simultaneous grunts. Then Mr. Quarterpage spoke.

"It is one of the original fifty burgess tickets of Market Milcaster, young sir, which gave its holder special and greatly valued privileges in respect to attendance at our once famous race-meeting, now unfortunately a thing of the past," he added. "Fifty — aye, forty! — years ago, to be in possession of one of those tickets was — was — "

"A grand thing!" said one of the old gentlemen.

"Mr. Lummis is right," said Mr. Quarterpage. "It was a grand thing — a very grand thing. Those tickets, sir, were treasured — are treasured. And yet you, a stranger, show us one! You got it, sir — "

Spargo saw that it was now necessary to cut matters short.

"I found this ticket — under mysterious circumstances — in London," he answered. "I want to trace it. I want to know who its original owner was. That is why I have come to Market Milcaster."

Mr. Quarterpage slowly looked round the circle of faces.

"Wonderful!" he said. "Wonderful! He found this ticket — one of our famous fifty — in London, and under mysterious circumstances. He wants to trace it — he wants to know to whom it belonged! That is why he has come to Market Milcaster. Most extraordinary! Gentlemen, I appeal to you if this is not the most extraordinary event that has happened in Market Milcaster for — I don't know how many years?"

There was a general murmur of assent, and Spargo found everybody looking at him as if he had just announced that he had come to buy the whole town.

"But — why?" he asked, showing great surprise. "Why?"

"Why?" exclaimed Mr. Quarterpage. "Why? He asks — why? Because, young gentleman, it is the greatest surprise to me, and to these friends of mine, too, every man jack of 'em, to hear that any one of our fifty tickets ever passed out of the possession of any of the fifty families to whom they belonged! And unless I am vastly, greatly, most unexplainably mistaken, young sir, you are not a member of any Market Milcaster family."

"No, I'm not," admitted Spargo. And he was going to add that until the previous evening he had never even heard of Market Milcaster, but he wisely refrained. "No, I'm certainly not," he added.

Mr. Quarterpage waved his long pipe.

"I believe," he said, "I believe that if the evening were not drawing to a close—it is already within a few minutes of our departure, young gentleman—I believe, I say, that if I had time, I could, from memory, give the names of the fifty families who held those tickets when the race-meeting came to an end. I believe I could!"

"I'm sure you could!" asserted the little man in the loud suit. "Never was such a memory as yours, never!"

"Especially for anything relating to the old racing matters," said the fat man. "Mr. Quarterpage is a walking encyclopaedia."

"My memory is good," said Mr. Quarterpage. "It's the greatest blessing I have in my declining years. Yes, I am sure I could do that, with a little thought. And what's more, nearly every one of those fifty families is still in the town, or if not in the town, close by it, or if not close by it, I know where they are. Therefore, I cannot make out how this young gentleman—from London, did you say, sir?"

"From London," answered Spargo.

"This young gentleman from London comes to be in possession of one of our tickets," continued Mr. Quarterpage. "It is—wonderful! But I tell you what, young gentleman from London, if you will do me the honour to breakfast with me in the morning, sir, I will show you my racing books and papers and we will speedily discover who the original holder of that ticket was. My name, sir, is Quarterpage—Benjamin Quarterpage—and I reside at the ivy-covered house exactly opposite this inn, and my breakfast hour is nine o'clock sharp, and I shall bid you heartily welcome!"

Spargo made his best bow.

"Sir," he said, "I am greatly obliged by your kind invitation, and I shall consider it an honour to wait upon you to the moment."

Accordingly, at five minutes to nine next morning, Spargo found himself in an old-fashioned parlour, looking out upon a delightful garden, gay with summer flowers, and being introduced by Mr. Quarterpage, Senior, to Mr. Quarterpage, Junior—a pleasant gentleman of sixty, always referred to by his father as something quite juvenile—and to Miss Quarterpage, a young-old lady of something a little less elderly than her brother, and to a breakfast table bounteously spread with all the choice fare of the season. Mr. Quarterpage, Senior, was as fresh and rosy as a cherub; it was a revelation to Spargo to encounter so old a man who was still in possession of such life and spirits, and of such a vigorous and healthy appetite.

Naturally, the talk over the breakfast table ran on Spargo's possession of the old silver ticket, upon which subject it was evident Mr. Quarterpage was still exercising his intellect. And Spargo, who had judged it well to enlighten his host as to who he was, and had exhibited a letter with which the editor of the *Watchman* had furnished him, told how in the exercise of his journalistic duties he had discovered the ticket in the lining of an old box. But he made no mention of the Marbury matter, being anxious to see first whither Mr. Quarterpage's revelations would lead him.

"You have no idea, Mr. Spargo," said the old gentleman, when, breakfast over, he and Spargo were closeted together in a little library in which were abundant evidences of the host's taste in sporting matters; "you have no idea of the value which was attached to the possession of one of those silver tickets. There is mine, as you see, securely framed and just as securely fastened to the wall. Those fifty silver tickets, my dear sir, were made when our old race-meeting was initiated, in the year 1781. They were made in the town by a local silversmith, whose great-great-grandson still carries on the business. The fifty were distributed amongst the fifty leading burgesses of the town to be kept in their families for ever — nobody ever anticipated in those days that our race-meeting would ever be discontinued. The ticket carried great privileges. It made its holder, and all members of his family, male and female, free of the stands, rings, and paddocks. It gave the holder himself and his eldest son, if of age, the right to a seat at our grand race banquet — at which, I may tell you, Mr. Spargo, Royalty itself has been present in the good old days. Consequently, as you see, to be the holder of a silver ticket was to be somebody."

"And when the race-meeting fell through?" asked Spargo. "What then?"

"Then, of course, the families who held the tickets looked upon them as heirlooms, to be taken great care of," replied Mr. Quarterpage. "They were dealt with as I dealt with mine — framed on velvet, and hung up — or locked away: I am sure that anybody who had one took the greatest care of it. Now, I said last night, over there at the 'Dragon,' that I could repeat the names of all the families who held these tickets. So I can. But here" — the old gentleman drew out a drawer and produced from it a parchment-bound book which he handled with great reverence — "here is a little volume of my own handwriting — memoranda relating to Market Milcaster Races — in which is a list of the original holders, together with another list showing who held the tickets when the races were given up. I make bold to say, Mr. Spargo, that by going through the second list, I could trace every ticket — except the one you have in your purse."

"Every one?" said Spargo, in some surprise.

"Every one! For as I told you," continued Mr. Quarterpage, "the families are either in the town (we're a conservative people here in Market Milcaster and we don't move far afield) or they're just outside the town, or they're not far away. I can't conceive how the ticket you have—and it's genuine enough—could ever get out of possession of one of these families, and—"

"Perhaps," suggested Spargo, "it never has been out of possession. I told you it was found in the lining of a box—that box belonged to a dead man."

"A dead man!" exclaimed Mr. Quarterpage. "A dead man! Who could—ah! Perhaps—perhaps I have an idea. Yes!—an idea. I remember something now that I had never thought of."

The old gentleman unfastened the clasp of his parchment-bound book, and turned over its pages until he came to one whereon was a list of names. He pointed this out to Spargo.

"There is the list of holders of the silver tickets at the time the race-meetings came to an end," he said. "If you were acquainted with this town you would know that those are the names of our best-known inhabitants—all, of course, burgesses. There's mine, you see—Quarterpage. There's Lummis, there's Kaye, there's Skene, there's Templeby—the gentlemen you saw last night. All good old town names. They all are—on this list. I know every family mentioned. The holders of that time are many of them dead; but their successors have the tickets. Yes—and now that I think of it, there's only one man who held a ticket when this list was made about whom I don't know anything—at least, anything recent. The ticket, Mr. Spargo, which you've found must have been his. But I thought—I thought somebody else had it!"

"And this man, sir? Who was he?" asked Spargo, intuitively conscious that he was coming to news. "Is his name there?"

The old man ran the tip of his finger down the list of names.

"There it is!" he said. "John Maitland."

Spargo bent over the fine writing.

"Yes, John Maitland," he observed. "And who was John Maitland?"

Mr. Quarterpage shook his head. He turned to another of the many drawers in an ancient bureau, and began to search amongst a mass of old newspapers, carefully sorted into small bundles and tied up.

"If you had lived in Market Milcaster one-and-twenty years ago, Mr. Spargo," he said, "you would have known who John Maitland was. For some time, sir, he was the best-known man in the place—aye, and in this corner of the world. But—aye, here it is—the newspaper of October 5th, 1891. Now, Mr. Spargo, you'll find in this old newspaper who John Maitland was, and all about him. Now, I'll tell you what to do. I've just got to go into my office for an hour to talk the day's business over with my son—you take this newspaper out into the garden there with one of these cigars, and read what'll you find in it, and when you've read that we'll have some more talk."

Spargo carried the old newspaper into the sunlit garden.

As soon as Spargo unfolded the paper he saw what he wanted on the middle page, headed in two lines of big capitals. He lighted a cigar and settled down to read.

"MARKET MILCASTER QUARTER SESSIONS

"TRIAL OF JOHN MAITLAND

"The Quarter Sessions for the Borough of Market Milcaster were held on Wednesday last, October 3rd, 1891, in the Town Hall, before the Recorder, Henry John Campernowne, Esq., K.C., who was accompanied on the bench by the Worshipful the Mayor of Market Milcaster (Alderman Pettiford), the Vicar of Market Milcaster (the Rev. P.B. Clabberton, M.A., R.D.), Alderman Banks, J.P., Alderman Peters, J.P., Sir Gervais Racton, J.P., Colonel Fludgate, J.P., Captain Murrill, J.P., and other magistrates and gentlemen. There was a crowded attendance of the public in anticipation of the trial of John Maitland, ex-manager of the Market Milcaster Bank, and the reserved portions of the Court were filled with the *élite* of the town and neighbourhood, including a considerable number of ladies who manifested the greatest interest in the proceedings.

"The Recorder, in charging the Grand Jury, said he regretted that the very pleasant and gratifying experience which had been his upon the occasion of his last two official visits to Market Milcaster — he referred to the fact that on both those occasions his friend the Worshipful Mayor had been able to present him with a pair of white gloves — was not to be repeated on the present occasion. It would be their sad and regrettable lot to have before them a fellow-townsman whose family had for generations occupied a foremost position in the life of the borough. That fellow-townsman was charged with one of the most serious offences known to a commercial nation like ours: the offence of embezzling the moneys of the bank of which he had for many years been the trusted manager, and with which he had been connected all his life since his school days. He understood that the prisoner who would shortly be put before the court on his trial was about to plead guilty, and there would accordingly be no need for him to direct the gentlemen of the Grand Jury on this matter — what he had to say respecting the gravity and even enormity of the offence he would reserve. The Recorder then addressed himself to the Grand Jury on the merits of two minor cases, which came before the court at a later period of the morning, after which they retired, and having formally returned a true bill against the prisoner, and a petty jury, chosen from well-known burgesses of the town having been duly sworn.

"JOHN MAITLAND, aged 42, bank manager, of the Bank House, High Street, Market Milcaster, was formally charged with embezzling, on April 23rd, 1891, the sum of £4,875 10s. 6d., the moneys of his employers, the Market Milcaster Banking Company Ltd., and converting the same to his own use. The prisoner, who appeared to feel his position most acutely, and who looked very pale and much worn, was represented by Mr. Charles Doolittle, the well-known barrister of Kingshaven; Mr. Stephens, K.C., appeared on behalf of the prosecution.

"Maitland, upon being charged, pleaded guilty.

"Mr. Stephens, K.C., addressing the Recorder, said that without any desire to unduly press upon the prisoner, who, he ventured to think, had taken a very wise course in pleading guilty to that particular count in the indictment with which he stood charged, he felt bound, in the interests of justice, to set forth to the Court some particulars of the defalcations which had arisen through the prisoner's much lamented dishonesty. He proposed to offer a clear and succinct account of the matter. The prisoner, John Maitland, was the last of an old Market Milcaster family — he was, in fact, he believed, with the exception of his own infant son, the very last of the race. His father had been manager of the bank before him. Maitland himself had entered the service of the bank at the age of eighteen, when he left the local Grammar School; he succeeded his father as manager at the age of thirty-two; he had therefore occupied this highest position of trust for ten years. His directors had the fullest confidence in him; they relied on his honesty and his honour; they gave him discretionary powers such as no bank-manager, probably, ever enjoyed or held before. In fact, he was so trusted that he was, to all intents and purposes, the Market Milcaster Banking Company; in other words he was allowed full control over everything, and given full licence to do what he liked. Whether the directors were wise in extending such liberty to even the most trusted servant, it was not for him (Mr. Stephens) to say; it was some consolation, under the circumstances, to know that the loss would fall upon the directors, inasmuch as they themselves held nearly the whole of the shares. But he had to speak of the loss — of the serious defalcations which Maitland had committed. The prisoner had wisely pleaded guilty to the first count of the indictment. But there were no less than seventeen counts in the indictment. He had pleaded guilty to embezzling a sum of £4,875 odd. But the total amount of the defalcations, comprised in the seventeen counts, was no less — it seemed a most amazing sum! — than £221,573 8s. 6d.! There was the fact — the banking company had been robbed of over two hundred thousand pounds by the prisoner in the dock before a mere accident, the most trifling chance, had revealed to the astounded directors that he was robbing them at all. And the most serious feature of the whole case was that not one penny of this money had been, or ever could be, recovered. He believed that the prisoner's learned counsel was about to urge upon the Court that the prisoner himself had been tricked and deceived by another man, unfortunately not before the Court – a man, he understood, also well known in Market Milcaster, who was now dead, and therefore could not be called, but whether he was so tricked or deceived was no excuse for his clever and wholesale robbing of his employers. He had thought it necessary to put these facts – which would not be denied – before the Court, in order that it might be known how heavy the defalcations really had been, and that they should be considered in dealing with the prisoner.

"The Recorder asked if there was no possibility of recovering any part of the vast sum concerned.

"Mr. Stephens replied that they were informed that there was not the remotest chance – the money, it was said by prisoner and those acting on his behalf, had utterly vanished with the death of the man to whom he had just made reference.

"Mr. Doolittle, on behalf of the prisoner, craved to address a few words to the Court in mitigation of sentence. He thanked Mr. Stephens for the considerate and eminently dispassionate manner in which he had outlined the main facts of the case. He had no desire to minimize the prisoner's guilt. But, on prisoner's behalf, he desired to tell the true story as to how these things came to be. Until as recently as three years previously the prisoner had never made the slightest deviation from the straight path of integrity. Unfortunately for him, and, he believed, for some others in Market Milcaster, there came to the town three years before the present proceedings, a man named Chamberlayne, who commenced business in the High Street as a stock-and-share broker. A man of good address and the most plausible manners, Chamberlayne attracted a good many people – amongst them his unfortunate client. It was matter of common knowledge that Chamberlayne had induced numerous persons in Market Milcaster to enter into financial transactions with him; it was matter of common repute that those transactions had not always turned out well for Chamberlayne's clients. Unhappily for himself, Maitland had great faith in Chamberlayne. He had begun to have transactions with him in a large way; they had gone on and on in a large way until he was involved to vast amounts. Believing thoroughly in Chamberlayne and his methods, he had entrusted him with very large sums of money.

"The Recorder interrupted Mr. Doolittle at this point to ask if he was to understand that Mr. Doolittle was referring to the prisoner's own money.

"Mr. Doolittle replied that he was afraid the large sums he referred to were the property of the bank. But the prisoner had such belief in Chamberlayne that he firmly anticipated that all would be well, and that these sums would be repaid, and that a vast profit would result from their use.

"The Recorder remarked that he supposed the prisoner intended to put the profit into his own pockets.

"Mr. Doolittle said at any rate the prisoner assured him that of the two hundred and twenty thousand pounds which was in question, Chamberlayne had had the immediate handling of at least two hundred thousand, and he, the prisoner, had not the ghost of a notion as to what Chamberlayne had done with it. Unfortunately for everybody, for the bank, for some other people, and especially for his unhappy client, Chamberlayne died, very suddenly, just as these proceedings were instituted, and so far it had been absolutely impossible to trace anything of the moneys concerned. He had died under mysterious circumstances, and there was just as much mystery about his affairs.

"The Recorder observed that he was still waiting to hear what Mr. Doolittle had to urge in mitigation of any sentence he, the Recorder, might think fit to pass.

"Mr. Doolittle said that he would trouble the Court with as few remarks as possible. All that he could urge on behalf of the unfortunate man in the dock was that until three years ago he had borne a most exemplary character, and had never committed a dishonest action. It had been his misfortune, his folly, to allow a plausible man to persuade him to these acts of dishonesty. That man had been called to another account, and the prisoner was left to bear the consequences of his association with him. It seemed as if Chamberlayne had made away with the money for his own purposes, and it might be that it would yet be recovered. He would only ask the Court to remember the prisoner's antecedents and his previous good conduct, and to bear in mind that whatever his near future might be he was, in a commercial sense, ruined for life.

"The Recorder, in passing sentence, said that he had not heard a single word of valid excuse for Maitland's conduct. Such dishonesty must be punished in the most severe fashion, and the prisoner must go to penal servitude for ten years.

"Maitland, who heard the sentence unmoved, was removed from the town later in the day to the county jail at Saxchester."

Spargo read all this swiftly; then went over it again, noting certain points in it. At last he folded up the newspaper and turned to the house — to see old Quarterpage beckoning to him from the library window.

"I perceive, sir," said Mr. Quarterpage, as Spargo entered the library, "that you have read the account of the Maitland trial."

"Twice," replied Spargo.

"And you have come to the conclusion that—but what conclusion have you come to?" asked Mr. Quarterpage.

"That the silver ticket in my purse was Maitland's property," said Spargo, who was not going to give all his conclusions at once.

"Just so," agreed the old gentleman. "I think so—I can't think anything else. But I was under the impression that I could have accounted for that ticket, just as I am sure I can account for the other forty-nine."

"Yes—and how?" asked Spargo.

Mr. Quarterpage turned to a corner cupboard and in silence produced a decanter and two curiously-shaped old wine-glasses. He carefully polished the glasses with a cloth which he took from a drawer, and set glasses and decanter on a table in the window, motioning Spargo to take a chair in proximity thereto. He himself pulled up his own elbow-chair.

"We'll take a glass of my old brown sherry," he said. "Though I say it as shouldn't, as the saying goes, I don't think you could find better brown sherry than that from Land's End to Berwick-upon-Tweed, Mr. Spargo—no, nor further north either, where they used to have good taste in liquor in my young days! Well, here's your good health, sir, and I'll tell you about Maitland."

"I'm curious," said Spargo. "And about more than Maitland. I want to know about a lot of things arising out of that newspaper report. I want to know something about the man referred to so much—the stockbroker, Chamberlayne."

"Just so," observed Mr. Quarterpage, smiling. "I thought that would touch your sense of the inquisitive. But Maitland first. Now, when Maitland went to prison, he left behind him a child, a boy, just then about two years old. The child's mother was dead. Her sister, a Miss Baylis, appeared on the scene—Maitland had married his wife from a distance—and took possession of the child and of Maitland's personal effects. He had been made bankrupt while he was awaiting his trial, and all his household goods were sold. But this Miss Baylis took some small personal things, and I always believed that she took the silver ticket. And she may have done, for anything I know to the contrary. Anyway, she took the child away, and there was an end of the Maitland family in Market Milcaster. Maitland, of course, was in due procedure of things removed to Dartmoor, and there he served his term. There were people who were very anxious to get hold of him when he came out—the bank people, for they believed that he knew more about the disposition of that money than he'd ever told, and they wanted to induce him to tell what they hoped he knew—between ourselves, Mr. Spargo, they were going to make it worth his while to tell."

Spargo tapped the newspaper, which he had retained while the old gentleman talked.

"Then they didn't believe what his counsel said—that Chamberlayne got all the money?" he asked.

Mr. Quarterpage laughed.

"No—nor anybody else!" he answered. "There was a strong idea in the town—you'll see why afterwards—that it was all a put-up job, and that Maitland cheerfully underwent his punishment knowing that there was a nice fortune waiting for him when he came out. And as I say, the bank people meant to get hold of him. But though they sent a special agent to meet him on his release, they never did get hold of him. Some mistake arose—when Maitland was released, he got clear away. Nobody's ever heard a word of him from that day to this. Unless Miss Baylis has."

"Where does this Miss Baylis live?" asked Spargo.

"Well, I don't know," replied Mr. Quarterpage. "She did live in Brighton when she took the child away, and her address was known, and I have it somewhere. But when the bank people sought her out after Maitland's release, she, too, had clean disappeared, and all efforts to trace her failed. In fact, according to the folks who lived near her in Brighton, she'd completely disappeared, with the child, five years before. So there wasn't a clue to Maitland. He served his time—made a model prisoner—they did find that much out!—earned the maximum remission, was released, and vanished. And for that very reason there's a theory about him in this very town to this very day!"

"What?" asked Spargo.

"This. That he's now living comfortably, luxuriously abroad on what he got from the bank," replied Mr. Quarterpage. "They say that the sister-in-law was in at the game; that when she disappeared with the child, she went abroad somewhere and made a home ready for Maitland, and that he went off to them as soon as he came out. Do you see?"

"I suppose that was possible," said Spargo.

"Quite possible, sir. But now," continued the old gentleman, replenishing the glasses, "now we come on to the Chamberlayne story. It's a good deal more to do with the Maitland story than appears at first sight, I'll tell it to you and you can form your own conclusions. Chamberlayne was a man who came to Market Milcaster—I don't know from where—in 1886—five years before the Maitland smash-up. He was then about Maitland's age—a man of thirty-seven or eight. He came as clerk to old Mr. Vallas, the rope and twine manufacturer: Vallas's place is still there, at the bottom of the High Street, near the river, though old Vallas is dead. He was a smart, cute, pushing chap, this Chamberlayne; he made himself indispensable to old Vallas, and old Vallas paid him a rare good salary. He settled down in the town, and he married a town girl, one of the Corkindales, the saddlers, when he'd been here three years. Unfortunately she died in childbirth within a year of their marriage. It was very soon after that that Chamberlayne threw up his post at Vallas's, and started business as a stock-and-share broker. He'd been a saving man; he'd got a nice bit of money with his wife; he always let it be known that he had money of his own, and he started in a good way. He was a man of the most plausible manners: he'd have coaxed butter out of a dog's throat if he'd wanted to. The moneyed men of the town believed in him—I believed in him myself, Mr. Spargo—I'd many a transaction with him, and I never lost aught by him—on the contrary, he did very well for me. He did well for most of his clients—there were, of course, ups and downs, but on the whole he satisfied his clients uncommonly well. But, naturally, nobody ever knew what was going on between him and Maitland."

"I gather from this report," said Spargo, "that everything came out suddenly—unexpectedly?"

"That was so, sir," replied Mr. Quarterpage. "Sudden? Unexpected? Aye, as a crack of thunder on a fine winter's day. Nobody had the ghost of a notion that anything was wrong. John Maitland was much respected in the town; much thought of by everybody; well known to everybody. I can assure you, Mr. Spargo, that it was no pleasant thing to have to sit on that grand jury as I did—I was its foreman, sir,—and hear a man sentenced that you'd regarded as a bosom friend. But there it was!"

"How was the thing discovered?" asked Spargo, anxious to get at facts.

"In this way," replied Mr. Quarterpage. "The Market Milcaster Bank is in reality almost entirely the property of two old families in the town, the Gutchbys and the Hostables. Owing to the death of his father, a young Hostable, fresh from college, came into the business. He was a shrewd, keen young fellow; he got some suspicion, somehow, about Maitland, and he insisted on the other partners consenting to a special investigation, and on their making it suddenly. And Maitland was caught before he had a chance. But we're talking about Chamberlayne."

"Yes, about Chamberlayne," agreed Spargo.

"Well, now, Maitland was arrested one evening," continued Mr. Quarterpage. "Of course, the news of his arrest ran through the town like wild-fire. Everybody was astonished; he was at that time — aye, and had been for years — a churchwarden at the Parish Church, and I don't think there could have been more surprise if we'd heard that the Vicar had been arrested for bigamy. In a little town like this, news is all over the place in a few minutes. Of course, Chamberlayne would hear that news like everybody else. But it was remembered, and often remarked upon afterwards, that from the moment of Maitland's arrest nobody in Market Milcaster ever had speech with Chamberlayne again. After his wife's death he'd taken to spending an hour or so of an evening across there at the 'Dragon,' where you saw me and my friends last night, but on that night he didn't go to the 'Dragon.' And next morning he caught the eight o'clock train to London. He happened to remark to the stationmaster as he got into the train that he expected to be back late that night, and that he should have a tiring day of it. But Chamberlayne didn't come back that night, Mr. Spargo. He didn't come back to Market Milcaster for four days, and when he did come back it was in a coffin!"

"Dead?" exclaimed Spargo. "That was sudden!"

"Very sudden," agreed Mr. Quarterpage. "Yes, sir, he came back in his coffin, did Chamberlayne. On the very evening on which he'd spoken of being back, there came a telegram here to say that he'd died very suddenly at the Cosmopolitan Hotel. That telegram came to his brother-in-law, Corkindale, the saddler — you'll find him down the street, opposite the Town Hall. It was sent to Corkindale by a nephew of Chamberlayne's, another Chamberlayne, Stephen, who lived in London, and was understood to be on the Stock Exchange there. I saw that telegram, Mr. Spargo, and it was a long one. It said that Chamberlayne had had a sudden seizure, and though a doctor had been got to him he'd died shortly afterwards. Now, as Chamberlayne had his nephew and friends in London, his brother-in-law, Tom Corkindale, didn't feel that there was any necessity for him to go up to town, so he just sent off a wire to Stephen Chamberlayne asking if there was aught he could do. And next morning came another wire from Stephen saying that no inquest would be necessary, as the doctor had been present and able to certify the cause of death, and would Corkindale make all arrangements for the funeral two days later. You see, Chamberlayne had bought a vault in our cemetery when he buried his wife, so naturally they wished to bury him in it, with her."

Spargo nodded. He was beginning to imagine all sorts of things and theories; he was taking everything in.

"Well," continued Mr. Quarterpage, "on the second day after that, they brought Chamberlayne's body down. Three of 'em came with it—Stephen Chamberlayne, the doctor who'd been called in, and a solicitor. Everything was done according to proper form and usage. As Chamberlayne had been well known in the town, a good number of townsfolk met the body at the station and followed it to the cemetery. Of course, many of us who had been clients of Chamberlayne's were anxious to know how he had come to such a sudden end. According to Stephen Chamberlayne's account, our Chamberlayne had wired to him and to his solicitor to meet him at the Cosmopolitan to do some business. They were awaiting him there when he arrived, and they had lunch together. After that, they got to their business in a private room. Towards the end of the afternoon, Chamberlayne was taken suddenly ill, and though they got a doctor to him at once, he died before evening. The doctor said he'd a diseased heart. Anyhow, he was able to certify the cause of his death, so there was no inquest and they buried him, as I have told you."

The old gentleman paused and, taking a sip at his sherry, smiled at some reminiscence which occurred to him.

"Well," he said, presently going on, "of course, on that came all the Maitland revelations, and Maitland vowed and declared that Chamberlayne had not only had nearly all the money, but that he was absolutely certain that most of it was in his hands in hard cash. But Chamberlayne, Mr. Spargo, had left practically nothing. All that could be traced was about three or four thousand pounds. He'd left everything to his nephew, Stephen. There wasn't a trace, a clue to the vast sums with which Maitland had entrusted him. And then people began to talk, and they said what some of them say to this very day!"

"What's that?" asked Spargo.

Mr. Quarterpage leaned forward and tapped his guest on the arm.

"That Chamberlayne never did die, and that that coffin was weighted with lead!" he answered.

This remarkable declaration awoke such a new conception of matters in Spargo's mind, aroused such infinitely new possibilities in his imagination, that for a full moment he sat silently staring at his informant, who chuckled with quiet enjoyment at his visitor's surprise.

"Do you mean to tell me," said Spargo at last, "that there are people in this town who still believe that the coffin in your cemetery which is said to contain Chamberlayne's body contains — lead?"

"Lots of 'em, my dear sir!" replied Mr. Quarterpage. "Lots of 'em! Go out in the street and asked the first six men you meet, and I'll go bail that four out of the six believe it."

"Then why, in the sacred name of common sense did no one ever take steps to make certain?" asked Spargo. "Why didn't they get an order for exhumation?"

"Because it was nobody's particular business to do so," answered Mr. Quarterpage. "You don't know country-town life, my dear sir. In towns like Market Milcaster folks talk and gossip a great deal, but they're always slow to do anything. It's a case of who'll start first — of initiative. And if they see it's going to cost anything — then they'll have nothing to do with it."

"But — the bank people?" suggested Spargo.

Mr. Quarterpage shook his head.

"They're amongst the lot who believe that Chamberlayne did die," he said. "They're very old-fashioned, conservative-minded people, the Gutchbys and the Hostables, and they accepted the version of the nephew, and the doctor, and the solicitor. But now I'll tell you something about those three. There was a man here in the town, a gentleman of your own profession, who came to edit that paper you've got on your knee. He got interested in this Chamberlayne case, and he began to make enquiries with the idea of getting hold of some good — what do you call it?"

"I suppose he'd call it 'copy,'" said Spargo.

"'Copy'—that was his term," agreed Mr. Quarterpage. "Well, he took the trouble to go to London to ask some quiet questions of the nephew, Stephen. That was just twelve months after Chamberlayne had been buried. But he found that Stephen Chamberlayne had left England—months before. Gone, they said, to one of the colonies, but they didn't know which. And the solicitor had also gone. And the doctor—couldn't be traced, no, sir, not even through the Medical Register. What do you think of all that, Mr. Spargo?"

"I think," answered Spargo, "that Market Milcaster folk are considerably slow. I should have had that death and burial enquired into. The whole thing looks to me like a conspiracy."

"Well, sir, it was, as I say, nobody's business," said Mr. Quarterpage. "The newspaper gentleman tried to stir up interest in it, but it was no good, and very soon afterwards he left. And there it is."

"Mr. Quarterpage," said Spargo, "what's your own honest opinion?"

The old gentleman smiled.

"Ah!" he said. "I've often wondered, Mr. Spargo, if I really have an opinion on that point. I think that what I probably feel about the whole affair is that there was a good deal of mystery attaching to it. But we seem, sir, to have gone a long way from the question of that old silver ticket which you've got in your purse. Now——"

"No!" said Spargo, interrupting his host with an accompanying wag of his forefinger. "No! I think we're coming nearer to it. Now you've given me a great deal of your time, Mr. Quarterpage, and told me a lot, and, first of all, before I tell you a lot, I'm going to show you something."

And Spargo took out of his pocket-book a carefully-mounted photograph of John Marbury—the original of the process-picture which he had had made for the *Watchman*. He handed it over.

"Do you recognize that photograph as that of anybody you know?" he asked. "Look at it well and closely."

Mr. Quarterpage put on a special pair of spectacles and studied the photograph from several points of view.

"No, sir," he said at last with a shake of the head. "I don't recognize it at all."

"Can't see in it any resemblance to any man you've ever known?" asked Spargo.

"No, sir, none!" replied Mr. Quarterpage. "None whatever."

"Very well," said Spargo, laying the photograph on the table between them. "Now, then, I want you to tell me what John Maitland was like when you knew him. Also, I want you to describe Chamberlayne as he was when he died, or was supposed to die. You remember them, of course, quite well?"

Mr. Quarterpage got up and moved to the door.

"I can do better than that," he said. "I can show you photographs of both men as they were just before Maitland's trial. I have a photograph of a small group of Market Milcaster notabilities which was taken at a municipal garden-party; Maitland and Chamberlayne are both in it. It's been put away in a cabinet in my drawing-room for many a long year, and I've no doubt it's as fresh as when it was taken."

He left the room and presently returned with a large mounted photograph which he laid on the table before his visitor.

"There you are, sir," he said. "Quite fresh, you see — it must be getting on to twenty years since that was taken out of the drawer that it's been kept in. Now, that's Maitland. And that's Chamberlayne."

Spargo found himself looking at a group of men who stood against an ivy-covered wall in the stiff attitudes in which photographers arrange masses of sitters. He fixed his attention on the two figures indicated by Mr. Quarterpage, and saw two medium-heighted, rather sturdily-built men about whom there was nothing very specially noticeable.

"Um!" he said, musingly. "Both bearded."

"Yes, they both wore beards — full beards," assented Mr. Quarterpage. "And you see, they weren't so much alike. But Maitland was a much darker man than Chamberlayne, and he had brown eyes, while Chamberlayne's were rather a bright blue."

"The removal of a beard makes a great difference," remarked Spargo. He looked at the photograph of Maitland in the group, comparing it with that of Marbury which he had taken from his pocket. "And twenty years makes a difference, too," he added musingly.

"To some people twenty years makes a vast difference, sir," said the old gentleman. "To others it makes none — I haven't changed much, they tell me, during the past twenty years. But I've known men change — age, almost beyond recognition! — in five years. It depends, sir, on what they go through."

Spargo suddenly laid aside the photographs, put his hands in his pockets, and looked steadfastly at Mr. Quarterpage.

"Look here!" he said. "I'm going to tell you what I'm after, Mr. Quarterpage. I'm sure you've heard all about what's known as the Middle Temple Murder — the Marbury case?"

"Yes, I've read of it," replied Mr. Quarterpage.

"Have you read the accounts of it in my paper, the *Watchman*?" asked Spargo.

Mr. Quarterpage shook his head.

"I've only read one newspaper, sir, since I was a young man," he replied. "I take the *Times*, sir — we always took it, aye, even in the days when newspapers were taxed."

"Very good," said Spargo. "But perhaps I can tell you a little more than you've read, for I've been working up that case ever since the body of the man known as John Marbury was found. Now, if you'll just give me your attention, I'll tell you the whole story from that moment until — now."

And Spargo, briefly, succinctly, re-told the story of the Marbury case from the first instant of his own connection with it until the discovery of the silver ticket, and Mr. Quarterpage listened in rapt attention, nodding his head from time to time as the younger man made his points.

"And now, Mr. Quarterpage," concluded Spargo, "this is the point I've come to. I believe that the man who came to the Anglo-Orient Hotel as John Marbury and who was undoubtedly murdered in Middle Temple Lane that night, was John Maitland — I haven't a doubt about it after learning what you tell me about the silver ticket. I've found out a great deal that's valuable here, and I think I'm getting nearer to a solution of the mystery. That is, of course, to find out who murdered John Maitland, or Marbury. What you have told me about the Chamberlayne affair has led me to think this — there may have been people, or a person, in London, who was anxious to get Marbury, as we'll call him, out of the way, and who somehow encountered him that night — anxious to silence him, I mean, because of the Chamberlayne affair. And I wondered, as there is so much mystery about him, and as he won't give any account of himself, if this man Aylmore was really Chamberlayne. Yes, I wondered that! But Aylmore's a tall, finely-built man, quite six feet in height, and his beard, though it's now getting grizzled, has been very dark, and Chamberlayne, you say, was a medium-sized, fair man, with blue eyes."

"That's so, sir," assented Mr. Quarterpage. "Yes, a middling-sized man, and fair — very fair. Deary me, Mr. Spargo! — this is a revelation. And you really think, sir, that John Maitland and John Marbury are one and the same person?"

"I'm sure of it, now," said Spargo. "I see it in this way. Maitland, on his release, went out to Australia, and there he stopped. At last he comes back, evidently well-to-do. He's murdered the very day of his arrival. Aylmore is the only man who knows anything of him — Aylmore won't tell all he knows; that's flat. But Aylmore's admitted that he knew him at some vague date, say from twenty-one to twenty-two or three years ago. Now, where did Aylmore know him? He says in London. That's a vague term. He won't say where — he won't say anything definite — he won't even say what he, Aylmore, himself was in those days. Do you recollect anything of anybody like Aylmore coming here to see Maitland, Mr. Quarterpage?"

"I don't," answered Mr. Quarterpage. "Maitland was a very quiet, retiring fellow, sir: he was about the quietest man in the town. I never remember that he had visitors; certainly I've no recollection of such a friend of his as this Aylmore, from your description of him, would be at that time."

"Did Maitland go up to London much in those days?" asked Spargo.

Mr. Quarterpage laughed.

"Well, now, to show you what a good memory I have," he said, "I'll tell you of something that occurred across there at the 'Dragon' only a few months before the Maitland affair came out. There were some of us in there one evening, and, for a rare thing, Maitland came in with Chamberlayne. Chamberlayne happened to remark that he was going up to town next day — he was always to and fro — and we got talking about London. And Maitland said in course of conversation, that he believed he was about the only man of his age in England — and, of course, he meant of his class and means — who'd never even seen London! And I don't think he ever went there between that time and his trial: in fact, I'm sure he didn't, for if he had, I should have heard of it."

"Well, that's queer," remarked Spargo. "It's very queer. For I'm certain Maitland and Marbury are one and the same person. My theory about that old leather box is that Maitland had that carefully planted before his arrest; that he dug it up when he came put of Dartmoor; that he took it off to Australia with him; that he brought it back with him; and that, of course, the silver ticket and the photograph had been in it all these years. Now — —"

At that moment the door of the library was opened, and a parlourmaid looked in at her master.

"There's the boots from the 'Dragon' at the front door, sir," she said. "He's brought two telegrams across from there for Mr. Spargo, thinking he might like to have them at once."

Spargo hurried out to the hall, took the two telegrams from the boots of the "Dragon," and, tearing open the envelopes, read the messages hastily. He went back to Mr. Quarterpage.

"Here's important news," he said as he closed the library door and resumed his seat. "I'll read these telegrams to you, sir, and then we can discuss them in the light of what we've been talking about this morning. The first is from our office. I told you we sent over to Australia for a full report about Marbury at the place he said he hailed from — Coolumbidgee. That report's just reached the *Watchman*, and they've wired it on to me. It's from the chief of police at Coolumbidgee to the editor of the *Watchman*, London: —

"John Marbury came to Coolumbidgee in the winter of 1898-9. He was unaccompanied. He appeared to be in possession of fairly considerable means and bought a share in a small sheep-farm from its proprietor, Andrew Robertson, who is still here, and who says that Marbury never told him anything about himself except that he had emigrated for health reasons and was a widower. He mentioned that he had had a son who was dead, and was now without relations. He lived a very quiet, steady life on the sheep-farm, never leaving it for many years. About six months ago, however, he paid a visit to Melbourne, and on returning told Robertson that he had decided to return to England in consequence of some news he had received, and must therefore sell his share in the farm. Robertson bought it from him for three thousand pounds, and Marbury shortly afterwards left for Melbourne. From what we could gather, Robertson thinks Marbury was probably in command of five or six thousand when he left Coolumbidgee. He told Robertson that he had met a man in Melbourne who had given him news that surprised him, but did not say what news. He had in his possession when he left Robertson exactly the luggage he brought with him when he came — a stout portmanteau and a small, square leather box. There are no effects of his left behind at Coolumbidgee."

"That's all," said Spargo, laying the first of the telegrams on the table. "And it seems to me to signify a good deal. But now here's more startling news. This is from Rathbury, the Scotland Yard detective that I told you of, Mr. Quarterpage—he promised, you know, to keep me posted in what went on in my absence. Here's what he says:

"Fresh evidence tending to incriminate Aylmore has come to hand. Authorities have decided to arrest him on suspicion. You'd better hurry back if you want material for to-morrow's paper."

Spargo threw that telegram down, too, waited while the old gentleman glanced at both of them with evident curiosity, and then jumped up.

"Well, I shall have to go, Mr. Quarterpage," he said. "I looked the trains out this morning so as to be in readiness. I can catch the 1.20 to Paddington—that'll get me in before half-past four. I've an hour yet. Now, there's another man I want to see in Market Milcaster. That's the photographer—or a photographer. You remember I told you of the photograph found with the silver ticket? Well, I'm calculating that that photograph was taken here, and I want to see the man who took it—if he's alive and I can find him."

Mr. Quarterpage rose and put on his hat.

"There's only one photographer in this town, sir," he said, "and he's been here for a good many years—Cooper. I'll take you to him—it's only a few doors away."

Spargo wasted no time in letting the photographer know what he wanted. He put a direct question to Mr. Cooper—an elderly man.

"Do you remember taking a photograph of the child of John Maitland, the bank manager, some twenty or twenty-one years ago?" he asked, after Mr. Quarterpage had introduced him as a gentleman from London who wanted to ask a few questions.

"Quite well, sir," replied Mr. Cooper. "As well as if it had been yesterday."

"Do you still happen to have a copy of it?" asked Spargo.

But Mr. Cooper had already turned to a row of file albums. He took down one labelled 1891, and began to search its pages. In a minute or two he laid it on his table before his callers.

"There you are, sir," he said. "That's the child!"

Spargo gave one glance at the photograph and turned to Mr. Quarterpage. "Just as I thought," he said. "That's the same photograph we found in the leather box with the silver ticket. I'm obliged to you, Mr. Cooper. Now, there's just one more question I want to ask. Did you ever supply any further copies of this photograph to anybody after the Maitland affair? — that is; after the family had left the town?"

"Yes," replied the photographer. "I supplied half a dozen copies to Miss Baylis, the child's aunt, who, as a matter of fact, brought him here to be photographed. And I can give you her address, too," he continued, beginning to turn over another old file. "I have it somewhere."

Mr. Quarterpage nudged Spargo.

"That's something I couldn't have done!" he remarked. "As I told you, she'd disappeared from Brighton when enquiries were made after Maitland's release."

"Here you are," said Mr. Cooper. "I sent six copies of that photograph to Miss Baylis in April, 1895. Her address was then 6, Chichester Square, Bayswater, W."

Spargo rapidly wrote this address down, thanked the photographer for his courtesy, and went out with Mr. Quarterpage. In the street he turned to the old gentleman with a smile.

"Well, I don't think there's much doubt about that!" he exclaimed. "Maitland and Marbury are the same man, Mr. Quarterpage. I'm as certain of that as that I see your Town Hall there."

"And what will you do next, sir?" enquired Mr. Quarterpage.

"Thank you — as I do — for all your kindness and assistance, and get off to town by this 1.20," replied Spargo. "And I shan't fail to let you know how things go on."

"One moment," said the old gentleman, as Spargo was hurrying away, "do you think this Mr. Aylmore really murdered Maitland?"

"No!" answered Spargo with emphasis. "I don't! And I think we've got a good deal to do before we find out who did."

Spargo purposely let the Marbury case drop out of his mind during his journey to town. He ate a hearty lunch in the train and talked with his neighbours; it was a relief to let his mind and attention turn to something else than the theme which had occupied it unceasingly for so many days. But at Reading the newspaper boys were shouting the news of the arrest of a Member of Parliament, and Spargo, glancing out of the window, caught sight of a newspaper placard:

THE MARBURY MURDER CASE ARREST OF MR. AYLMORE

He snatched a paper from a boy as the train moved out and; unfolding it, found a mere announcement in the space reserved for stop-press news:

"Mr. Stephen Aylmore, M.P., was arrested at two o'clock this afternoon, on his way to the House of Commons, on a charge of being concerned in the murder of John Marbury in Middle Temple Lane on the night of June 21st last. It is understood he will be brought up at Bow Street at ten o'clock tomorrow morning."

Spargo hurried to New Scotland Yard as soon as he reached Paddington. He met Rathbury coming away from his room. At sight of him, the detective turned back.

"Well, so there you are!" he said. "I suppose you've heard the news?"

Spargo nodded as he dropped into a chair.

"What led to it?" he asked abruptly. "There must have been something."

"There was something," he replied. "The thing — stick, bludgeon, whatever you like to call it, some foreign article — with which Marbury was struck down was found last night."

"Well?" asked Spargo.

"It was proved to be Aylmore's property," answered Rathbury. "It was a South American curio that he had in his rooms in Fountain Court."

"Where was it found?" asked Spargo.

Rathbury laughed.

"He was a clumsy fellow who did it, whether he was Aylmore or whoever he was!" he replied. "Do you know, it had been dropped into a sewer-trap in Middle Temple Lane—actually! Perhaps the murderer thought it would be washed out into the Thames and float away. But, of course, it was bound to come to light. A sewer man found it yesterday evening, and it was quickly recognized by the woman who cleans up for Aylmore as having been in his rooms ever since she knew them."

"What does Aylmore say about it?" asked Spargo. "I suppose he's said something?" "Says that the bludgeon is certainly his, and that he brought it from South America with him," announced Rathbury; "but that he doesn't remember seeing it in his rooms for some time, and thinks that it was stolen from them."

"Um!" said Spargo, musingly. "But—how do you know that was the thing that Marbury was struck down with?"

Rathbury smiled grimly.

"There's some of his hair on it—mixed with blood," he answered. "No doubt about that. Well—anything come of your jaunt westward?"

"Yes," replied Spargo. "Lots!"

"Good?" asked Rathbury.

"Extra good. I've found out who Marbury really was."

"No! Really?"

"No doubt, to my mind. I'm certain of it."

Rathbury sat down at his desk, watching Spargo with rapt attention.

"And who was he?" he asked.

"John Maitland, once of Market Milcaster," replied Spargo. "Ex-bank manager. Also ex-convict."

"Ex-convict!"

"Ex-convict. He was sentenced, at Market Milcaster Quarter Sessions, in autumn, 1891, to ten years' penal servitude, for embezzling the bank's money, to the tune of over two hundred thousand pounds. Served his term at Dartmoor. Went to Australia as soon, or soon after, he came out. That's who Marbury was—Maitland. Dead—certain!"

Rathbury still stared at his caller.

"Go on!" he said. "Tell all about it, Spargo. Let's hear every detail. I'll tell you all I know after. But what I know's nothing to that."

Spargo told him the whole story of his adventures at Market Milcaster, and the detective listened with rapt attention.

"Yes," he said at the end. "Yes—I don't think there's much doubt about that. Well, that clears up a lot, doesn't it?"

Spargo yawned.

"Yes, a whole slate full is wiped off there," he said. "I haven't so much interest in Marbury, or Maitland now. My interest is all in Aylmore."

Rathbury nodded.

"Yes," he said. "The thing to find out is—who is Aylmore, or who was he, twenty years ago?"

"Your people haven't found anything out, then?" asked Spargo.

"Nothing beyond the irreproachable history of Mr. Aylmore since he returned to this country, a very rich man, some ten years since," answered Rathbury, smiling. "They've no previous dates to go on. What are you going to do next, Spargo?"

"Seek out that Miss Baylis," replied Spargo.

"You think you could get something there?" asked Rathbury.

"Look here!" said Spargo. "I don't believe for a second Aylmore killed Marbury. I believe I shall get at the truth by following up what I call the Maitland trail. This Miss Baylis must know something—if she's alive. Well, now I'm going to report at the office. Keep in touch with me, Rathbury."

He went on then to the *Watchman* office, and as he got out of his taxi-cab at its door, another cab came up and set down Mr. Aylmore's daughters.

Jessie Aylmore came forward to meet Spargo with ready confidence; the elder girl hung back diffidently.

"May we speak to you?" said Jessie. "We have come on purpose to speak to you. Evelyn didn't want to come, but I made her come."

Spargo shook hands silently with Evelyn Aylmore and motioned them both to follow him. He took them straight upstairs to his room and bestowed them in his easiest chairs before he addressed them.

"I've only just got back to town," he said abruptly. "I was sorry to hear the news about your father. That's what's brought you here, of course. But—I'm afraid I can't do much."

"I told you that we had no right to trouble Mr. Spargo, Jessie," said Evelyn Aylmore. "What can he do to help us?"

Jessie shook her head impatiently.

"The Watchman's about the most powerful paper in London, isn't it?" she said. "And isn't Mr. Spargo writing all these articles about the Marbury case? Mr. Spargo, you must help us!"

Spargo sat down at his desk and began turning over the letters and papers which had accumulated during his absence.

"To be absolutely frank with you," he said, presently, "I don't see how anybody's going to help, so long as your father keeps up that mystery about the past."

"That," said Evelyn, quietly, "is exactly what Ronald says, Jessie. But we can't make our father speak, Mr. Spargo. That he is as innocent as we are of this terrible crime we are certain, and we don't know why he wouldn't answer the questions put to him at the inquest. And—we know no more than you know or anyone knows, and though I have begged my father to speak, he won't say a word. We saw his danger: Ronald—Mr. Breton—told us, and we implored him to tell everything he knew about Mr. Marbury. But so far he has simply laughed at the idea that he had anything to do with the murder, or could be arrested for it, and now — — "

"And now he's locked up," said Spargo in his usual matter-of-fact fashion. "Well, there are people who have to be saved from themselves, you know. Perhaps you'll have to save your father from the consequences of his own—shall we say obstinacy? Now, look here, between ourselves, how much do you know about your father's—past?"

The two sisters looked at each other and then at Spargo.

"Nothing," said the elder.

"Absolutely nothing!" said the younger.

"Answer a few plain questions," said Spargo. "I'm not going to print your replies, nor make use of them in any way: I'm only asking the questions with a desire to help you. Have you any relations in England?"

"None that we know of," replied Evelyn.

"Nobody you could go to for information about the past?" asked Spargo.

"No—nobody!"

Spargo drummed his fingers on his blotting-pad. He was thinking hard.

"How old is your father?" he asked suddenly.

"He was fifty-nine a few weeks ago," answered Evelyn.

"And how old are you, and how old is your sister?" demanded Spargo.

"I am twenty, and Jessie is nearly nineteen."

"Where were you born?"

"Both of us at San Gregorio, which is in the San José province of Argentina, north of Monte Video."

"Your father was in business there?"

"He was in business in the export trade, Mr. Spargo. There's no secret about that. He exported all sorts of things to England and to France—skins, hides, wools, dried salts, fruit. That's how he made his money."

"You don't know how long he'd been there when you were born?"

"No."

"Was he married when he went out there?"

"No, he wasn't. We do know that. He's told us the circumstances of his marriage, because they were romantic. When he sailed from England to Buenos Ayres, he met on the steamer a young lady who, he said, was like himself, relationless and nearly friendless. She was going out to Argentina as a governess. She and my father fell in love with each other, and they were married in Buenos Ayres soon after the steamer arrived."

"And your mother is dead?"

"My mother died before we came to England. I was eight years old, and Jessie six, then."

"And you came to England—how long after that?"

"Two years."

"So that you've been in England ten years. And you know nothing whatever of your father's past beyond what you've told me?"

"Nothing—absolutely nothing."

"Never heard him talk of—you see, according to your account, your father was a man of getting on to forty when he went out to Argentina. He must have had a career of some sort in this country. Have you never heard him speak of his boyhood? Did he never talk of old times, or that sort of thing?"

"I never remember hearing my father speak of any period antecedent to his marriage," replied Evelyn.

"I once asked him a question about his childhood." said Jessie. "He answered that his early days had not been very happy ones, and that he had done his best to forget them. So I never asked him anything again."

"So that it really comes to this," remarked Spargo. "You know nothing whatever about your father, his family, his fortunes, his life, beyond what you yourselves have observed since you were able to observe? That's about it, isn't it?"

"I should say that that is exactly it," answered Evelyn.

"Just so," said Spargo. "And therefore, as I told your sister the other day, the public will say that your father has some dark secret behind him, and that Marbury had possession of it, and that your father killed him in order to silence him. That isn't my view. I not only believe your father to be absolutely innocent, but I believe that he knows no more than a child unborn of Marbury's murder, and I'm doing my best to find out who that murderer was. By the by, since you'll see all about it in tomorrow morning's *Watchman*, I may as well tell you that I've found out who Marbury really was. He— —"

At this moment Spargo's door was opened and in walked Ronald Breton. He shook his head at sight of the two sisters.

"I thought I should find you here," he said. "Jessie said she was coming to see you, Spargo. I don't know what good you can do—I don't see what good the most powerful newspaper in the world can do. My God!—everything's about as black as ever it can be. Mr. Aylmore—I've just come away from him; his solicitor, Stratton, and I have been with him for an hour—is obstinate as ever—he will not tell more than he has told. Whatever good can you do, Spargo, when he won't speak about that knowledge of Marbury which he must have?"

"Oh, well!" said Spargo. "Perhaps we can give him some information about Marbury. Mr. Aylmore has forgotten that it's not such a difficult thing to rake up the past as he seems to think it is. For example, as I was just telling these young ladies, I myself have discovered who Marbury really was."

Breton started.

"You have? Without doubt?" he exclaimed.

"Without reasonable doubt. Marbury was an ex-convict."

Spargo watched the effect of this sudden announcement. The two girls showed no sign of astonishment or of unusual curiosity; they received the news with as much unconcern as if Spargo had told them that Marbury was a famous musician. But Ronald Breton started, and it seemed to Spargo that he saw a sense of suspicion dawn in his eyes.

"Marbury—an ex-convict!" he exclaimed. "You mean that?"

"Read your *Watchman* in the morning," said Spargo. "You'll find the whole story there—I'm going to write it tonight when you people have gone. It'll make good reading."

Evelyn and Jessie Aylmore took Spargo's hint and went away, Spargo seeing them to the door with another assurance of his belief in their father's innocence and his determination to hunt down the real criminal. Ronald Breton went down with them to the street and saw them into a cab, but in another minute he was back in Spargo's room as Spargo had expected. He shut the door carefully behind him and turned to Spargo with an eager face.

"I say, Spargo, is that really so?" he asked. "About Marbury being an ex-convict?"

"That's so, Breton. I've no more doubt about it than I have that I see you. Marbury was in reality one John Maitland, a bank manager, of Market Milcaster, who got ten years' penal servitude in 1891 for embezzlement."

"In 1891? Why—that's just about the time that Aylmore says he knew him!"

"Exactly. And—it just strikes me," said Spargo, sitting down at his desk and making a hurried note, "it just strikes me—didn't Aylmore say he knew Marbury in London?"

"Certainly," replied Breton. "In London."

"Um!" mused Spargo. "That's queer, because Maitland had never been in London up to the time of his going to Dartmoor, whatever he may have done when he came out of Dartmoor, and, of course, Aylmore had gone to South America long before that. Look here, Breton," he continued, aloud, "have you access to Aylmore? Will you, can you, see him before he's brought up at Bow Street tomorrow?"

"Yes," answered Breton. "I can see him with his solicitor."

"Then listen," said Spargo. "Tomorrow morning you'll find the whole story of how I proved Marbury's identity with Maitland in the *Watchman*. Read it as early as you can; get an interview with Aylmore as early as you can; make him read it, every word, before he's brought up. Beg him if he values his own safety and his daughters' peace of mind to throw away all that foolish reserve, and to tell all he knows about Maitland twenty years ago. He should have done that at first. Why, I was asking his daughters some questions before you came in—they know absolutely nothing of their father's history previous to the time when they began to understand things! Don't you see that Aylmore's career, previous to his return to England, is a blank past!"

"I know—I know!" said Breton. "Yes—although I've gone there a great deal, I never heard Aylmore speak of anything earlier than his Argentine experiences. And yet, he must have been getting on when he went out there."

"Thirty-seven or eight, at least," remarked Spargo. "Well, Aylmore's more or less of a public man, and no public man can keep his life hidden nowadays. By the by, how did you get to know the Aylmores?"

"My guardian, Mr. Elphick, and I met them in Switzerland," answered Breton. "We kept up the acquaintance after our return."

"Mr. Elphick still interesting himself in the Marbury case?" asked Spargo.

"Very much so. And so is old Cardlestone, at the foot of whose stairs the thing came off. I dined with them last night and they talked of little else," said Breton.

"And their theory—"

"Oh, still the murder for the sake of robbery!" replied Breton. "Old Cardlestone is furious that such a thing could have happened at his very door. He says that there ought to be a thorough enquiry into every tenant of the Temple."

"Longish business that," observed Spargo. "Well, run away now, Breton—I must write."

"Shall you be at Bow Street tomorrow morning?" asked Breton as he moved to the door. "It's to be at ten-thirty."

"No, I shan't!" replied Spargo. "It'll only be a remand, and I know already just as much as I should hear there. I've got something much more important to do. But you'll remember what I asked of you—get Aylmore to read my story in the *Watchman*, and beg him to speak out and tell all he knows—all!"

And when Breton had gone, Spargo again murmured those last words: "All he knows—all!"

Next day, a little before noon, Spargo found himself in one of those pretentious yet dismal Bayswater squares, which are almost entirely given up to the trade, calling, or occupation of the lodging and boarding-house keeper. They are very pretentious, those squares, with their many-storied houses, their stuccoed frontages, and their pilastered and balconied doorways; innocent country folk, coming into them from the neighbouring station of Paddington, take them to be the residences of the dukes and earls who, of course, live nowhere else but in London. They are further encouraged in this belief by the fact that young male persons in evening dress are often seen at the doorways in more or less elegant attitudes. These, of course, are taken by the country folk to be young lords enjoying the air of Bayswater, but others, more knowing, are aware that they are Swiss or German waiters whose linen might be cleaner.

Spargo gauged the character of the house at which he called as soon as the door was opened to him. There was the usual smell of eggs and bacon, of fish and chops; the usual mixed and ancient collection of overcoats, wraps, and sticks in the hall; the usual sort of parlourmaid to answer the bell. And presently, in answer to his enquiries, there was the usual type of landlady confronting him, a more than middle-aged person who desired to look younger, and made attempts in the way of false hair, teeth, and a little rouge, and who wore that somewhat air and smile which in its wearer — under these circumstances — always means that she is considering whether you will be able to cheat her or whether she will be able to see you.

"You wish to see Miss Baylis?" said this person, examining Spargo closely. "Miss Baylis does not often see anybody."

"I hope," said Spargo politely, "that Miss Baylis is not an invalid?"

"No, she's not an invalid," replied the landlady; "but she's not as young as she was, and she's an objection to strangers. Is it anything I can tell her?"

"No," said Spargo. "But you can, if you please, take her a message from me. Will you kindly give her my card, and tell her that I wish to ask her a question about John Maitland of Market Milcaster, and that I should be much obliged if she would give me a few minutes."

"Perhaps you will sit down," said the landlady. She led Spargo into a room which opened out upon a garden; in it two or three old ladies, evidently inmates, were sitting. The landlady left Spargo to sit with them and to amuse himself by watching them knit or sew or read the papers, and he wondered if they always did these things every day, and if they would go on doing them until a day would come when they would do them no more, and he was beginning to feel very dreary when the door opened and a woman entered whom Spargo, after one sharp glance at her, decided to be a person who was undoubtedly out of the common. And as she slowly walked across the room towards him he let his first glance lengthen into a look of steady inspection.

The woman whom Spargo thus narrowly inspected was of very remarkable appearance. She was almost masculine; she stood nearly six feet in height; she was of a masculine gait and tread, and spare, muscular, and athletic. What at once struck Spargo about her face was the strange contrast between her dark eyes and her white hair; the hair, worn in abundant coils round a well-shaped head, was of the most snowy whiteness; the eyes of a real coal-blackness, as were also the eyebrows above them. The features were well-cut and of a striking firmness; the jaw square and determined. And Spargo's first thought on taking all this in was that Miss Baylis seemed to have been fitted by Nature to be a prison wardress, or the matron of a hospital, or the governess of an unruly girl, and he began to wonder if he would ever manage to extract anything out of those firmly-locked lips.

Miss Baylis, on her part, looked Spargo over as if she was half-minded to order him to instant execution. And Spargo was so impressed by her that he made a profound bow and found a difficulty in finding his tongue.

"Mr. Spargo?" she said in a deep voice which seemed peculiarly suited to her. "Of, I see, the *Watchman*? You wish to speak to me?"

Spargo again bowed in silence. She signed him to the window near which they were standing.

"Open the casement, if you please," she commanded him. "We will walk in the garden. This is not private."

Spargo obediently obeyed her orders; she swept through the opened window and he followed her. It was not until they had reached the bottom of the garden that she spoke again.

"I understand that you desire to ask me some question about John Maitland, of Market Milcaster?" she said. "Before you put it. I must ask you a question. Do you wish any reply I may give you for publication?"

"Not without your permission," replied Spargo. "I should not think of publishing anything you may tell me except with your express permission."

She looked at him gloomily, seemed to gather an impression of his good faith, and nodded her head.

"In that case," she said, "what do you want to ask?"

"I have lately had reason for making certain enquiries about John Maitland," answered Spargo. "I suppose you read the newspapers and possibly the *Watchman*, Miss Baylis?"

But Miss Baylis shook her head.

"I read no newspapers," she said. "I have no interest in the affairs of the world. I have work which occupies all my time: I give my whole devotion to it."

"Then you have not recently heard of what is known as the Marbury case—a case of a man who was found murdered?" asked Spargo.

"I have not," she answered. "I am not likely to hear such things."

Spargo suddenly realized that the power of the Press is not quite as great nor as far-reaching as very young journalists hold it to be, and that there actually are, even in London, people who can live quite cheerfully without a newspaper. He concealed his astonishment and went on.

"Well," he said, "I believe that the murdered man, known to the police as John Marbury, was, in reality, your brother-in-law, John Maitland. In fact, Miss Baylis, I'm absolutely certain of it!"

He made this declaration with some emphasis, and looked at his stern companion to see how she was impressed. But Miss Baylis showed no sign of being impressed.

"I can quite believe that, Mr. Spargo," she said coldly. "It is no surprise to me that John Maitland should come to such an end. He was a thoroughly bad and unprincipled man, who brought the most terrible disgrace on those who were, unfortunately, connected with him. He was likely to die a bad man's death."

"I may ask you a few questions about him?" suggested Spargo in his most insinuating manner.

"You may, so long as you do not drag my name into the papers," she replied. "But pray, how do you know that I have the sad shame of being John Maitland's sister-in-law?"

"I found that out at Market Milcaster," said Spargo. "The photographer told me — Cooper."

"Ah!" she exclaimed.

"The questions I want to ask are very simple," said Spargo. "But your answers may materially help me. You remember Maitland going to prison, of course?"

Miss Baylis laughed — a laugh of scorn.

"Could I ever forget it?" she exclaimed.

"Did you ever visit him in prison?" asked Spargo.

"Visit him in prison!" she said indignantly. "Visits in prison are to be paid to those who deserve them, who are repentant; not to scoundrels who are hardened in their sin!"

"All right. Did you ever see him after he left prison?"

"I saw him, for he forced himself upon me — I could not help myself. He was in my presence before I was aware that he had even been released."

"What did he come for?" asked Spargo.

"To ask for his son — who had been in my charge," she replied.

"That's a thing I want to know about," said Spargo. "Do you know what a certain lot of people in Market Milcaster say to this day, Miss Baylis? — they say that you were in at the game with Maitland; that you had a lot of the money placed in your charge; that when Maitland went to prison, you took the child away, first to Brighton, then abroad — disappeared with him — and that you made a home ready for Maitland when he came out. That's what's said by some people in Market Milcaster."

Miss Baylis's stern lips curled.

"People in Market Milcaster!" she exclaimed. "All the people I ever knew in Market Milcaster had about as many brains between them as that cat on the wall there. As for making a home for John Maitland, I would have seen him die in the gutter, of absolute want, before I would have given him a crust of dry bread!"

"You appear to have a terrible dislike of this man," observed Spargo, astonished at her vehemence.

"I had — and I have," she answered. "He tricked my sister into a marriage with him when he knew that she would rather have married an honest man who worshipped her; he treated her with quiet, infernal cruelty; he robbed her and me of the small fortunes our father left us."

"Ah!" said Spargo. "Well, so you say Maitland came to you, when he came out of prison, to ask for his boy. Did he take the boy?"

"No — the boy was dead."

"Dead, eh? Then I suppose Maitland did not stop long with you?"

Miss Baylis laughed her scornful laugh.

"I showed him the door!" she said.

"Well, did he tell you that he was going to Australia?" enquired Spargo.

"I should not have listened to anything that he told me, Mr. Spargo," she answered.

"Then, in short," said Spargo, "you never heard of him again?"

"I never heard of him again," she declared passionately, "and I only hope that what you tell me is true, and that Marbury really was Maitland!"

Spargo, having exhausted the list of questions which he had thought out on his way to Bayswater, was about to take his leave of Miss Baylis, when a new idea suddenly occurred to him, and he turned back to that formidable lady.

"I've just thought of something else," he said. "I told you that I'm certain Marbury was Maitland, and that he came to a sad end — murdered."

"And I've told you," she replied scornfully, "that in my opinion no end could be too bad for him."

"Just so — I understand you," said Spargo. "But I didn't tell you that he was not only murdered but robbed — robbed of probably a good deal. There's good reason to believe that he had securities, bank notes, loose diamonds, and other things on him to the value of a large amount. He'd several thousand pounds when he left Coolumbidgee, in New South Wales, where he'd lived quietly for some years."

Miss Baylis smiled sourly.

"What's all this to me?" she asked.

"Possibly nothing. But you see, that money, those securities, may be recovered. And as the boy you speak of is dead, there surely must be somebody who's entitled to the lot. It's worth having, Miss Baylis, and there's strong belief on the part of the police that it will turn up."

This was a bit of ingenious bluff on the part of Spargo; he watched its effect with keen eyes. But Miss Baylis was adamant, and she looked as scornful as ever.

"I say again what's all that to me?" she exclaimed.

"Well, but hadn't the dead boy any relatives on his father's side?" asked Spargo. "I know you're his aunt on the mother's side, and as you're indifferent perhaps, I can find some on the other side. It's very easy to find all these things out, you know."

Miss Baylis, who had begun to stalk back to the house in gloomy and majestic fashion, and had let Spargo see plainly that this part of the interview was distasteful to her, suddenly paused in her stride and glared at the young journalist.

"Easy to find all these things out?" she repeated.

Spargo caught, or fancied he caught, a note of anxiety in her tone. He was quick to turn his fancy to practical purpose.

"Oh, easy enough!" he said. "I could find out all about Maitland's family through that boy. Quite, quite easily!"

Miss Baylis had stopped now, and stood glaring at him. "How?" she demanded.

"I'll tell you," said Spargo with cheerful alacrity. "It is, of course, the easiest thing in the world to trace all about his short life. I suppose I can find the register of his birth at Market Milcaster, and you, of course, will tell me where he died. By the by, when did he die, Miss Baylis?"

But Miss Baylis was going on again to the house.

"I shall tell you nothing more," she said angrily. "I've told you too much already, and I believe all you're here for is to get some news for your paper. But I will, at any rate tell you this—when Maitland went to prison his child would have been defenceless but for me; he'd have had to go to the workhouse but for me; he hadn't a single relation in the world but me, on either father's or mother's side. And even at my age, old woman as I am, I'd rather beg my bread in the street, I'd rather starve and die, than touch a penny piece that had come from John Maitland! That's all."

Then without further word, without offering to show Spargo the way out, she marched in at the open window and disappeared. And Spargo, knowing no other way, was about to follow her when he heard a sudden rustling sound in the shadow by which they had stood, and the next moment a queer, cracked, horrible voice, suggesting all sorts of things, said distinctly and yet in a whisper:

"Young man!"

Spargo turned and stared at the privet hedge behind him. It was thick and bushy, and in its full summer green, but it seemed to him that he saw a nondescript shape behind. "Who's there?" he demanded. "Somebody listening?"

There was a curious cackle of laughter from behind the hedge; then the cracked, husky voice spoke again.

"Young man, don't you move or look as if you were talking to anybody. Do you know where the 'King of Madagascar' public-house is in this quarter of the town, young man?"

"No!" answered Spargo. "Certainly not!"

"Well, anybody'll tell you when you get outside, young man," continued the queer voice of the unseen person. "Go there, and wait at the corner by the 'King of Madagascar,' and I'll come there to you at the end of half an hour. Then I'll tell you something, young man—I'll tell you something. Now run away, young man, run away to the 'King of Madagascar'—I'm coming!"

The voice ended in low, horrible cachinnation which made Spargo feel queer. But he was young enough to be in love with adventure, and he immediately turned on his heel without so much as a glance at the privet hedge, and went across the garden and through the house, and let himself out at the door. And at the next corner of the square he met a policeman and asked him if he knew where the "King of Madagascar" was.

"First to the right, second to the left," answered the policeman tersely. "You can't miss it anywhere round there—it's a landmark."

And Spargo found the landmark—a great, square-built tavern—easily, and he waited at a corner of it wondering what he was going to see, and intensely curious about the owner of the queer voice, with all its suggestions of he knew not what. And suddenly there came up to him an old woman and leered at him in a fashion that made him suddenly realize how dreadful old age may be.

Spargo had never seen such an old woman as this in his life. She was dressed respectably, better than respectably. Her gown was good; her bonnet was smart; her smaller fittings were good. But her face was evil; it showed unmistakable signs of a long devotion to the bottle; the old eyes leered and ogled, the old lips were wicked. Spargo felt a sense of disgust almost amounting to nausea, but he was going to hear what the old harridan had to say and he tried not to look what he felt.

"Well?" he said, almost roughly. "Well?"

"Well, young man, there you are," said his new acquaintance. "Let us go inside, young man; there's a quiet little place where a lady can sit and take her drop of gin—I'll show you. And if you're good to me, I'll tell you something about that cat that you were talking to just now. But you'll give me a little matter to put in my pocket, young man? Old ladies like me have a right to buy little comforts, you know, little comforts."

Spargo followed this extraordinary person into a small parlour within; the attendant who came in response to a ring showed no astonishment at her presence; he also seemed to know exactly what she required, which was a certain brand of gin, sweetened, and warm. And Spargo watched her curiously as with shaking hand she pushed up the veil which hid little of her wicked old face, and lifted the glass to her mouth with a zest which was not thirst but pure greed of liquor. Almost instantly he saw a new light steal into her eyes, and she laughed in a voice that grew clearer with every sound she made.

"Ah, young man!" she said with a confidential nudge of the elbow that made Spargo long to get up and fly. "I wanted that! It's done me good. When I've finished that, you'll pay for another for me — and perhaps another? They'll do me still more good. And you'll give me a little matter of money, won't you, young man?"

"Not till I know what I'm giving it for," replied Spargo.

"You'll be giving it because I'm going to tell you that if it's made worth my while I can tell you, or somebody that sent you, more about Jane Baylis than anybody in the world. I'm not going to tell you that now, young man — I'm sure you don't carry in your pocket what I shall want for my secret, not you, by the look of you! I'm only going to show you that I have the secret. Eh?"

"Who are you?" asked Spargo.

The woman leered and chuckled. "What are you going to give me, young man?" she asked.

Spargo put his fingers in his pocket and pulled out two half-sovereigns.

"Look here," he said, showing his companion the coins, "if you can tell me anything of importance you shall have these. But no trifling, now. And no wasting of time. If you have anything to tell, out with it!"

The woman stretched out a trembling, claw-like hand.

"But let me hold one of those, young man!" she implored. "Let me hold one of the beautiful bits of gold. I shall tell you all the better if I hold one of them. Let me — there's a good young gentleman."

Spargo gave her one of the coins, and resigned himself to his fate, whatever it might be.

"You won't get the other unless you tell something," he said. "Who are you, anyway?"

The woman, who had begun mumbling and chuckling over the half-sovereign, grinned horribly.

"At the boarding-house yonder, young man, they call me Mother Gutch," she answered; "but my proper name is Mrs. Sabina Gutch, and once upon a time I was a good-looking young woman. And when my husband died I went to Jane Baylis as housekeeper, and when she retired from that and came to live in that boarding-house where we live now, she was forced to bring me with her and to keep me. Why had she to do that, young man?"

"Heaven knows!" answered Spargo.

"Because I've got a hold on her, young man—I've got a secret of hers," continued Mother Gutch. "She'd be scared to death if she knew I'd been behind that hedge and had heard what she said to you, and she'd be more than scared if she knew that you and I were here, talking. But she's grown hard and near with me, and she won't give me a penny to get a drop of anything with, and an old woman like me has a right to her little comforts, and if you'll buy the secret, young man, I'll split on her, there and then, when you pay the money."

"Before I talk about buying any secret," said Spargo, "you'll have to prove to me that you've a secret to sell that's worth my buying."

"And I will prove it!" said Mother Gutch with sudden fierceness. "Touch the bell, and let me have another glass, and then I'll tell you. Now," she went on, more quietly—Spargo noticed that the more she drank, the more rational she became, and that her nerves seemed to gain strength and her whole appearance to be improved—"now, you came to her to find out about her brother-in-law, Maitland, that went to prison, didn't you?"

"Well?" demanded Spargo.

"And about that boy of his?" she continued.

"You heard all that was said," answered Spargo. "I'm waiting to hear what you have to say."

But Mother Gutch was resolute in having her own way. She continued her questions:

"And she told you that Maitland came and asked for the boy, and that she told him the boy was dead, didn't she?" she went on.

"Well?" said Spargo despairingly. "She did. What then?"

Mother Gutch took an appreciative pull at her glass and smiled knowingly. "What then?" she chuckled. "All lies, young man, the boy isn't dead—any more than I am. And my secret is—"

"Well?" demanded Spargo impatiently. "What is it?"

"This!" answered Mother Gutch, digging her companion in the ribs, "I know what she did with him!"

Spargo turned on his disreputable and dissolute companion with all his journalistic energies and instincts roused. He had not been sure, since entering the "King of Madagascar," that he was going to hear anything material to the Middle Temple Murder; he had more than once feared that this old gin-drinking harridan was deceiving him, for the purpose of extracting drink and money from him. But now, at the mere prospect of getting important information from her, he forgot all about Mother Gutch's unfortunate propensities, evil eyes, and sodden face; he only saw in her somebody who could tell him something. He turned on her eagerly.

"You say that John Maitland's son didn't die!" he exclaimed.

"The boy did not die," replied Mother Gutch.

"And that you know where he is?" asked Spargo.

Mother Gutch shook her head.

"I didn't say that I know where he is, young man," she replied. "I said I knew what she did with him."

"What, then?" demanded Spargo.

Mother Gutch drew herself up in a vast assumption of dignity, and favoured Spargo with a look.

"That's the secret, young man," she said. "I'm willing to sell that secret, but not for two half-sovereigns and two or three drops of cold gin. If Maitland left all that money you told Jane Baylis of, when I was listening to you from behind the hedge, my secret's worth something."

Spargo suddenly remembered his bit of bluff to Miss Baylis. Here was an unexpected result of it.

"Nobody but me can help you to trace Maitland's boy," continued Mother Gutch, "and I shall expect to be paid accordingly. That's plain language, young man."

Spargo considered the situation in silence for a minute or two. Could this wretched, bibulous old woman really be in possession of a secret which would lead to the solving of the mystery of the Middle Temple Murder? Well, it would be a fine thing for the *Watchman* if the clearing up of everything came through one of its men. And the *Watchman* was noted for being generous even to extravagance in laying out money on all sorts of objects: it had spent money like water on much less serious matters than this.

"How much do you want for your secret?" he suddenly asked, turning to his companion.

Mother Gutch began to smooth out a pleat in her gown. It was really wonderful to Spargo to find how very sober and normal this old harridan had become; he did not understand that her nerves had been all a-quiver and on edge when he first met her, and that a resort to her favourite form of alcohol in liberal quantity had calmed and quickened them; secretly he was regarding her with astonishment as the most extraordinary old person he had ever met, and he was almost afraid of her as he waited for her decision. At last Mother Gutch spoke.

"Well, young man," she said, "having considered matters, and having a right to look well to myself, I think that what I should prefer to have would be one of those annuities. A nice, comfortable annuity, paid weekly — none of your monthlies or quarterlies, but regular and punctual, every Saturday morning. Or Monday morning, as was convenient to the parties concerned — but punctual and regular. I know a good many ladies in my sphere of life as enjoys annuities, and it's a great comfort to have 'em paid weekly."

It occurred to Spargo that Mrs. Gutch would probably get rid of her weekly dole on the day it was paid, whether that day happened to be Monday or Saturday, but that, after all, was no concern of his, so he came back to first principles.

"Even now you haven't said how much," he remarked.

"Three pound a week," replied Mother Gutch. "And cheap, too!"

Spargo thought hard for two minutes. The secret might—might!—lead to something big. This wretched old woman would probably drink herself to death within a year or two. Anyhow, a few hundreds of pounds was nothing to the *Watchman*. He glanced at his watch. At that hour—for the next hour—the great man of the *Watchman* would be at the office. He jumped to his feet, suddenly resolved and alert.

"Here, I'll take you to see my principals," he said. "We'll run along in a taxi-cab."

"With all the pleasure in the world, young man," replied Mother Gutch; "when you've given me that other half-sovereign. As for principals, I'd far rather talk business with masters than with men—though I mean no disrespect to you." Spargo, feeling that he was in for it, handed over the second half-sovereign, and busied himself in ordering a taxi-cab. But when that came round he had to wait while Mrs. Gutch consumed a third glass of gin and purchased a flask of the same beverage to put in her pocket. At last he got her off, and in due course to the *Watchman* office, where the hall-porter and the messenger boys stared at her in amazement, well used as they were to seeing strange folk, and he got her to his own room, and locked her in, and then he sought the presence of the mighty.

What Spargo said to his editor and to the great man who controlled the fortunes and workings of the *Watchman* he never knew. It was probably fortunate for him that they were both thoroughly conversant with the facts of the Middle Temple Murder, and saw that there might be an advantage in securing the revelations of which Spargo had got the conditional promise. At any rate, they accompanied Spargo to his room, intent on seeing, hearing and bargaining with the lady he had locked up there.

Spargo's room smelt heavily of unsweetened gin, but Mother Gutch was soberer than ever. She insisted upon being introduced to proprietor and editor in due and proper form, and in discussing terms with them before going into any further particulars. The editor was all for temporizing with her until something could be done to find out what likelihood of truth there was in her, but the proprietor, after sizing her up in his own shrewd fashion, took his two companions out of the room.

"We'll hear what the old woman has to say on her own terms," he said. "She may have something to tell that is really of the greatest importance in this case: she certainly has something to tell. And, as Spargo says, she'll probably drink herself to death in about as short a time as possible. Come back—let's hear her story." So they returned to the gin-scented atmosphere, and a formal document was drawn out by which the proprietor of the *Watchman* bound himself to pay Mrs. Gutch the sum of three pounds a week for life (Mrs. Gutch insisting on the insertion of the words "every Saturday morning, punctual and regular") and then Mrs. Gutch was invited to tell her tale. And Mrs. Gutch settled herself to do so, and Spargo prepared to take it down, word for word.

"Which the story, as that young man called it, is not so long as a monkey's tail nor so short as a Manx cat's, gentlemen," said Mrs. Gutch; "but full of meat as an egg. Now, you see, when that Maitland affair at Market Milcaster came off, I was housekeeper to Miss Jane Baylis at Brighton. She kept a boarding-house there, in Kemp Town, and close to the sea-front, and a very good thing she made out of it, and had saved a nice bit, and having, like her sister, Mrs. Maitland, had a little fortune left her by her father, as was at one time a publican here in London, she had a good lump of money. And all that money was in this here Maitland's hands, every penny. I very well remember the day when the news came about that affair of Maitland robbing the bank. Miss Baylis, she was like a mad thing when she saw it in the paper, and before she'd seen it an hour she was off to Market Milcaster. I went up to the station with her, and she told me then before she got in the train that Maitland had all her fortune and her savings, and her sister's, his wife's, too, and that she feared all would be lost."

"Mrs. Maitland was then dead," observed Spargo without looking up from his writing-block.

"She was, young man, and a good thing, too," continued Mrs. Gutch. "Well, away went Miss Baylis, and no more did I hear or see for nearly a week, and then back she comes, and brings a little boy with her—which was Maitland's. And she told me that night that she'd lost every penny she had in the world, and that her sister's money, what ought to have been the child's, was gone, too, and she said her say about Maitland. However, she saw well to that child; nobody could have seen better. And very soon after, when Maitland was sent to prison for ten years, her and me talked about things. 'What's the use,' says I to her, 'of your letting yourself get so fond of that child, and looking after it as you do, and educating it, and so on?' I says. 'Why not?' says she. 'Tisn't yours,' I says, 'you haven't no right to it,' I says. 'As soon as ever its father comes out,' says I,' he'll come and claim it, and you can't do nothing to stop him.' Well, gentlemen, if you'll believe me, never did I see a woman look as she did when I says all that. And she up and swore that Maitland should never see or touch the child again—not under no circumstances whatever."

Mrs. Gutch paused to take a little refreshment from her pocket-flask, with an apologetic remark as to the state of her heart. She resumed, presently, apparently refreshed.

"Well, gentlemen, that notion, about Maitland's taking the child away from her seemed to get on her mind, and she used to talk to me at times about it, always saying the same thing—that Maitland should never have him. And one day she told me she was going to London to see lawyers about it, and she went, and she came back, seeming more satisfied, and a day or two afterwards, there came a gentleman who looked like a lawyer, and he stopped a day or two, and he came again and again, until one day she came to me, and she says, 'You don't know who that gentleman is that's come so much lately?' she says. 'Not I,' I says, 'unless he's after you.' 'After me!' she says, tossing her head: 'That's the gentleman that ought to have married my poor sister if that scoundrel Maitland hadn't tricked her into throwing him over!' 'You don't say so!' I says. 'Then by rights he ought to have been the child's pa!' 'He's going to be a father to the boy,' she says. 'He's going to take him and educate him in the highest fashion, and make a gentleman of him,' she says, 'for his mother's sake.' 'Mercy on us!' says I. 'What'll Maitland say when he comes for him?' 'Maitland'll never come for him,' she says, 'for I'm going to leave here, and the boy'll be gone before then. This is all being done,' she says, 'so that the child'll never know his father's shame—he'll never know who his father was.' And true enough, the boy was taken away, but Maitland came before she'd gone, and she told him the child was dead, and I never see a man so cut up. However, it wasn't no concern of mine. And so there's so much of the secret, gentlemen, and I would like to know if I ain't giving good value."

"Very good," said the proprietor. "Go on." But Spargo intervened.

"Did you ever hear the name of the gentleman who took the boy away?" he asked.

"Yes, I did," replied Mrs. Gutch. "Of course I did. Which it was Elphick."

Spargo dropped his pen on the desk before him with a sharp clatter that made Mrs. Gutch jump. A steady devotion to the bottle had made her nerves to be none of the strongest, and she looked at the startler of them with angry malevolence.

"Don't do that again, young man!" she exclaimed sharply. "I can't a-bear to be jumped out of my skin, and it's bad manners. I observed that the gentleman's name was Elphick."

Spargo contrived to get in a glance at his proprietor and his editor — a glance which came near to being a wink.

"Just so — Elphick," he said. "A law gentleman I think you said, Mrs. Gutch?"

"I said," answered Mrs. Gutch, "as how he looked like a lawyer gentleman. And since you're so particular, young man, though I wasn't addressing you but your principals, he was a lawyer gentleman. One of the sort that wears wigs and gowns — ain't I seen his picture in Jane Baylis's room at the boarding-house where you saw her this morning?"

"Elderly man?" asked Spargo.

"Elderly he will be now," replied the informant; "but when he took the boy away he was a middle-aged man. About his age," she added, pointing to the editor in a fashion which made that worthy man wince and the proprietor desire to laugh unconsumedly; "and not so very unlike him neither, being one as had no hair on his face."

"Ah!" said Spargo. "And where did this Mr. Elphick take the boy, Mrs. Gutch?"

But Mrs. Gutch shook her head.

"Ain't no idea," she said. "He took him. Then, as I told you, Maitland came, and Jane Baylis told him that the boy was dead. And after that she never even told me anything about the boy. She kept a tight tongue. Once or twice I asked her, and she says, 'Never you mind,' she says; 'he's all right for life, if he lives to be as old as Methusalem.' And she never said more, and I never said more. But," continued Mrs. Gutch, whose pocket-flask was empty, and who began to wipe tears away, "she's treated me hard has Jane Baylis, never allowing me a little comfort such as a lady of my age should have, and when I hears the two of you a-talking this morning the other side of that privet hedge, thinks I, 'Now's the time to have my knife into you, my fine madam!' And I hope I done it."

Spargo looked at the editor and the proprietor, nodding his head slightly. He meant them to understand that he had got all he wanted from Mother Gutch.

"What are you going to do, Mrs. Gutch, when you leave here?" he asked. "You shall be driven straight back to Bayswater, if you like."

"Which I shall be obliged for, young man," said Mrs. Gutch, "and likewise for the first week of the annuity, and will call every Saturday for the same at eleven punctual, or can be posted to me on a Friday, whichever is agreeable to you gentlemen. And having my first week in my purse, and being driven to Bayswater, I shall take my boxes and go to a friend of mine where I shall be hearty welcome, shaking the dust of my feet off against Jane Baylis and where I've been living with her."

"Yes, but, Mrs. Gutch," said Spargo, with some anxiety, "if you go back there tonight, you'll be very careful not to tell Miss Baylis that you've been here and told us all this?"

Mrs. Gutch rose, dignified and composed.

"Young man," she said, "you mean well, but you ain't used to dealing with ladies. I can keep my tongue as still as anybody when I like. I wouldn't tell Jane Baylis my affairs—my new affairs, gentlemen, thanks to you—not for two annuities, paid twice a week!"

"Take Mrs. Gutch downstairs, Spargo, and see her all right, and then come to my room," said the editor. "And don't you forget, Mrs. Gutch—keep a quiet tongue in your head—no more talk—or there'll be no annuities on Saturday mornings."

So Spargo took Mother Gutch to the cashier's department and paid her her first week's money, and he got her a taxi-cab, and paid for it, and saw her depart, and then he went to the editor's room, strangely thoughtful. The editor and the proprietor were talking, but they stopped when Spargo entered and looked at him eagerly. "I think we've done it," said Spargo quietly.

"What, precisely, have we found out?" asked the editor.

"A great deal more than I'd anticipated," answered Spargo, "and I don't know what fields it doesn't open out. If you look back, you'll remember that the only thing found on Marbury's body was a scrap of grey paper on which was a name and address—Ronald Breton, King's Bench Walk."

"Well?"

"Breton is a young barrister. Also he writes a bit—I have accepted two or three articles of his for our literary page."

"Well?"

"Further, he is engaged to Miss Aylmore, the eldest daughter of Aylmore, the Member of Parliament who has been charged at Bow Street today with the murder of Marbury."

"I know. Well, what then, Spargo?"

"But the most important matter," continued Spargo, speaking very deliberately, "is this—that is, taking that old woman's statement to be true, as I personally believe it is—that Breton, as he has told me himself (I have seen a good deal of him) was brought up by a guardian. That guardian is Mr. Septimus Elphick, the barrister."

The proprietor and the editor looked at each other. Their faces wore the expression of men thinking on the same lines and arriving at the same conclusion. And the proprietor suddenly turned on Spargo with a sharp interrogation: "You think then——"

Spargo nodded.

"I think that Mr. Septimus Elphick is the Elphick, and that Breton is the young Maitland of whom Mrs. Gutch has been talking," he answered.

The editor got up, thrust his hands in his pockets, and began to pace the room.

"If that's so," he said, "if that's so, the mystery deepens. What do you propose to do, Spargo?"

"I think," said Spargo, slowly, "I think that without telling him anything of what we have learnt, I should like to see young Breton and get an introduction from him to Mr. Elphick. I can make a good excuse for wanting an interview with him. If you will leave it in my hands — "

"Yes, yes!" said the proprietor, waving a hand. "Leave it entirely in Spargo's hands."

"Keep me informed," said the editor. "Do what you think. It strikes me you're on the track."

Spargo left their presence, and going back to his own room, still faintly redolent of the personality of Mrs. Gutch, got hold of the reporter who had been present at Bow Street when Aylmore was brought up that morning. There was nothing new; the authorities had merely asked for another remand. So far as the reporter knew, Aylmore had said nothing fresh to anybody.

Spargo went round to the Temple and up to Ronald Breton's chambers. He found the young barrister just preparing to leave, and looking unusually grave and thoughtful. At sight of Spargo he turned back from his outer door, beckoned the journalist to follow him, and led him into an inner room.

"I say, Spargo!" he said, as he motioned his visitor to take a chair. "This is becoming something more than serious. You know what you told me to do yesterday as regards Aylmore?"

"To get him to tell all? — Yes," said Spargo.

Breton shook his head.

"Stratton — his solicitor, you know — and I saw him this morning before the police-court proceedings," he continued. "I told him of my talk with you; I even went as far as to tell him that his daughters had been to the *Watchman* office. Stratton and I both begged him to take your advice and tell all, everything, no matter at what cost to his private feelings. We pointed out to him the serious nature of the evidence against him; how he had damaged himself by not telling the whole truth at once; how he had certainly done a great deal to excite suspicion against himself; how, as the evidence stands at present, any jury could scarcely do less than convict him. And it was all no good, Spargo!"

"He won't say anything?"

"He'll say no more. He was adamant. 'I told the entire truth in respect to my dealings with Marbury on the night he met his death at the inquest,' he said, over and over again, 'and I shall say nothing further on any consideration. If the law likes to hang an innocent man on such evidence as that, let it!' And he persisted in that until we left him. Spargo, I don't know what's to be done."

"And nothing happened at the police-court?"

"Nothing—another remand. Stratton and I saw Aylmore again before he was removed. He left us with a sort of sardonic remark—'If you all want to prove me innocent,' he said, 'find the guilty man.'"

"Well, there was a tremendous lot of common sense in that," said Spargo.

"Yes, of course, but how, how, how is it going to be done?" exclaimed Breton. "Are you any nearer—is Rathbury any nearer? Is there the slightest clue that will fasten the guilt on anybody else?"

Spargo gave no answer to these questions. He remained silent a while, apparently thinking.

"Was Rathbury in court?" he suddenly asked.

"He was," replied Breton. "He was there with two or three other men who I suppose were detectives, and seemed to be greatly interested in Aylmore."

"If I don't see Rathbury tonight I'll see him in the morning," said Spargo. He rose as if to go, but after lingering a moment, sat down again. "Look here," he continued, "I don't know how this thing stands in law, but would it be a very weak case against Aylmore if the prosecution couldn't show some motive for his killing Marbury?"

Breton smiled.

"There's no necessity to prove motive in murder," he said. "But I'll tell you what, Spargo—if the prosecution can show that Aylmore had a motive for getting rid of Marbury, if they could prove that it was to Aylmore's advantage to silence him—why, then, I don't think he's a chance."

"I see. But so far no motive, no reason for his killing Marbury has been shown."

"I know of none."

Spargo rose and moved to the door.

"Well, I'm off," he said. Then, as if he suddenly recollected something, he turned back. "Oh, by the by," he said, "isn't your guardian, Mr. Elphick, a big authority on philately?"

"One of the biggest. Awful enthusiast."

"Do you think he'd tell me a bit about those Australian stamps which Marbury showed to Criedir, the dealer?"

"Certain, he would—delighted. Here"—and Breton scribbled a few words on a card—"there's his address and a word from me. I'll tell you when you can always find him in, five nights out of seven—at nine o'clock, after he's dined. I'd go with you tonight, but I must go to Aylmore's. The two girls are in terrible trouble." "Give them a message from me," said Spargo as they went out together. "Tell them to keep up their hearts and their courage."

Spargo went round again to the Temple that night at nine o'clock, asking himself over and over again two questions — the first, how much does Elphick know? the second, how much shall I tell him?

The old house in the Temple to which he repaired and in which many a generation of old fogies had lived since the days of Queen Anne, was full of stairs and passages, and as Spargo had forgotten to get the exact number of the set of chambers he wanted, he was obliged to wander about in what was a deserted building. So wandering, he suddenly heard steps, firm, decisive steps coming up a staircase which he himself had just climbed. He looked over the banisters down into the hollow beneath. And there, marching up resolutely, was the figure of a tall, veiled woman, and Spargo suddenly realized, with a sharp quickening of his pulses, that for the second time that day he was beneath one roof with Miss Baylis.

Spargo's mind acted quickly. Knowing what he now knew, from his extraordinary dealings with Mother Gutch, he had no doubt whatever that Miss Baylis had come to see Mr. Elphick — come, of course, to tell Mr. Elphick that he, Spargo, had visited her that morning, and that he was on the track of the Maitland secret history. He had never thought of it before, for he had been busily engaged since the departure of Mother Gutch; but, naturally, Miss Baylis and Mr. Elphick would keep in communication with each other. At any rate, here she was, and her destination was, surely, Elphick's chambers. And the question for him, Spargo, was — what to do?

What Spargo did was to remain in absolute silence, motionless, tense, where he was on the stair, and to trust to the chance that the woman did not look up. But Miss Baylis neither looked up nor down: she reached a landing, turned along a corridor with decision, and marched forward. A moment later Spargo heard a sharp double knock on a door: a moment after that he heard a door heavily shut; he knew then that Miss Baylis had sought and gained admittance — somewhere.

To find out precisely where that somewhere was drew Spargo down to the landing which Miss Baylis had just left. There was no one about—he had not, in fact, seen a soul since he entered the building. Accordingly he went along the corridor into which he had seen Miss Baylis turn. He knew that all the doors in that house were double ones, and that the outer oak in each was solid and substantial enough to be sound proof. Yet, as men will under such circumstances, he walked softly; he said to himself, smiling at the thought, that he would be sure to start if somebody suddenly opened a door on him. But no hand opened any door, and at last he came to the end of the corridor and found himself confronting a small board on which was painted in white letters on a black ground, Mr. Elphick's Chambers.

Having satisfied himself as to his exact whereabouts, Spargo drew back as quietly as he had come. There was a window half-way along the corridor from which, he had noticed as he came along, one could catch a glimpse of the Embankment and the Thames; to this he withdrew, and leaning on the sill looked out and considered matters. Should he go and—if he could gain admittance—beard these two conspirators? Should he wait until the woman came out and let her see that he was on the track? Should he hide again until she went, and then see Elphick alone?

In the end Spargo did none of these things immediately. He let things slide for the moment. He lighted a cigarette and stared at the river and the brown sails, and the buildings across on the Surrey side. Ten minutes went by—twenty minutes—nothing happened. Then, as half-past nine struck from all the neighbouring clocks, Spargo flung away a second cigarette, marched straight down the corridor and knocked boldly at Mr. Elphick's door.

Greatly to Spargo's surprise, the door was opened before there was any necessity to knock again. And there, calmly confronting him, a benevolent, yet somewhat deprecating expression on his spectacled and placid face, stood Mr. Elphick, a smoking cap on his head, a tasseled smoking jacket over his dress shirt, and a short pipe in his hand.

Spargo was taken aback: Mr. Elphick apparently was not. He held the door well open, and motioned the journalist to enter.

"Come in, Mr. Spargo," he said. "I was expecting you. Walk forward into my sitting-room."

Spargo, much astonished at this reception, passed through an ante-room into a handsomely furnished apartment full of books and pictures. In spite of the fact that it was still very little past midsummer there was a cheery fire in the grate, and on a table set near a roomy arm-chair was set such creature comforts as a spirit-case, a syphon, a tumbler, and a novel—from which things Spargo argued that Mr. Elphick had been taking his ease since his dinner. But in another armchair on the opposite side of the hearth was the forbidding figure of Miss Baylis, blacker, gloomier, more mysterious than ever. She neither spoke nor moved when Spargo entered: she did not even look at him. And Spargo stood staring at her until Mr. Elphick, having closed his doors, touched him on the elbow, and motioned him courteously to a seat.

"Yes, I was expecting you, Mr. Spargo," he said, as he resumed his own chair. "I have been expecting you at any time, ever since you took up your investigation of the Marbury affair, in some of the earlier stages of which you saw me, you will remember, at the mortuary. But since Miss Baylis told me, twenty minutes ago, that you had been to her this morning I felt sure that it would not be more than a few hours before you would come to me."

"Why, Mr. Elphick, should you suppose that I should come to you at all?" asked Spargo, now in full possession of his wits.

"Because I felt sure that you would leave no stone unturned, no corner unexplored," replied Mr. Elphick. "The curiosity of the modern pressman is insatiable."

Spargo stiffened.

"I have no curiosity, Mr. Elphick," he said. "I am charged by my paper to investigate the circumstances of the death of the man who was found in Middle Temple Lane, and, if possible, to track his murderer, and——"

Mr. Elphick laughed slightly and waved his hand.

"My good young gentleman!" he said. "You exaggerate your own importance. I don't approve of modern journalism nor of its methods. In your own case you have got hold of some absurd notion that the man John Marbury was in reality one John Maitland, once of Market Milcaster, and you have been trying to frighten Miss Baylis here into——"

Spargo suddenly rose from his chair. There was a certain temper in him which, when once roused, led him to straight hitting, and it was roused now. He looked the old barrister full in the face.

"Mr. Elphick," he said, "you are evidently unaware of all that I know. So I will tell you what I will do. I will go back to my office, and I will write down what I do know, and give the true and absolute proofs of what I know, and, if you will trouble yourself to read the *Watchman* tomorrow morning, then you, too, will know."

"Dear me — dear me!" said Mr. Elphick, banteringly. "We are so used to ultra-sensational stories from the *Watchman* that — but I am a curious and inquisitive old man, my good young sir, so perhaps you will tell me in a word what it is you do know, eh?"

Spargo reflected for a second. Then he bent forward across the table and looked the old barrister straight in the face.

"Yes," he said quietly. "I will tell you what I know beyond doubt. I know that the man murdered under the name of John Marbury was, without doubt, John Maitland, of Market Milcaster, and that Ronald Breton is his son, whom you took from that woman!"

If Spargo had desired a complete revenge for the cavalier fashion in which Mr. Elphick had treated it he could not have been afforded a more ample one than that offered to him by the old barrister's reception of this news. Mr. Elphick's face not only fell, but changed; his expression of almost sneering contempt was transformed to one clearly resembling abject terror; he dropped his pipe, fell back in his chair, recovered himself, gripped the chair's arms, and stared at Spargo as if the young man had suddenly announced to him that in another minute he must be led to instant execution. And Spargo, quick to see his advantage, followed it up.

"That is what I know, Mr. Elphick, and if I choose, all the world shall know it tomorrow morning!" he said firmly. "Ronald Breton is the son of the murdered man, and Ronald Breton is engaged to be married to the daughter of the man charged with the murder. Do you hear that? It is not matter of suspicion, or of idea, or of conjecture, it is fact — fact!"

Mr. Elphick slowly turned his face to Miss Baylis. He gasped out a few words.

"You — did — not — tell — me — this!"

Then Spargo, turning to the woman, saw that she, too, was white to the lips and as frightened as the man.

"I — didn't know!" she muttered. "He didn't tell me. He only told me this morning what — what I've told you."

Spargo picked up his hat.

"Good-night, Mr. Elphick," he said.

But before he could reach the door the old barrister had leapt from his chair and seized him with trembling hands. Spargo turned and looked at him. He knew then that for some reason or other he had given Mr. Septimus Elphick a thoroughly bad fright.

"Well?" he growled.

"My dear young gentleman!" implored Mr. Elphick. "Don't go! I'll — I'll do anything for you if you won't go away to print that. I'll — I'll give you a thousand pounds!"

Spargo shook him off.

"That's enough!" he snarled. "Now, I am off! What, you'd try to bribe me?"

Mr. Elphick wrung his hands.

"I didn't mean that — indeed I didn't!" he almost wailed. "I — I don't know what I meant. Stay, young gentleman, stay a little, and let us — let us talk. Let me have a word with you — as many words as you please. I implore you!"

Spargo made a fine pretence of hesitation.

"If I stay," he said, at last, "it will only be on the strict condition that you answer — and answer truly — whatever questions I like to ask you. Otherwise — — "

He made another move to the door, and again Mr. Elphick laid beseeching hands on him.

"Stay!" he said. "I'll answer anything you like!"

Spargo sat down again in the chair which he had just left, and looked at the two people upon whom his startling announcement had produced such a curious effect. And he recognized as he looked at them that, while they were both frightened, they were frightened in different ways. Miss Baylis had already recovered her composure; she now sat sombre and stern as ever, returning Spargo's look with something of indifferent defiance; he thought he could see that in her mind a certain fear was battling with a certain amount of wonder that he had discovered the secret. It seemed to him that so far as she was concerned the secret had come to an end; it was as if she said in so many words that now the secret was out he might do his worst.

But upon Mr. Septimus Elphick the effect was very different. He was still trembling from excitement; he groaned as he sank into his chair and the hand with which he poured out a glass of spirits shook; the glass rattled against his teeth when he raised it to his lips. The half-contemptuous fashion of his reception of Spargo had now wholly disappeared; he was a man who had received a shock, and a bad one. And Spargo, watching him keenly, said to himself: This man knows a great deal more than, a great deal beyond, the mere fact that Marbury was Maitland, and that Ronald Breton is in reality Maitland's son; he knows something which he never wanted anybody to know, which he firmly believed it impossible anybody ever could know. It was as if he had buried something deep, deep down in the lowest depths, and was as astounded as he was frightened to find that it had been at last flung up to the broad light of day.

"I shall wait," suddenly said Spargo, "until you are composed, Mr. Elphick. I have no wish to distress you. But I see, of course, that the truths which I have told you are of a sort that cause you considerable — shall we say fear?"

Elphick took another stiff pull at his liquor. His hand had grown steadier, and the colour was coming back to his face.

"If you will let me explain," he said. "If you will hear what was done for the boy's sake — eh?"

"That," answered Spargo, "is precisely what I wish. I can tell you this — I am the last man in the world to wish harm of any sort to Mr. Breton."

Miss Baylis relieved her feelings with a scornful sniff. "He says that!" she exclaimed, addressing the ceiling. "He says that, knowing that he means to tell the world in his rag of a paper that Ronald Breton, on whom every care has been lavished, is the son of a scoundrel, an ex-convict, a— —"

Elphick lifted his hand.

"Hush — hush!" he said imploringly. "Mr. Spargo means well, I am sure — I am convinced. If Mr. Spargo will hear me— —"

But before Spargo could reply, a loud insistent knocking came at the outer door. Elphick started nervously, but presently he moved across the room, walking as if he had received a blow, and opened the door. A boy's voice penetrated into the sitting-room.

"If you please, sir, is Mr. Spargo, of the *Watchman*, here? He left this address in case he was wanted."

Spargo recognized the voice as that of one of the office messenger boys, and jumping up, went to the door.

"What is it, Rawlins?" he asked.

"Will you please come back to the office, sir, at once? There's Mr. Rathbury there and says he must see you instantly."

"All right," answered Spargo. "I'm coming just now."

He motioned the lad away, and turned to Elphick.

"I shall have to go," he said. "I may be kept. Now, Mr. Elphick, can I come to see you tomorrow morning?"

"Yes, yes, tomorrow morning!" replied Elphick eagerly. "Tomorrow morning, certainly. At eleven — eleven o'clock. That will do?"

"I shall be here at eleven," said Spargo. "Eleven sharp."

He was moving away when Elphick caught him by the sleeve.

"A word — just a word!" he said. "You — you have not told the — the boy — Ronald — of what you know? You haven't?"

"I haven't," replied Spargo.

Elphick tightened his grip on Spargo's sleeve. He looked into his face beseechingly.

"Promise me—promise me, Mr. Spargo, that you won't tell him until you have seen me in the morning!" he implored. "I beg you to promise me this."

Spargo hesitated, considering matters.

"Very well—I promise," he said.

"And you won't print it?" continued Elphick, still clinging to him. "Say you won't print it tonight?"

"I shall not print it tonight," answered Spargo. "That's certain."

Elphick released his grip on the young man's arm.

"Come—at eleven tomorrow morning," he said, and drew back and closed the door.

Spargo ran quickly to the office and hurried up to his own room. And there, calmly seated in an easy-chair, smoking a cigar, and reading an evening newspaper, was Rathbury, unconcerned and outwardly as imperturbable as ever. He greeted Spargo with a careless nod and a smile.

"Well," he said, "how's things?"

Spargo, half-breathless, dropped into his desk-chair.

"You didn't come here to tell me that," he said.

Rathbury laughed.

"No," he said, throwing the newspaper aside, "I didn't. I came to tell you my latest. You're at full liberty to stick it into your paper tonight: it may just as well be known."

"Well?" said Spargo.

Rathbury took his cigar out of his lips and yawned.

"Aylmore's identified," he said lazily.

Spargo sat up, sharply.

"Identified!"

"Identified, my son. Beyond doubt."

"But as whom—as what?" exclaimed Spargo.

Rathbury laughed.

"He's an old lag—an ex-convict. Served his time partly at Dartmoor. That, of course, is where he met Maitland or Marbury. D'ye see? Clear as noontide now, Spargo."

Spargo sat drumming his fingers on the desk before him. His eyes were fixed on a map of London that hung on the opposite wall; his ears heard the throbbing of the printing-machines far below. But what he really saw was the faces of the two girls; what he really heard was the voices of two girls …

"Clear as noontide—as noontide," repeated Rathbury with great cheerfulness.

Spargo came back to the earth of plain and brutal fact.

"What's clear as noontide?" he asked sharply.

"What? Why, the whole thing! Motive—everything," answered Rathbury. "Don't you see, Maitland and Aylmore (his real name is Ainsworth, by the by) meet at Dartmoor, probably, or, rather, certainly, just before Aylmore's release. Aylmore goes abroad, makes money, in time comes back, starts new career, gets into Parliament, becomes big man. In time, Maitland, who, after his time, has also gone abroad, also comes back. The two meet. Maitland probably tries to blackmail Aylmore or threatens to let folk know that the flourishing Mr. Aylmore, M.P., is an ex-convict. Result—Aylmore lures him to the Temple and quiets him. Pooh!— the whole thing's clear as noontide, as I say. As—noontide!"

Spargo drummed his fingers again.

"How?" he asked quietly. "How came Aylmore to be identified?"

"My work," said Rathbury proudly. "My work, my son. You see, I thought a lot. And especially after we'd found out that Marbury was Maitland."

"You mean after I'd found out," remarked Spargo.

Rathbury waved his cigar.

"Well, well, it's all the same," he said. "You help me, and I help you, eh? Well, as I say, I thought a considerable lot. I thought— now, where did Maitland, or Marbury, know or meet Aylmore twenty or twenty-two years ago? Not in London, because we knew Maitland never was in London—at any rate, before his trial, and we haven't the least proof that he was in London after. And why won't Aylmore tell? Clearly because it must have been in some undesirable place. And then, all of a sudden, it flashed on me in a moment of—what do you writing fellows call those moments, Spargo?"

"Inspiration, I should think," said Spargo. "Direct inspiration."

"That's it. In a moment of direct inspiration, it flashed on me — why, twenty years ago, Maitland was in Dartmoor — they must have met there! And so, we got some old warders who'd been there at that time to come to town, and we gave 'em opportunities to see Aylmore and to study him. Of course, he's twenty years older, and he's grown a beard, but they began to recall him, and then one man remembered that if he was the man they thought he'd a certain birth-mark. And — he has!"

"Does Aylmore know that he's been identified?" asked Spargo.

Rathbury pitched his cigar into the fireplace and laughed.

"Know!" he said scornfully. "Know? He's admitted it. What was the use of standing out against proof like that. He admitted it tonight in my presence. Oh, he knows all right!"

"And what did he say?"

Rathbury laughed contemptuously.

"Say? Oh, not much. Pretty much what he said about this affair — that when he was convicted the time before he was an innocent man. He's certainly a good hand at playing the innocent game."

"And of what was he convicted?"

"Oh, of course, we know all about it — now. As soon as we found out who he really was, we had all the particulars turned up. Aylmore, or Ainsworth (Stephen Ainsworth his name really is) was a man who ran a sort of what they call a Mutual Benefit Society in a town right away up in the North — Cloudhampton — some thirty years ago. He was nominally secretary, but it was really his own affair. It was patronized by the working classes — Cloudhampton's a purely artisan population — and they stuck a lot of their brass, as they call it, in it. Then suddenly it came to smash, and there was nothing. He — Ainsworth, or Aylmore — pleaded that he was robbed and duped by another man, but the court didn't believe him, and he got seven years. Plain story you see, Spargo, when it all comes out, eh?"

"All stories are quite plain — when they come out," observed Spargo. "And he kept silence now, I suppose, because he didn't want his daughters to know about his past?"

"Just so," agreed Rathbury. "And I don't know that I blame him. He thought, of course, that he'd go scot-free over this Marbury affair. But he made his mistake in the initial stages, my boy—oh, yes!"

Spargo got up from his desk and walked around his room for a few minutes, Rathbury meanwhile finding and lighting another cigar. At last Spargo came back and clapped a hand on the detective's shoulder.

"Look here, Rathbury!" he said. "It's very evident that you're now going on the lines that Aylmore did murder Marbury. Eh?"

Rathbury looked up. His face showed astonishment.

"After evidence like that!" he exclaimed. "Why, of course. There's the motive, my son, the motive!"

Spargo laughed.

"Rathbury!" he said. "Aylmore no more murdered Marbury than you did!"

The detective got up and put on his hat.

"Oh!" he said. "Perhaps you know who did, then?"

"I shall know in a few days," answered Spargo.

Rathbury stared wonderingly at him. Then he suddenly walked to the door. "Good-night!" he said gruffly.

"Good-night, Rathbury," replied Spargo and sat down at his desk.

But that night Spargo wrote nothing for the *Watchman*. All he wrote was a short telegram addressed to Aylmore's daughters. There were only three words on it—*Have no fear.*

Alone of all the London morning newspapers, the *Watchman* appeared next day destitute of sensationalism in respect to the Middle Temple Murder. The other daily journals published more or less vivid accounts of the identification of Mr. Stephen Aylmore, M.P. for the Brookminster Division, as the *ci-devant* Stephen Ainsworth, ex-convict, once upon a time founder and secretary of the Hearth and Home Mutual Benefit Society, the headquarters of which had been at Cloudhampton, in Daleshire; the fall of which had involved thousands of honest working folk in terrible distress if not in absolute ruin. Most of them had raked up Ainsworth's past to considerable journalistic purpose: it had been an easy matter to turn up old files, to recount the fall of the Hearth and Home, to tell anew the story of the privations of the humble investors whose small hoards had gone in the crash; it had been easy, too, to set out again the history of Ainsworth's arrest, trial, and fate. There was plenty of romance in the story: it was that of a man who by his financial ability had built up a great industrial insurance society; had — as was alleged — converted the large sums entrusted to him to his own purposes; had been detected and punished; had disappeared, after his punishment, so effectually that no one knew where he had gone; had come back, comparatively a few years later, under another name, a very rich man, and had entered Parliament and been, in a modest way, a public character without any of those who knew him in his new career suspecting that he had once worn a dress liberally ornamented with the broad arrow. Fine copy, excellent copy: some of the morning newspapers made a couple of columns of it.

But the *Watchman*, up to then easily ahead of all its contemporaries in keeping the public informed of all the latest news in connection with the Marbury affair, contented itself with a brief announcement. For after Rathbury had left him, Spargo had sought his proprietor and his editor, and had sat long in consultation with them, and the result of their talk had been that all the *Watchman* thought fit to tell its readers next morning was contained in a curt paragraph:

"We understand that Mr. Stephen Aylmore, M.P., who is charged with the murder of John Marbury, or Maitland, in the Temple on June 21st last, was yesterday afternoon identified by certain officials as Stephen Ainsworth, who was sentenced to a term of penal servitude in connection with the Hearth and Home Mutual Benefit Society funds nearly thirty years ago."

Coming down to Fleet Street that morning, Spargo, strolling jauntily along the front of the Law Courts, encountered a fellow-journalist, a man on an opposition newspaper, who grinned at him in a fashion which indicated derision.

"Left behind a bit, that rag of yours, this morning, Spargo, my boy!" he remarked elegantly. "Why, you've missed one of the finest opportunities I ever heard of in connection with that Aylmore affair. A miserable paragraph!—why, I worked off a column and a half in ours! What were you doing last night, old man?"

"Sleeping," said Spargo and went by with a nod. "Sleeping!"

He left the other staring at him, and crossed the road to Middle Temple Lane. It was just on the stroke of eleven as he walked up the stairs to Mr. Elphick's chambers; precisely eleven as he knocked at the outer door. It is seldom that outer doors are closed in the Temple at that hour, but Elphick's door was closed fast enough. The night before it had been promptly opened, but there was no response to Spargo's first knock, nor to his second, nor to his third. And half-unconsciously he murmured aloud: "Elphick's door is closed!"

It never occurred to Spargo to knock again: instinct told him that Elphick's door was closed because Elphick was not there; closed because Elphick was not going to keep the appointment. He turned and walked slowly back along the corridor. And just as he reached the head of the stairs Ronald Breton, pale and anxious, came running up them, and at sight of Spargo paused, staring questioningly at him. As if with a mutual sympathy the two young men shook hands.

"I'm glad you didn't print more than those two or three lines in the *Watchman* this morning," said Breton. "It was—considerate. As for the other papers!—Aylmore assured me last night, Spargo, that though he did serve that term at Dartmoor he was innocent enough! He was scapegoat for another man who disappeared."

Then, as Spargo merely nodded, he added, awkwardly:

"And I'm obliged to you, too, old chap, for sending that wire to the two girls last night—it was good of you. They want all the comfort they can get, poor things! But—what are you doing here, Spargo?"

Spargo leant against the head of the stairs and folded his hands.

"I came here," he said, "to keep an appointment with Mr. Elphick—an appointment which he made when I called on him, as you suggested, at nine o'clock. The appointment—a most important one—was for eleven o'clock."

Breton glanced at his watch.

"Come on, then," he said. "It's well past that now, and my guardian's a very martinet in the matter of punctuality."

But Spargo did not move. Instead, he shook his head, regarding Breton with troubled eyes.

"So am I," he answered. "I was trained to it. Your guardian isn't there, Breton."

"Not there? If he made an appointment for eleven? Nonsense—I never knew him miss an appointment!"

"I knocked three times—three separate times," answered Spargo.

"You should have knocked half a dozen times—he may have overslept himself. He sits up late—he and old Cardlestone often sit up half the night, talking stamps or playing piquet," said Breton. "Come on—you'll see!"

Spargo shook his head again.

"He's not there, Breton," he said. "He's gone!"

Breton stared at the journalist as if he had just announced that he had seen Mr. Septimus Elphick riding down Fleet Street on a dromedary. He seized Spargo's elbow.

"Come on!" he said. "I have a key to Mr. Elphick's door, so that I can go in and out as I like. I'll soon show you whether he's gone or not."

Spargo followed the young barrister down the corridor.

"All the same," he said meditatively as Breton fitted a key to the latch, "he's not there, Breton. He's—off!"

"Good heavens, man, I don't know what you're talking about!" exclaimed Breton, opening the door and walking into the lobby. "Off! Where on earth should he be off to, when he's made an appointment with you for eleven, and — Hullo!"

He had opened the door of the room in which Spargo had met Elphick and Miss Baylis the night before, and was walking in when he pulled himself up on the threshold with a sharp exclamation.

"Good God!" he cried. "What — what's all this?"

Spargo quietly looked over Breton's shoulder. It needed but one quick glance to show him that much had happened in that quiet room since he had quitted it the night before. There stood the easy-chair in which he had left Elphick; there, close by it, but pushed aside, as if by a hurried hand, was the little table with its spirit case, its syphon, its glass, in which stale liquid still stood; there was the novel, turned face downwards; there, upon the novel, was Elphick's pipe. But the rest of the room was in dire confusion. The drawers of a bureau had been pulled open and never put back; papers of all descriptions, old legal-looking documents, old letters, littered the centre-table and the floor; in one corner of the room a black japanned box had been opened, its contents strewn about, and the lid left yawning. And in the grate, and all over the fender there were masses of burned and charred paper; it was only too evident that the occupant of the chambers, wherever he might have disappeared to, had spent some time before his disappearance in destroying a considerable heap of documents and papers, and in such haste that he had not troubled to put matters straight before he went.

Breton stared at this scene for a moment in utter consternation. Then he made one step towards an inner door, and Spargo followed him. Together they entered an inner room—a sleeping apartment. There was no one in it, but there were evidences that Elphick had just as hastily packed a bag as he had destroyed his papers. The clothes which Spargo had seen him wearing the previous evening were flung here, there, everywhere: the gorgeous smoking-jacket was tossed unceremoniously in one corner, a dress-shirt, in the bosom of which valuable studs still glistened, in another. One or two suitcases lay about, as if they had been examined and discarded in favour of something more portable; here, too, drawers, revealing stocks of linen and underclothing, had been torn open and left open; open, too, swung the door of a wardrobe, revealing a quantity of expensive clothing. And Spargo, looking around him, seemed to see all that had happened—the hasty, almost frantic search for and tearing up and burning of papers; the hurried change of clothing, of packing necessaries into a bag that could be carried, and then the flight the getting away, the——

"What on earth does all this mean?" exclaimed Breton. "What is it, Spargo?"

"I mean exactly what I told you," answered Spargo. "He's off! Off!"

"Off! But why off? What—my guardian!—as quiet an old gentleman as there is in the Temple—off!" cried Breton. "For what reason, eh? It isn't—good God, Spargo, it isn't because of anything you said to him last night!"

"I should say it is precisely because of something that I said to him last night," replied Spargo. "I was a fool ever to let him out of my sight."

Breton turned on his companion and gasped.

"Out—of—your—sight!" he exclaimed. "Why—why—you don't mean to say that Mr. Elphick has anything to do with this Marbury affair? For God's sake, Spargo——"

Spargo laid a hand on the young barrister's shoulder.

"I'm afraid you'll have to hear a good deal, Breton," he said. "I was going to talk to you today in any case. You see——"

Before Spargo could say more a woman, bearing the implements which denote the charwoman's profession, entered the room and immediately cried out at what she saw. Breton turned on her almost savagely.

"Here, you!" he said. "Have you seen anything of Mr. Elphick this morning?"

The charwoman rolled her eyes and lifted her hands.

"Me, sir! Not a sign of him, sir. Which I never comes here much before half-past eleven, sir, Mr. Elphick being then gone out to his breakfast. I see him yesterday morning, sir, which he was then in his usual state of good health, sir, if any thing's the matter with him now. No, sir, I ain't seen nothing of him."

Breton let out another exclamation of impatience.

"You'd better leave all this," he said. "Mr. Elphick's evidently gone away in a hurry, and you mustn't touch anything here until he comes back. I'm going to lock up the chambers: if you've a key of them give it to me."

The charwoman handed over a key, gave another astonished look at the rooms, and vanished, muttering, and Breton turned to Spargo.

"What do you say?" he demanded. "I must hear—a good deal! Out with it, then, man, for Heaven's sake."

But Spargo shook his head.

"Not now, Breton," he answered. "Presently, I tell you, for Miss Aylmore's sake, and your own, the first thing to do is to get on your guardian's track. We must—must, I say!—and at once."

Breton stood staring at Spargo for a moment as if he could not credit his own senses. Then he suddenly motioned Spargo out of the room.

"Come on!" he said. "I know who'll know where he is, if anybody does."

"Who, then?" asked Spargo, as they hurried out.

"Cardlestone," answered Breton, grimly. "Cardlestone!"

Chapter 30 REVELATION

There was as much bright sunshine that morning in Middle Temple Lane as ever manages to get into it, and some of it was shining in the entry into which Spargo and Breton presently hurried. Full of haste as he was Breton paused at the foot of the stair. He looked down at the floor and at the wall at its side.

"Wasn't it there?" he said in a low voice, pointing at the place he looked at. "Wasn't it there, Spargo, just there, that Marbury, or, rather, Maitland, was found?"

"It was just there," answered Spargo.

"You saw him?"

"I saw him."

"Soon—afterwards?"

"Immediately after he was found. You know all that, Breton. Why do you ask now?"

Breton, who was still staring at the place on which he had fixed his eyes on walking into the entry, shook his head.

"Don't know," he answered. "I—but come on—let's see if old Cardlestone can tell us anything."

There was another charwoman, armed with pails and buckets, outside Cardlestone's door, into which she was just fitting a key. It was evident to Spargo that she knew Breton, for she smiled at him as she opened the door.

"I don't think Mr. Cardlestone'll be in, sir," she said. "He's generally gone out to breakfast at this time—him and Mr. Elphick goes together."

"Just see," said Breton. "I want to see him if he is in." The charwoman entered the chambers and immediately screamed.

"Quite so," remarked Spargo. "That's what I expected to hear. Cardlestone, you see, Breton, is also—off!"

Breton made no reply. He rushed after the charwoman, with Spargo in close attendance.

"Good God—another!" groaned Breton.

If the confusion in Elphick's rooms had been bad, that in Cardlestone's chambers was worse. Here again all the features of the previous scene were repeated—drawers had been torn open, papers thrown about; the hearth was choked with light ashes; everything was at sixes and sevens. An open door leading into an inner room showed that Cardlestone, like Elphick, had hastily packed a bag; like Elphick had changed his clothes, and had thrown his discarded garments anywhere, into any corner. Spargo began to realize what had taken place—Elphick, having made his own preparations for flight, had come to Cardlestone, and had expedited him, and they had fled together. But—why?

The charwoman sat down in the nearest chair and began to moan and sob; Breton strode forward, across the heaps of papers and miscellaneous objects tossed aside in that hurried search and clearing up, into the inner room. And Spargo, looking about him, suddenly caught sight of something lying on the floor at which he made a sharp clutch. He had just secured it and hurried it into his pocket when Breton came back.

"I don't know what all this means, Spargo," he said, almost wearily. "I suppose you do. Look here," he went on, turning to the charwoman, "stop that row—that'll do no good, you know. I suppose Mr. Cardlestone's gone away in a hurry. You'd better—what had she better do, Spargo?"

"Leave things exactly as they are, lock up the chambers, and as you're a friend of Mr. Cardlestone's give you the key," answered Spargo, with a significant glance. "Do that, now, and let's go—I've something to do." Once outside, with the startled charwoman gone away, Spargo turned to Breton.

"I'll tell you all I know, presently, Breton," he said. "In the meantime, I want to find out if the lodge porter saw Mr. Elphick or Mr. Cardlestone leave. I must know where they've gone—if I can only find out. I don't suppose they went on foot."

"All right," responded Breton, gloomily. "We'll go and ask. But this is all beyond me. You don't mean to say——"

"Wait a while," answered Spargo. "One thing at once," he continued, as they walked up Middle Temple Lane. "This is the first thing. You ask the porter if he's seen anything of either of them—he knows you."

The porter, duly interrogated, responded with alacrity.

"Anything of Mr. Elphick this morning, Mr. Breton?" he answered. "Certainly, sir. I got a taxi for Mr. Elphick and Mr. Cardlestone early this morning—soon after seven. Mr. Elphick said they were going to Paris, and they'd breakfast at Charing Cross before the train left."

"Say when they'd be back?" asked Breton, with an assumption of entire carelessness.

"No, sir, Mr. Elphick didn't," answered the porter. "But I should say they wouldn't be long because they'd only got small suit-cases with them—such as they'd put a day or two's things in, sir."

"All right," said Breton. He turned away towards Spargo who had already moved off. "What next?" he asked. "Charing Cross, I suppose!"

Spargo smiled and shook his head.

"No," he answered. "I've no use for Charing Cross. They haven't gone to Paris. That was all a blind. For the present let's go back to your chambers. Then I'll talk to you."

Once within Breton's inner room, with the door closed upon them, Spargo dropped into an easy-chair and looked at the young barrister with earnest attention.

"Breton!" he said. "I believe we're coming in sight of land. You want to save your prospective father-in-law, don't you?"

"Of course!" growled Breton. "That goes without saying. But——"

"But you may have to make some sacrifices in order to do it," said Spargo. "You see——"

"Sacrifices!" exclaimed Breton. "What——"

"You may have to sacrifice some ideas—you may find that you'll not be able to think as well of some people in the future as you have thought of them in the past. For instance—Mr. Elphick."

Breton's face grew dark.

"Speak plainly, Spargo!" he said. "It's best with me."

"Very well," replied Spargo. "Mr. Elphick, then, is in some way connected with this affair."

"You mean the—murder?"

"I mean the murder. So is Cardlestone. Of that I'm now dead certain. And that's why they're off. I startled Elphick last night. It's evident that he immediately communicated with Cardlestone, and that they made a rapid exit. Why?"

"Why? That's what I'm asking you! Why? Why? Why?"

"Because they're afraid of something coming out. And being afraid, their first instinct is to—run. They've run at the first alarm. Foolish—but instinctive."

Breton, who had flung himself into the elbow-chair at his desk, jumped to his feet and thumped his blotting-pad.

"Spargo!" he exclaimed. "Are you telling me that you accuse my guardian and his friend, Mr. Cardlestone. of being— murderers?"

"Nothing of the sort. I am accusing Mr. Elphick and Mr. Cardlestone of knowing more about the murder than they care to tell or want to tell. I am also accusing them, and especially your guardian, of knowing all about Maitland, alias Marbury. I made him confess last night that he knew this dead man to be John Maitland."

"You did!"

"I did. And now, Breton, since it's got to come out, well have the truth. Pull yourself together—get your nerves ready, for you'll have to stand a shock or two. But I know what I'm talking about—I can prove every word I'm going to say to you. And first let me ask you a few questions. Do you know anything about your parentage?"

"Nothing—beyond what Mr. Elphick has told me."

"And what was that?"

"That my parents were old friends of his, who died young, leaving me unprovided for, and that he took me up and looked after me."

"And he's never given you any documentary evidence of any sort to prove the truth of that story?"

"Never! I never questioned his statement. Why should I?"

"You never remember anything of your childhood—I mean of any person who was particularly near you in your childhood?"

"I remember the people who brought me up from the time I was three years old. And I have just a faint, shadowy recollection of some woman, a tall, dark woman, I think, before that."

"Miss Baylis," said Spargo to himself. "All right, Breton," he went on aloud. "I'm going to tell you the truth. I'll tell it to you straight out and give you all the explanations afterwards. Your real name is not Breton at all. Your real name is Maitland, and you're the only child of the man who was found murdered at the foot of Cardlestone's staircase!"

Spargo had been wondering how Breton would take this, and he gazed at him with some anxiety as he got out the last words. What would he do? — what would he say? — what — —

Breton sat down quietly at his desk and looked Spargo hard between the eyes.

"Prove that to me, Spargo," he said, in hard, matter-of-fact tones. "Prove it to me, every word. Every word, Spargo!"

Spargo nodded.

"I will — every word," he answered. "It's the right thing. Listen, then."

It was a quarter to twelve, Spargo noticed, throwing a glance at the clock outside, as he began his story; it was past one when he brought it to an end. And all that time Breton listened with the keenest attention, only asking a question now and then; now and then making a brief note on a sheet of paper which he had drawn to him.

"That's all," said Spargo at last.

"It's plenty," observed Breton laconically.

He sat staring at his notes for a moment; then he looked up at Spargo. "What do you really think?" he asked.

"About — what?" said Spargo.

"This flight of Elphick's and Cardlestone's."

"I think, as I said, that they knew something which they think may be forced upon them. I never saw a man in a greater fright than that I saw Elphick in last night. And it's evident that Cardlestone shares in that fright, or they wouldn't have gone off in this way together."

"Do you think they know anything of the actual murder?"

Spargo shook his head.

"I don't know. Probably. They know something. And — look here!"

Spargo put his hand in his breast pocket and drew something out which he handed to Breton, who gazed at it curiously.

"What's this?" he demanded. "Stamps?"

"That, from the description of Criedir, the stamp-dealer, is a sheet of those rare Australian stamps which Maitland had on him — carried on him. I picked it up just now in Cardlestone's room, when you were looking into his bedroom."

"But that, after all, proves nothing. Those mayn't be the identical stamps. And whether they are or not — —" "What are the probabilities?" interrupted Spargo sharply. "I believe that those are the stamps which Maitland — your father! — had on him, and I want to know how they came to be in Cardlestone's rooms. And I will know."

Breton handed the stamps back.

"But the general thing, Spargo?" he said. "If they didn't murder — I can't realize the thing yet! — my father — —"

"If they didn't murder your father, they know who did!" exclaimed Spargo. "Now, then, it's time for more action. Let Elphick and Cardlestone alone for the moment — they'll be tracked easily enough. I want to tackle something else for the moment. How do you get an authority from the Government to open a grave?"

"Order from the Home Secretary, which will have to be obtained by showing the very strongest reasons why it should be made."

"Good! We'll give the reasons. I want to have a grave opened."

"A grave opened! Whose grave?"

"The grave of the man Chamberlayne at Market Milcaster," replied Spargo.

Breton started.

"His? In Heaven's name, why?" he demanded.

Spargo laughed as he got up.

"Because I believe it's empty," he answered. "Because I believe that Chamberlayne is alive, and that his other name is — Cardlestone!"

Chapter 31 THE PENITENT WINDOW-CLEANER

That afternoon Spargo had another of his momentous interviews with his proprietor and his editor. The first result was that all three drove to the offices of the legal gentleman who catered for the *Watchman* when it wanted any law, and that things were put in shape for an immediate application to the Home Office for permission to open the Chamberlayne grave at Market Milcaster; the second was that on the following morning there appeared in the *Watchman* a notice which set half the mouths of London a-watering. That notice; penned by Spargo, ran as follows: —

"ONE THOUSAND POUNDS REWARD.

"WHEREAS, on some date within the past twelve months, there was stolen, abstracted, or taken from the chambers in Fountain Court, Temple, occupied by Mr. Stephen Aylmore, M.P., under the name of Mr. Anderson, a walking-stick, or stout staff, of foreign make, and of curious workmanship, which stick was probably used in the murder of John Marbury, or Maitland, in Middle Temple Lane, on the night of June 21-22 last, and is now in the hands of the police:

"This is to give notice that the Proprietor of the *Watchman* newspaper will pay the above-mentioned reward (ONE THOUSAND POUNDS STERLING) at once and in cash to whosoever will prove that he or she stole, abstracted, or took away the said stick from the said chambers, and will further give full information as to his or her disposal of the same, and the Proprietor of the *Watchman* moreover engages to treat any revelation affecting the said stick in the most strictly private and confidential manner, and to abstain from using it in any way detrimental to the informant, who should call at the *Watchman* office, and ask for Mr. Frank Spargo at any time between eleven and one o'clock midday, and seven and eleven o'clock in the evening."

"And you really expect to get some information through that?" asked Breton, who came into Spargo's room about noon on the day on which the promising announcement came out. "You really do?"

"Before today is out," said Spargo confidently. "There is more magic in a thousand-pound reward than you fancy, Breton. I'll have the history of that stick before midnight."

"How are you to tell that you won't be imposed upon?" suggested Breton. "Anybody can say that he or she stole the stick."

"Whoever comes here with any tale of a stick will have to prove to me how he or she got the stick and what was done with the stick," said Spargo. "I haven't the least doubt that that stick was stolen or taken away from Aylmore's rooms in Fountain Court, and that it got into the hands of — "

"Yes, of whom?"

"That's what I want to know in some fashion. I've an idea, already. But I can afford to wait for definite information. I know one thing — when I get that information — as I shall — we shall be a long way on the road towards establishing Aylmore's innocence."

Breton made no remark upon this. He was looking at Spargo with a meditative expression.

"Spargo," he said, suddenly, "do you think you'll get that order for the opening of the grave at Market Milcaster?"

"I was talking to the solicitors over the 'phone just now," answered Spargo. "They've every confidence about it. In fact, it's possible it may be made this afternoon. In that case, the opening will be made early tomorrow morning."

"Shall you go?" asked Breton.

"Certainly. And you can go with me, if you like. Better keep in touch with us all day in case we hear. You ought to be there — you're concerned."

"I should like to go — I will go," said Breton. "And if that grave proves to be — empty — I'll — I'll tell you something."

Spargo looked up with sharp instinct.

"You'll tell me something? Something? What?"

"Never mind — wait until we see if that coffin contains a dead body or lead and sawdust. If there's no body there — — "

At that moment one of the senior messenger boys came in and approached Spargo. His countenance, usually subdued to an official stolidity, showed signs of something very like excitement.

"There's a man downstairs asking for you, Mr. Spargo," he said. "He's been hanging about a bit, sir, — seems very shy about coming up. He won't say what he wants, and he won't fill up a form, sir. Says all he wants is a word or two with you."

"Bring him up at once!" commanded Spargo. He turned to Breton when the boy had gone. "There!" he said, laughing. "This is the man about the stick — you see if it isn't."

"You're such a cock-sure chap, Spargo," said Breton. "You're always going on a straight line."

"Trying to, you mean," retorted Spargo. "Well, stop here, and hear what this chap has to say: it'll no doubt be amusing."

The messenger boy, deeply conscious that he was ushering into Spargo's room an individual who might shortly carry away a thousand pounds of good *Watchman* money in his pocket, opened the door and introduced a shy and self-conscious young man, whose nervousness was painfully apparent to everybody and deeply felt by himself. He halted on the threshold, looking round the comfortably-furnished room, and at the two well-dressed young men which it framed as if he feared to enter on a scene of such grandeur.

"Come in, come in!" said Spargo, rising and pointing to an easy-chair at the side of his desk. "Take a seat. You've called about that reward, of course."

The man in the chair eyed the two of them cautiously, and not without suspicion. He cleared his throat with a palpable effort.

"Of course," he said. "It's all on the strict private. Name of Edward Mollison, sir."

"And where do you live, and what do you do?" asked Spargo.

"You might put it down Rowton House, Whitechapel," answered Edward Mollison. "Leastways, that's where I generally hang out when I can afford it. And — window-cleaner. Leastways, I was window cleaning when — when — — "

"When you came in contact with the stick we've been advertising about," suggested Spargo. "Just so. Well, Mollison — what about the stick?"

Mollison looked round at the door, and then at the windows, and then at Breton.

"There ain't no danger of me being got into trouble along of that stick?" he asked. "'Cause if there is, I ain't a-going to say a word — no, not for no thousand pounds! Me never having been in no trouble of any sort, guv'nor — though a poor man."

"Not the slightest danger in the world, Mollison," replied Spargo. "Not the least. All you've got to do is to tell the truth — and prove that it is the truth. So it was you who took that queer-looking stick out of Mr. Aylmore's rooms in Fountain Court, was it?"

Mollison appeared to find this direct question soothing to his feelings. He smiled weakly.

"It was cert'nly me as took it, sir," he said. "Not that I meant to pinch it — not me! And, as you might say, I didn't take it, when all's said and done. It was — put on me."

"Put on you, was it?" said Spargo. "That's interesting. And how was it put on you?"

Mollison grinned again and rubbed his chin.

"It was this here way," he answered. "You see, I was working at that time — near on to nine months since, it is — for the Universal Daylight Window Cleaning Company, and I used to clean a many windows here and there in the Temple, and them windows at Mr. Aylmore's — only I knew them as Mr. Anderson's — among 'em. And I was there one morning, early it was, when the charwoman she says to me, 'I wish you'd take these two or three hearthrugs,' she says, 'and give 'em a good beating,' she says. And me being always a ready one to oblige, 'All right!' I says, and takes 'em. 'Here's something to wallop 'em with,' she says, and pulls that there old stick out of a lot that was in a stand in a corner of the lobby. And that's how I came to handle it, sir."

"I see," said Spargo. "A good explanation. And when you had beaten the hearthrugs — what then?"

Mollison smiled his weak smile again.

"Well, sir, I looked at that there stick and I see it was something uncommon," he answered. "And I thinks — 'Well, this Mr. Anderson, he's got a bundle of sticks and walking canes up there — hell never miss this old thing,' I thinks. And so I left it in a corner when I'd done beating the rugs, and when I went away with my things I took it with me."

"You took it with you?" said Spargo. "Just so. To keep as a curiosity, I suppose?"

Mollison's weak smile turned to one of cunning. He was obviously losing his nervousness; the sound of his own voice and the reception of his news was imparting confidence to him.

"Not half!" he answered. "You see, guv'nor, there was an old cove as I knew in the Temple there as is, or was, 'cause I ain't been there since, a collector of antikities, like, and I'd sold him a queer old thing, time and again. And, of course, I had him in my eye when I took the stick away — see?"

"I see. And you took the stick to him?"

"I took it there and then," replied Mollison. "Pitched him a tale, I did, about it having been brought from foreign parts by Uncle Simon — which I never had no Uncle Simon. Made out it was a rare curiosity — which it might ha' been one, for all I know."

"Exactly. And the old cove took a fancy to it, eh?"

"Bought it there and then," answered Mollison, with something very like a wink.

"Ah! Bought it there and then. And how much did he give you for it?" asked Spargo. "Something handsome, I hope?"

"Couple o' quid," replied Mollison. "Me not wishing to part with a family heirloom for less."

"Just so. And do you happen to be able to tell me the old cove's name and his address, Mollison?" asked Spargo.

"I do, sir. Which they've painted on his entry — the fifth or sixth as you go down Middle Temple Lane," answered Mollison. "Mr. Nicholas Cardlestone, first floor up the staircase."

Spargo rose from his seat without as much as a look at Breton.

"Come this way, Mollison," he said. "We'll go and see about your little reward. Excuse me, Breton."

Breton kicked his heels in solitude for half an hour. Then Spargo came back.

"There — that's one matter settled, Breton," he said. "Now for the next. The Home Secretary's made the order for the opening of the grave at Market Milcaster. I'm going down there at once, and I suppose you're coming. And remember, if that grave's empty — —"

"If that grave's empty," said Breton, "I'll tell you — a good deal."

There travelled down together to Market Milcaster late that afternoon, Spargo, Breton, the officials from the Home Office, entrusted with the order for the opening of the Chamberlayne grave, and a solicitor acting on behalf of the proprietor of the *Watchman*. It was late in the evening when they reached the little town, but Spargo, having looked in at the parlour of the "Yellow Dragon" and ascertained that Mr. Quarterpage had only just gone home, took Breton across the street to the old gentleman's house. Mr. Quarterpage himself came to the door, and recognized Spargo immediately. Nothing would satisfy him but that the two should go in; his family, he said, had just retired, but he himself was going to take a final nightcap and a cigar, and they must share it.

"For a few minutes only then, Mr. Quarterpage," said Spargo as they followed the old man into his dining-room. "We have to be up at daybreak. And — possibly — you, too, would like to be up just as early."

Mr. Quarterpage looked an enquiry over the top of a decanter which he was handling.

"At daybreak?" he exclaimed.

"The fact is," said Spargo, "that grave of Chamberlayne's is going to be opened at daybreak. We have managed to get an order from the Home Secretary for the exhumation of Chamberlayne's body: the officials in charge of it have come down in the same train with us; we're all staying across there at the 'Dragon.' The officials have gone to make the proper arrangements with your authorities. It will be at daybreak, or as near it as can conveniently be managed. And I suppose, now that you know of it, you'll be there?"

"God bless me!" exclaimed Mr. Quarterpage. "You've really done that! Well, well, so we shall know the truth at last, after all these years. You're a very wonderful young man, Mr. Spargo, upon my word. And this other young gentleman?"

Spargo looked at Breton, who had already given him permission to speak. "Mr. Quarterpage," he said, "this young gentleman is, without doubt, John Maitland's son. He's the young barrister, Mr. Ronald Breton, that I told you of, but there's no doubt about his parentage. And I'm sure you'll shake hands with him and wish him well."

Mr. Quarterpage set down decanter and glass and hastened to give Breton his hand.

"My dear young sir!" he exclaimed. "That I will indeed! And as to wishing you well—ah, I never wished anything but well to your poor father. He was led away, sir, led away by Chamberlayne. God bless me, what a night of surprises! Why, Mr. Spargo, supposing that coffin is found empty—what then?"

"Then," answered Spargo, "then I think we shall be able to put our hands on the man who is supposed to be in it."

"You think my father was worked upon by this man Chamberlayne, sir?" observed Breton a few minutes later when they had all sat down round Mr. Quarterpage's hospitable hearth. "You think he was unduly influenced by him?"

Mr. Quarterpage shook his head sadly.

"Chamberlayne, my dear young sir," he answered. "Chamberlayne was a plausible and a clever fellow. Nobody knew anything about him until he came to this town, and yet before he had been here very long he had contrived to ingratiate himself with everybody—of course, to his own advantage. I firmly believe that he twisted your father round his little finger. As I told Mr. Spargo there when he was making his enquiries of me a short while back, it would never have been any surprise to me to hear—definitely, I mean, young gentlemen—that all this money that was in question went into Chamberlayne's pockets. Dear me—dear me!—and you really believe that Chamberlayne is actually alive, Mr. Spargo?"

Spargo pulled out his watch. "We shall all know whether he was buried in that grave before another six hours are over, Mr. Quarterpage," he said.

He might well have spoken of four hours instead of six, for it was then nearly midnight, and before three o'clock Spargo and Breton, with the other men who had accompanied them from London were out of the "Yellow Dragon" and on their way to the cemetery just outside the little town. Over the hills to the eastward the grey dawn was slowly breaking: the long stretch of marshland which lies between Market Milcaster and the sea was white with fog: on the cypresses and acacias of the cemetery hung veils and webs of gossamer: everything around them was quiet as the dead folk who lay beneath their feet. And the people actively concerned went quietly to work, and those who could do nothing but watch stood around in silence.

"In all my long life of over ninety years," whispered old Quarterpage, who had met them at the cemetery gates, looking fresh and brisk in spite of his shortened rest, "I have never seen this done before. It seems a strange, strange thing to interfere with a dead man's last resting-place—a dreadful thing."

"If there is a dead man there," said Spargo.

He himself was mainly curious about the details of this exhumation; he had no scruples, sentimental or otherwise, about the breaking in upon the dead. He watched all that was done. The men employed by the local authorities, instructed over-night, had fenced in the grave with canvas; the proceedings were accordingly conducted in strict privacy; a man was posted to keep away any very early passersby, who might be attracted by the unusual proceedings. At first there was nothing to do but wait, and Spargo occupied himself by reflecting that every spadeful of earth thrown out of that grave was bringing him nearer to the truth; he had an unconquerable intuition that the truth of at any rate one phase of the Marbury case was going to be revealed to them. If the coffin to which they were digging down contained a body, and that the body of the stockbroker, Chamberlayne, then a good deal of his, Spargo's, latest theory, would be dissolved to nothingness. But if that coffin contained no body at all, then—"

"They're down to it!" whispered Breton.

Presently they all went and looked down into the grave. The workmen had uncovered the coffin preparatory to lifting it to the surface; one of them was brushing the earth away from the name-plate. And in the now strong light they could all read the lettering on it.

JAMES CARTWRIGHT CHAMBERLAYNE Born 1852 Died 1891

Spargo turned away as the men began to lift the coffin out of the grave.

"We shall know now!" he whispered to Breton. "And yet—what is it we shall know if——"

"If what?" said Breton. "If—what?"

But Spargo shook his head. This was one of the great moments he had lately been working for, and the issues were tremendous.

"Now for it!" said the *Watchman's* solicitor in an undertone. "Come, Mr. Spargo, now we shall see."

They all gathered round the coffin, set on low trestles at the graveside, as the workmen silently went to work on the screws. The screws were rusted in their sockets; they grated as the men slowly worked them out. It seemed to Spargo that each man grew slower and slower in his movements; he felt that he himself was getting fidgety. Then he heard a voice of authority.

"Lift the lid off!"

A man at the head of the coffin, a man at the foot suddenly and swiftly raised the lid: the men gathered round craned their necks with a quick movement.

Sawdust!

The coffin was packed to the brim with sawdust, tightly pressed down. The surface lay smooth, undisturbed, levelled as some hand had levelled it long years before. They were not in the presence of death, but of deceit.

Somebody laughed faintly. The sound of the laughter broke the spell. The chief official present looked round him with a smile.

"It is evident that there were good grounds for suspicion," he remarked. "Here is no dead body, gentlemen. See if anything lies beneath the sawdust," he added, turning to the workmen. "Turn it out!"

The workmen began to scoop out the sawdust with their hands; one of them, evidently desirous of making sure that no body was in the coffin, thrust down his fingers at various places along its length. He, too, laughed.

"The coffin's weighted with lead!" he remarked. "See!"

And tearing the sawdust aside, he showed those around him that at three intervals bars of lead had been tightly wedged into the coffin where the head, the middle, and the feet of a corpse would have rested.

"Done it cleverly," he remarked, looking round. "You see how these weights have been adjusted. When a body's laid out in a coffin, you know, all the weight's in the end where the head and trunk rest. Here you see the heaviest bar of lead is in the middle; the lightest at the feet. Clever!"

"Clear out all the sawdust," said some one. "Let's see if there's anything else."

There was something else. At the bottom of the coffin two bundles of papers, tied up with pink tape. The legal gentlemen present immediately manifested great interest in these. So did Spargo, who, pulling Breton along with him, forced his way to where the officials from the Home Office and the solicitor sent by the *Watchman* were hastily examining their discoveries.

The first bundle of papers opened evidently related to transactions at Market Milcaster: Spargo caught glimpses of names that were familiar to him, Mr. Quarterpage's amongst them. He was not at all astonished to see these things. But he was something more than astonished when, on the second parcel being opened, a quantity of papers relating to Cloudhampton and the Hearth and Home Mutual Benefit Society were revealed. He gave a hasty glance at these and drew Breton aside.

"It strikes me we've found a good deal more than we ever bargained for!" he exclaimed. "Didn't Aylmore say that the real culprit at Cloudhampton was another man—his clerk or something of that sort?"

"He did," agreed Breton. "He insists on it."

"Then this fellow Chamberlayne must have been the man," said Spargo. "He came to Market Milcaster from the north. What'll be done with those papers?" he asked, turning to the officials.

"We are going to seal them up at once, and take them to London," replied the principal person in authority. "They will be quite safe, Mr. Spargo; have no fear. We don't know what they may reveal."

"You don't, indeed!" said Spargo. "But I may as well tell you that I have a strong belief that they'll reveal a good deal that nobody dreams of, so take the greatest care of them."

Then, without waiting for further talk with any one, Spargo hurried Breton out of the cemetery. At the gate, he seized him by the arm.

"Now, then, Breton!" he commanded. "Out with it!"

"With what?"

"You promised to tell me something—a great deal, you said—if we found that coffin empty. It is empty. Come on—quick!"

"All right. I believe I know where Elphick and Cardlestone can be found. That's all."

"All! It's enough. Where, then, in heaven's name?"

"Elphick has a queer little place where he and Cardlestone sometimes go fishing—right away up in one of the wildest parts of the Yorkshire moors. I expect they've gone there. Nobody knows even their names there—they could go and lie quiet there for— ages."

"Do you know the way to it?"

"I do—I've been there."

Spargo motioned him to hurry.

"Come on, then," he said. "We're going there by the very first train out of this. I know the train, too—we've just time to snatch a mouthful of breakfast and to send a wire to the *Watchman*, and then we'll be off. Yorkshire!—Gad, Breton, that's over three hundred miles away!"

Chapter 33 FORESTALLED

Travelling all that long summer day, first from the south-west of England to the Midlands, then from the Midlands to the north, Spargo and Breton came late at night to Hawes' Junction, on the border of Yorkshire and Westmoreland, and saw rising all around them in the half-darkness the mighty bulks of the great fells which rise amongst that wild and lonely stretch of land. At that hour of the night and amidst that weird silence, broken only by the murmur of some adjacent waterfall the scene was impressive and suggestive; it seemed to Spargo as if London were a million miles away, and the rush and bustle of human life a thing of another planet. Here and there in the valleys he saw a light, but such lights were few and far between; even as he looked some of them twinkled and went out. It was evident that he and Breton were presently to be alone with the night.

"How far?" he asked Breton as they walked away from the station.

"We'd better discuss matters," answered Breton. "The place is in a narrow valley called Fossdale, some six or seven miles away across these fells, and as wild a walk as any lover of such things could wish for. It's half-past nine now, Spargo: I reckon it will take us a good two and a half hours, if not more, to do it. Now, the question is — Do we go straight there, or do we put up for the night? There's an inn here at this junction: there's the Moor Cock Inn a mile or so along the road which we must take before we turn off to the moorland and the fells. It's going to be a black night — look at those masses of black cloud gathering there! — and possibly a wet one, and we've no waterproofs. But it's for you to say — I'm game for whatever you like."

"Do you know the way?" asked Spargo.

"I've been the way. In the daytime I could go straight ahead. I remember all the landmarks. Even in the darkness I believe I can find my way. But it's rough walking."

"We'll go straight there," said Spargo. "Every minute's precious. But — can we get a mouthful of bread and cheese and a glass of ale first?"

"Good idea! We'll call in at the 'Moor Cock.' Now then, while we're on this firm road, step it out lively."

The "Moor Cock" was almost deserted at that hour: there was scarcely a soul in it when the two travellers turned in to its dimly-lighted parlour. The landlord, bringing the desired refreshment, looked hard at Breton.

"Come our way again then, sir?" he remarked with a sudden grin of recognition.

"Ah, you remember me?" said Breton.

"I call in mind when you came here with the two old gents last year," replied the landlord. "I hear they're here again—Tom Summers was coming across that way this morning, and said he'd seen 'em at the little cottage. Going to join 'em, I reckon, sir?"

Breton kicked Spargo under the table.

"Yes, we're going to have a day or two with them," he answered. "Just to get a breath of your moorland air."

"Well, you'll have a roughish walk over there tonight, gentlemen," said the landlord. "There's going to be a storm. And it's a stiffish way to make out at this time o'night."

"Oh, we'll manage," said Breton, nonchalantly. "I know the way, and we're not afraid of a wet skin."

The landlord laughed, and sitting down on his long settle folded his arms and scratched his elbows.

"There was a gentleman—London gentleman by his tongue—came in here this afternoon, and asked the way to Fossdale," he observed. "He'll be there long since—he'd have daylight for his walk. Happen he's one of your party?—he asked where the old gentlemen's little cottage was."

Again Spargo felt his shin kicked and made no sign. "One of their friends, perhaps," answered Breton. "What was he like?"

The landlord ruminated. He was not good at description and was conscious of the fact.

"Well, a darkish, serious-faced gentleman," he said. "Stranger hereabouts, at all events. Wore a grey suit—something like your friend's there. Yes—he took some bread and cheese with him when he heard what a long way it was."

"Wise man," remarked Breton. He hastily finished his own bread and cheese, and drank off the rest of his pint of ale. "Come on," he said, "let's be stepping."

Outside, in the almost tangible darkness, Breton clutched Spargo's arm. "Who's the man?" he said. "Can you think, Spargo?"

"Can't" answered Spargo. "I was trying to, while that chap was talking. But—it's somebody that's got in before us. Not Rathbury, anyhow—he's not serious-faced. Heavens, Breton, however are you going to find your way in this darkness?"

"You'll see presently. We follow the road a little. Then we turn up the fell side there. On the top, if the night clears a bit, we ought to see Great Shunnor Fell and Lovely Seat—they're both well over two thousand feet, and they stand up well. We want to make for a point clear between them. But I warn you, Spargo, it's stiff going!"

"Go ahead!" said Spargo. "It's the first time in my life I ever did anything of this sort, but we're going on if it takes us all night. I couldn't sleep in any bed now that I've heard there's somebody ahead of us. Go first, old chap, and I'll follow."

Breton went steadily forward along the road. That was easy work, but when he turned off and began to thread his way up the fell-side by what was obviously no more than a sheep-track, Spargo's troubles began. It seemed to him that he was walking as in a nightmare; all that he saw was magnified and heightened; the darkening sky above; the faint outlines of the towering hills; the gaunt spectres of fir and pine; the figure of Breton forging stolidly and surely ahead. Now the ground was soft and spongy under his feet; now it was stony and rugged; more than once he caught an ankle in the wire-like heather and tripped, bruising his knees. And in the end he resigned himself to keeping his eye on Breton, outlined against the sky, and following doggedly in his footsteps.

"Was there no other way than this?" he asked after a long interval of silence. "Do you mean to say those two—Elphick and Cardlestone—would take this way?"

"There is another way—down the valley, by Thwaite Bridge and Hardraw," answered Breton, "but it's miles and miles round. This is a straight cut across country, and in daylight it's a delightful walk. But at night—Gad!—here's the rain, Spargo!"

The rain came down as it does in that part of the world, with a suddenness that was as fierce as it was heavy. The whole of the grey night was blotted out; Spargo was only conscious that he stood in a vast solitude and was being gradually drowned. But Breton, whose sight was keener, and who had more knowledge of the situation dragged his companion into the shelter of a group of rocks. He laughed a little as they huddled closely together.

"This is a different sort of thing to pursuing detective work in Fleet Street, Spargo," he said. "You would come on, you know."

"I'm going on if we go through cataracts and floods," answered Spargo. "I might have been induced to stop at the 'Moor Cock' overnight if we hadn't heard of that chap in front. If he's after those two he's somebody who knows something. What I can't make out is — who he can be."

"Nor I," said Breton. "I can't think of anybody who knows of this retreat. But — has it ever struck you, Spargo, that somebody beside yourself may have been investigating?"

"Possible," replied Spargo. "One never knows. I only wish we'd been a few hours earlier. For I wanted to have the first word with those two."

The rain ceased as suddenly as it had come. Just as suddenly the heavens cleared. And going forward to the top of the ridge which they were then crossing, Breton pointed an arm to something shining far away below them.

"You see that?" he said. "That's a sheet of water lying between us and Cotterdale. We leave that on our right hand, climb the fell beyond it, drop down into Cotterdale, cross two more ranges of fell, and come down into Fossdale under Lovely Seat. There's a good two hours and a half stiff pull yet, Spargo. Think you can stick it?"

Spargo set his teeth.

"Go on!" he said.

Up hill, down dale, now up to his ankles in peaty ground, now tearing his shins, now bruising his knees, Spargo, yearning for the London lights, the well-paved London streets, the convenient taxi-cab, even the humble omnibus, plodded forward after his guide. It seemed to him that they had walked for ages and had traversed a whole continent of mountains and valley when at last Breton, halting on the summit of a wind-swept ridge, laid one hand on his companion's shoulder and pointed downward with the other.

"There!" he said. "There!"

Spargo looked ahead into the night. Far away, at what seemed to him to be a considerable distance, he saw the faint, very faint glimmer of a light—a mere spark of a light.

"That's the cottage," said Breton, "Late as it is, you see, they're up. And here's the roughest bit of the journey. It'll take me all my time to find the track across this moor, Spargo, so step carefully after me—there are bogs and holes hereabouts."

Another hour had gone by ere the two came to the cottage. Sometimes the guiding light had vanished, blotted out by intervening rises in the ground; always, when they saw it again, they were slowly drawing nearer to it. And now when they were at last close to it, Spargo realized that he found himself in one of the loneliest places he had ever been capable of imagining—so lonely and desolate a spot he had certainly never seen. In the dim light he could see a narrow, crawling stream, making its way down over rocks and stones from the high ground of Great Shunnor Fell. Opposite to the place at which they stood, on the edge of the moorland, a horseshoe like formation of ground was backed by a ring of fir and pine; beneath this protecting fringe of trees stood a small building of grey stone which looked as if it had been originally built by some shepherd as a pen for the moorland sheep. It was of no more than one storey in height, but of some length; a considerable part of it was hidden by shrubs and brushwood. And from one uncurtained, blindless window the light of a lamp shone boldly into the fading darkness without.

Breton pulled up on the edge of the crawling stream.

"We've got to get across there, Spargo," he said. "But as we're already soaked to the knee it doesn't matter about getting another wetting. Have you any idea how long we've been walking?"

"Hours—days—years!" replied Spargo.

"I should say quite four hours," said Breton. "In that case, it's well past two o'clock, and the light will be breaking in another hour or so. Now, once across this stream, what shall we do?"

"What have we come to do? Go to the cottage, of course!"

"Wait a bit. No need to startle them. By the fact they've got a light, I take it that they're up. Look there!"

As he spoke, a figure crossed the window passing between it and the light.

"That's not Elphick, nor yet Cardlestone," said Spargo. "They're medium-heighted men. That's a tallish man."

"Then it's the man the landlord of the 'Moor Cock' told us about," said Breton. "Now, look here—I know every inch of this place. When we're across let me go up to the cottage, and I'll take an observation through that window and see who's inside. Come on."

He led Spargo across the stream at a place where a succession of boulders made a natural bridge, and bidding him keep quiet, went up the bank to the cottage. Spargo, watching him, saw him make his way past the shrubs and undergrowth until he came to a great bush which stood between the lighted window and the projecting porch of the cottage. He lingered in the shadow of this bush but for a short moment; then came swiftly and noiselessly back to his companion. His hand fell on Spargo's arm with a clutch of nervous excitement.

"Spargo!" he whispered. "Who on earth do you think the other man is?"

Spargo, almost irritable from desire to get at close grips with the objects of his long journey, shook off Breton's hand with a growl of resentment.

"And how on earth can I waste time guessing?" he exclaimed. "Who is he?"

Breton laughed softly.

"Steady, Spargo, steady!" he said. "It's Myerst — the Safe Deposit man. Myerst!"

Spargo started as if something had bitten him.

"Myerst!" he almost shouted. "Myerst! Good Lord! — why did I never think of him? Myerst! Then — — "

"I don't know why you should have thought of him," said Breton. "But — he's there."

Spargo took a step towards the cottage: Breton pulled him back.

"Wait!" he said. "We've got to discuss this. I'd better tell you what they're doing."

"What are they doing, then?" demanded Spargo impatiently.

"Well," answered Breton. "They're going through a quantity of papers. The two old gentlemen look very ill and very miserable. Myerst is evidently laying down the law to them in some fashion or other. I've formed a notion, Spargo."

"What notion?"

"Myerst is in possession of whatever secret they have, and he's followed them down here to blackmail them. That's my notion."

Spargo thought awhile, pacing up and down the river bank.

"I daresay you're right," he said. "Now, what's to be done?"

Breton, too, considered matters.

"I wish," he said at last, "I wish we could get in there and overhear what's going on. But that's impossible — I know that cottage. The only thing we can do is this — we must catch Myerst unawares. He's here for no good. Look here!"

And reaching round to his hip-pocket Breton drew out a Browning revolver and wagged it in his hand with a smile.

"That's a useful thing to have, Spargo," he remarked. "I slipped it into my pocket the other day, wondering why on earth I did it. Now it'll come in handy. For anything we know Myerst may be armed."

"Well?" said Spargo.

"Come up to the cottage. If things turn out as I think they will, Myerst, when he's got what he wants, will be off. Now, you shall get where I did just now, behind that bush, and I'll station myself in the doorway. You can report to me, and when Myerst comes out I'll cover him. Come on, Spargo; it's beginning to get light already."

Breton cautiously led the way along the river bank, making use of such cover as the willows and alders afforded. Together, he and Spargo made their way to the front of the cottage. Arrived at the door, Breton posted himself in the porch, motioning to Spargo to creep in behind the bushes and to look through the window. And Spargo noiselessly followed his directions and slightly parting the branches which concealed him looked in through the uncurtained glass.

The interior into which he looked was rough and comfortless in the extreme. There were the bare accessories of a moorland cottage; rough chairs and tables, plastered walls, a fishing rod or two piled in a corner; some food set out on a side table. At the table in the middle of the floor the three men sat. Cardlestone's face was in the shadow; Myerst had his back to the window; old Elphick bending over the table was laboriously writing with shaking fingers. And Spargo twisted his head round to his companion.

"Elphick," he said, "is writing a cheque. Myerst has another cheque in his hand. Be ready! — when he gets that second cheque I guess he'll be off."

Breton smiled grimly and nodded. A moment later Spargo whispered again.

"Look out, Breton! He's coming."

Breton drew back into the angle of the porch; Spargo quitted his protecting bush and took the other angle. The door opened. And they heard Myerst's voice, threatening, commanding in tone.

"Now, remember all I've said! And don't you forget — I've the whip hand of both of you — the whip hand!"

Then Myerst turned and stepped out into the grey light—to find himself confronted by an athletic young man who held the muzzle of an ugly revolver within two inches of the bridge of his nose and in a remarkably firm and steady grip. Another glance showed him the figure of a second business-like looking young man at his side, whose attitude showed a desire to grapple with him.

"Good-morning, Mr. Myerst," said Breton with cold and ironic politeness. "We are glad to meet you so unexpectedly. And—I must trouble you to put up your hands. Quick!"

Myerst made one hurried movement of his right hand towards his hip, but a sudden growl from Breton made him shift it just as quickly above his head, whither the left followed it. Breton laughed softly.

"That's wise, Mr. Myerst," he said, keeping his revolver steadily pointed at his prisoner's nose. "Discretion will certainly be the better part of your valour on this occasion. Spargo—may I trouble you to see what Mr. Myerst carries in his pockets? Go through them carefully. Not for papers or documents—just now. We can leave that matter—we've plenty of time. See if he's got a weapon of any sort on him, Spargo—that's the important thing."

Considering that Spargo had never gone through the experience of searching a man before, he made sharp and creditable work of seeing what the prisoner carried. And he forthwith drew out and exhibited a revolver, while Myerst, finding his tongue, cursed them both, heartily and with profusion.

"Excellent!" said Breton, laughing again. "Sure he's got nothing else on him that's dangerous, Spargo? All right. Now, Mr. Myerst, right about face! Walk into the cottage, hands up, and remember there are two revolvers behind your back. March!"

Myerst obeyed this peremptory order with more curses. The three walked into the cottage. Breton kept his eye on his captive; Spargo gave a glance at the two old men. Cardlestone, white and shaking, was lying back in his chair; Elphick, scarcely less alarmed, had risen, and was coming forward with trembling limbs.

"Wait a moment," said Breton, soothingly. "Don't alarm yourself. We'll deal with Mr. Myerst here first. Now, Myerst, my man, sit down in that chair—it's the heaviest the place affords. Into it, now! Spargo, you see that coil of rope there. Tie Myerst up—hand and foot—to that chair. And tie him well. All the knots to be double, Spargo, and behind him."

Myerst suddenly laughed. "You damned young bully!" he exclaimed. "If you put a rope round me, you're only putting ropes round the necks of these two old villains. Mark that, my fine fellows!"

"We'll see about that later," answered Breton. He kept Myerst covered while Spargo made play with the rope. "Don't be afraid of hurting him, Spargo," he said. "Tie him well and strong. He won't shift that chair in a hurry."

Spargo spliced his man to the chair in a fashion that would have done credit to a sailor. He left Myerst literally unable to move either hand or foot, and Myerst cursed him from crown to heel for his pains. "That'll do," said Breton at last. He dropped his revolver into his pocket and turned to the two old men. Elphick averted his eyes and sank into a chair in the darkest corner of the room: old Cardlestone shook as with palsy and muttered words which the two young men could not catch. "Guardian," continued Breton, "don't be frightened! And don't you be frightened, either, Mr. Cardlestone. There's nothing to be afraid of, just yet, whatever there may be later on. It seems to me that Mr. Spargo and I came just in time. Now, guardian, what was this fellow after?"

Old Elphick lifted his head and shook it; he was plainly on the verge of tears; as for Cardlestone, it was evident that his nerve was completely gone. And Breton pointed Spargo to an old corner cupboard.

"Spargo," he said, "I'm pretty sure you'll find whisky in there. Give them both a stiff dose: they've broken up. Now, guardian," he continued, when Spargo had carried out this order, "what was he after? Shall I suggest it? Was it—blackmail?"

Cardlestone began to whimper; Elphick nodded his head. "Yes, yes!" he muttered. "Blackmail! That was it—blackmail. He—he got money—papers—from us. They're on him."

Breton turned on the captive with a look of contempt.

"I thought as much, Mr. Myerst," he said. "Spargo, let's see what he has on him."

Spargo began to search the prisoner's pockets. He laid out everything on the table as he found it. It was plain that Myerst had contemplated some sort of flight or a long, long journey. There was a quantity of loose gold; a number of bank-notes of the more easily negotiated denominations; various foreign securities, realizable in Paris. And there was an open cheque, signed by Cardlestone for ten thousand pounds, and another, with Elphick's name at the foot, also open, for half that amount. Breton examined all these matters as Spargo handed them out. He turned to old Elphick.

"Guardian," he said, "why have you or Mr. Cardlestone given this man these cheques and securities? What hold has he on you?"

Old Cardlestone began to whimper afresh; Elphick turned a troubled face on his ward.

"He—he threatened to accuse us of the murder of Marbury!" he faltered. "We—we didn't see that we had a chance."

"What does he know of the murder of Marbury and of you in connection with it?" demanded Breton. "Come—tell me the truth now."

"He's been investigating—so he says," answered Elphick. "He lives in that house in Middle Temple Lane, you know, in the top-floor rooms above Cardlestone's. And—and he says he's the fullest evidence against Cardlestone—and against me as an accessory after the fact."

"And—it's a lie?" asked Breton.

"A lie!" answered Elphick. "Of course, it's a lie. But—he's so clever that—that——"

"That you don't know how you could prove it otherwise," said Breton. "Ah! And so this fellow lives over Mr. Cardlestone there, does he? That may account for a good many things. Now we must have the police here." He sat down at the table and drew the writing materials to him. "Look here, Spargo," he continued. "I'm going to write a note to the superintendent of police at Hawes—there's a farm half a mile from here where I can get a man to ride down to Hawes with the note. Now, if you want to send a wire to the *Watchman*, draft it out, and he'll take it with him."

Elphick began to move in his corner.

"Must the police come?" he said. "Must——"

"The police must come," answered Breton firmly. "Go ahead with your wire, Spargo, while I write this note."

Three quarters of an hour later, when Breton came back from the farm, he sat down at Elphick's side and laid his hand on the old man's.

"Now, guardian," he said, quietly, "you've got to tell us the truth."

It had been apparent to Spargo, from the moment of his entering the cottage, that the two old men were suffering badly from shock and fright: Cardlestone still sat in his corner shivering and trembling; he looked incapable of explaining anything; Elphick was scarcely more fitted to speak. And when Breton issued his peremptory invitation to his guardian to tell the truth, Spargo intervened.

"Far better leave him alone, Breton," he said in a low voice. "Don't you see the old chap's done up? They're both done up. We don't know what they've gone through with this fellow before we came, and it's certain they've had no sleep. Leave it all till later — after all, we've found them and we've found him." He jerked his thumb over his shoulder in Myerst's direction, and Breton involuntarily followed the movement. He caught the prisoner's eye, and Myerst laughed.

"I daresay you two young men think yourselves very clever," he said sneeringly. "Don't you, now?"

"We've been clever enough to catch you, anyway," retorted Breton. "And now we've got you we'll keep you till the police can relieve us of you."

"Oh!" said Myerst, with another sneering laugh. "And on what charge do you propose to hand me over to the police? It strikes me you'll have some difficulty in formulating one, Mr. Breton."

"Well see about that later," said Breton. "You've extorted money by menaces from these gentlemen, at any rate."

"Have I? How do you know they didn't entrust me with these cheques as their agent?" exclaimed Myerst. "Answer me that! Or, rather, let them answer if they dare. Here you, Cardlestone, you Elphick — didn't you give me these cheques as your agent? Speak up now, and quick!"

Spargo, watching the two old men, saw them both quiver at the sound of Myerst's voice; Cardlestone indeed, began to whimper softly.

"Look here, Breton," he said, whispering, "this scoundrel's got some hold on these two old chaps—they're frightened to death of him. Leave them alone: it would be best for them if they could get some rest. Hold your tongue, you!" he added aloud, turning to Myerst. "When we want you to speak we'll tell you."

But Myerst laughed again.

"All very high and mighty, Mr. Spargo of the *Watchman!*" he sneered. "You're another of the cock-sure lot. And you're very clever, but not clever enough. Now, look here! Supposing—"

Spargo turned his back on him. He went over to old Cardlestone and felt his hands. And he turned to Breton with a look of concern.

"I say!" he exclaimed. "He's more than frightened—he's ill! What's to be done?"

"I asked the police to bring a doctor along with them," answered Breton. "In the meantime, let's put him to bed—there are beds in that inner room. We'll get him to bed and give him something hot to drink—that's all I can think of for the present."

Between them they managed to get Cardlestone to his bed, and Spargo, with a happy thought, boiled water on the rusty stove and put hot bottles to his feet. When that was done they persuaded Elphick to lie down in the inner room. Presently both old men fell asleep, and then Breton and Spargo suddenly realized that they themselves were hungry and wet and weary.

"There ought to be food in the cupboard," said Breton, beginning to rummage. "They've generally had a good stock of tinned things. Here we are, Spargo—these are tongues and sardines. Make some hot coffee while I open one of these tins."

The prisoner watched the preparations for a rough and ready breakfast with eyes that eventually began to glisten.

"I may remind you that I'm hungry, too," he said as Spargo set the coffee on the table. "And you've no right to starve me, even if you've the physical ability to keep me tied up. Give me something to eat, if you please."

"You shan't starve," said Breton, carelessly. He cut an ample supply of bread and meat, filled a cup with coffee and placed cup and plate before Myerst. "Untie his right arm, Spargo," he continued. "I think we can give him that liberty. We've got his revolver, anyhow."

For a while the three men ate and drank in silence. At last Myerst pushed his plate away. He looked scrutinizingly at his two captors. "Look here!" he said. "You think you know a lot about all this affair, Spargo, but there's only one person who knows all about it. That's me!"

"We're taking that for granted," said Spargo. "We guessed as much when we found you here. You'll have ample opportunity for explanation, you know, later on."

"I'll explain now, if you care to hear," said Myerst with another of his cynical laughs. "And if I do, I'll tell you the truth. I know you've got an idea in your heads that isn't favourable to me, but you're utterly wrong, whatever you may think. Look here! — I'll make you a fair offer. There are some cigars in my case there — give me one, and mix me a drink of that whisky — a good 'un — and I'll tell you what I know about this matter. Come on! — anything's better than sitting here doing nothing."

The two young men looked at each other. Then Breton nodded. "Let him talk if he likes," he said. "We're not bound to believe him. And we may hear something that's true. Give him his cigar and his drink."

Myerst took a stiff pull at the contents of the tumbler which Spargo presently set before him. He laughed as he inhaled the first fumes of his cigar.

"As it happens, you'll hear nothing but the truth," he observed. "Now that things are as they are, there's no reason why I shouldn't tell the truth. The fact is, I've nothing to fear. You can't give me in charge, for it so happens that I've got a power of attorney from these two old chaps inside there to act for them in regard to the money they entrusted me with. It's in an inside pocket of that letter-case, and if you look at it, Breton, you'll see it's in order. I'm not even going to dare you to interfere with or destroy it — you're a barrister, and you'll respect the law. But that's a fact — and if anybody's got a case against anybody, I have against you two for assault and illegal detention. But I'm not a vindictive man, and — — "

Breton took up Myerst's letter-case and examined its contents. And presently he turned to Spargo.

"He's right!" he whispered. "This is quite in order." He turned to Myerst. "All the same," he said, addressing him, "we shan't release you, because we believe you're concerned in the murder of John Marbury. We're justified in holding you on that account."

"All right, my young friend," said Myerst. "Have your own stupid way. But I said I'd tell you the plain truth. Well, the plain truth is that I know no more of the absolute murder of your father than I know of what is going on in Timbuctoo at this moment! I do not know who killed John Maitland. That's a fact! It may have been the old man in there who's already at his own last gasp, or it mayn't. I tell you I don't know — though, like you, Spargo, I've tried hard to find out. That's the truth — I do not know."

"You expect us to believe that?" exclaimed Breton incredulously.

"Believe it or not, as you like — it's the truth," answered Myerst. "Now, look here — I said nobody knew as much of this affair as I know, and that's true also. And here's the truth of what I know. The old man in that room, whom you know as Nicholas Cardlestone, is in reality Chamberlayne, the stockbroker, of Market Milcaster, whose name was so freely mentioned when your father was tried there. That's another fact!"

"How," asked Breton, sternly, "can you prove it? How do you know it?"

"Because," replied Myerst, with a cunning grin, "I helped to carry out his mock death and burial — I was a solicitor in those days, and my name was — something else. There were three of us at it: Chamberlayne's nephew; a doctor of no reputation; and myself. We carried it out very cleverly, and Chamberlayne gave us five thousand pounds apiece for our trouble. It was not the first time that I had helped him and been well paid for my help. The first time was in connection with the Cloudhampton Hearth and Home Mutual Benefit Society affair — Aylmore, or Ainsworth, was as innocent as a child in that! — Chamberlayne was the man at the back. But, unfortunately, Chamberlayne didn't profit — he lost all he got by it, pretty quick. That was why be transferred his abilities to Market Milcaster."

"You can prove all this, I suppose?" remarked Spargo.

"Every word—every letter! But about the Market Milcaster affair: Your father, Breton, was right in what he said about Chamberlayne having all the money that was got from the bank. He had—and he engineered that mock death and funeral so that he could disappear, and he paid us who helped him generously, as I've told you. The thing couldn't have been better done. When it was done, the nephew disappeared; the doctor disappeared; Chamberlayne disappeared. I had bad luck—to tell you the truth, I was struck off the rolls for a technical offence. So I changed my name and became Mr. Myerst, and eventually what I am now. And it was not until three years ago that I found Chamberlayne. I found him in this way: After I became secretary to the Safe Deposit Company, I took chambers in the Temple, above Cardlestone's. And I speedily found out who he was. Instead of going abroad, the old fox—though he was a comparatively young 'un, then!—had shaved off his beard, settled down in the Temple and given himself up to his two hobbies, collecting curiosities and stamps. There he'd lived quietly all these years, and nobody had ever recognized or suspected him. Indeed, I don't see how they could; he lived such a quiet, secluded life, with his collections, his old port, and his little whims and fads. But—I knew him!"

"And you doubtless profited by your recognition," suggested Breton.

"I certainly did. He was glad to pay me a nice sum every quarter to hold my tongue," replied Myerst, "and I was glad to take it and, naturally, I gained a considerable knowledge of him. He had only one friend—Mr. Elphick, in there. Now, I'll you about him."

"Only if you are going to speak respectfully of him," said Breton sternly.

"I've no reason to do otherwise. Elphick is the man who ought to have married your mother. When things turned out as they did, Elphick took you and brought you up as he has done, so that you should never know of your father's disgrace. Elphick never knew until last night that Cardlestone is Chamberlayne. Even the biggest scoundrels have friends—Elphick's very fond of Cardlestone. He——"

Spargo turned sharply on Myerst.

"You say Elphick didn't know until last night!" he exclaimed. "Why, then, this running away? What were they running from?"

"I have no more notion than you have, Spargo," replied Myerst. "I tell you one or other of them knows something that I don't. Elphick, I gather, took fright from you, and went to Cardlestone—then they both vanished. It may be that Cardlestone did kill Maitland—I don't know. But I'll tell you what I know about the actual murder—for I do know a good deal about it, though, as I say, I don't know who killed Maitland. Now, first, you know all that about Maitland's having papers and valuables and gold on him? Very well—I've got all that. The whole lot is locked up—safely—and I'm willing to hand it over to you, Breton, when we go back to town, and the necessary proof is given—as it will be—that you're Maitland's son."

Myerst paused to see the effect of this announcement, and laughed when he saw the blank astonishment which stole over his hearers' faces.

"And still more," he continued, "I've got all the contents of that leather box which Maitland deposited with me—that's safely locked up, too, and at your disposal. I took possession of that the day after the murder. Then, for purposes of my own, I went to Scotland Yard, as Spargo there is aware. You see, I was playing a game—and it required some ingenuity."

"A game!" exclaimed Breton. "Good heavens—what game?"

"I never knew until I had possession of all these things that Marbury was Maitland of Market Milcaster," answered Myerst. "When I did know then I began to put things together and to pursue my own line, independent of everybody. I tell you I had all Maitland's papers and possessions, by that time—except one thing. That packet of Australian stamps. And—I found out that those stamps were in the hands of—Cardlestone!"

Myerst paused, to take a pull at his glass, and to look at the
two amazed listeners with a smile of conscious triumph.

"In the hands of Cardlestone," he repeated. "Now, what did I
argue from that? Why, of course, that Maitland had been to
Cardlestone's rooms that night. Wasn't he found lying dead at the
foot of Cardlestone's stairs? Aye — but who found him? Not the
porter — not the police — not you, Master Spargo, with all your
cleverness. The man who found Maitland lying dead there that
night was — I!"

In the silence that followed, Spargo, who had been making
notes of what Myerst said, suddenly dropped his pencil and
thrusting his hands in his pockets sat bolt upright with a look which
Breton, who was watching him seriously, could not make out. It
was the look of a man whose ideas and conceptions are being
rudely upset. And Myerst, too, saw it and he laughed, more
sneeringly than ever.

"That's one for you, Spargo!" he said. "That surprises you —
that makes you think. Now what do you think? — if one may ask."

"I think," said Spargo, "that you are either a consummate
liar, or that this mystery is bigger than before."

"I can lie when it's necessary," retorted Myerst. "Just now it
isn't necessary. I'm telling you the plain truth: there's no reason why
I shouldn't. As I've said before, although you two young bullies
have tied me up in this fashion, you can't do anything against me.
I've a power of attorney from those two old men in there, and that's
enough to satisfy anybody as to my possession of their cheques and
securities. I've the whip hand of you, my sons, in all ways. And
that's why I'm telling you the truth — to amuse myself during this
period of waiting. The plain truth, my sons!"

"In pursuance of which," observed Breton, drily, "I think you
mentioned that you were the first person to find my father lying
dead?"

"I was. That is—as far as I can gather. I'll tell you all about it. As I said, I live over Cardlestone. That night I came home very late—it was well past one o'clock. There was nobody about—as a matter of fact, no one has residential chambers in that building but Cardlestone and myself. I found the body of a man lying in the entry. I struck a match and immediately recognized my visitor of the afternoon—John Marbury. Now, although I was so late in going home, I was as sober as a man can be, and I think pretty quickly at all times. I thought at double extra speed just then. And the first thing I did was to strip the body of every article it had on it— money, papers, everything. All these things are safely locked up— they've never been tracked. Next day, using my facilities as secretary to the Safe Deposit Company, I secured the things in that box. Then I found out who the dead man really was. And then I deliberately set to work to throw dust in the eyes of the police and of the newspapers, and particularly in the eyes of young Master Spargo there. I had an object."

"What?" asked Breton.

"What! Knowing all I did, I firmly believed that Marbury, or, rather, Maitland, had been murdered by either Cardlestone or Elphick. I put it to myself in this way, and my opinion was strengthened as you, Spargo, inserted news in your paper— Maitland, finding himself in the vicinity of Cardlestone after leaving Aylmore's rooms that night, turned into our building, perhaps just to see where Cardlestone lived. He met Cardlestone accidentally, or he perhaps met Cardlestone and Elphick together—they recognized each other. Maitland probably threatened to expose Cardlestone, or, rather, Chamberlayne—nobody, of course, could know what happened, but my theory was that Chamberlayne killed him. There, at any rate, was the fact that Maitland was found murdered at Chamberlayne's very threshold. And, in the course of a few days, I proved, to my own positive satisfaction, by getting access to Chamberlayne's rooms in his absence that Maitland had been there, had been in those rooms. For I found there, in Chamberlayne's desk, the rare Australian stamps of which Criedir told at the inquest. That was proof positive."

Spargo looked at Breton. They knew what Myerst did not know—that the stamps of which he spoke were lying in Spargo's breast pocket, where they had lain since he had picked them up from the litter and confusion of Chamberlayne's floor.

"Why," asked Breton, after a pause, "why did you never accuse Cardlestone, or Chamberlayne, of the murder?"

"I did! I have accused him a score of times—and Elphick, too," replied Myerst with emphasis. "Not at first, mind you—I never let Chamberlayne know that I ever suspected him for some time. I had my own game to play. But at last—not so many days ago—I did. I accused them both. That's how I got the whip hand of them. They began to be afraid—by that time Elphick had got to know all about Cardlestone's past as Chamberlayne. And as I tell you, Elphick's fond of Cardlestone. It's queer, but he is. He—wants to shield him."

"What did they say when you accused them?" asked Breton. "Let's keep to that point—never mind their feelings for one another."

"Just so, but that feeling's a lot more to do with this mystery than you think, my young friend," said Myerst. "What did they say, you ask? Why, they strenuously denied it, Cardlestone swore solemnly to me that he had no part or lot in the murder of Maitland. So did Elphick. But—they know something about the murder. If those two old men can't tell you definitely who actually struck John Maitland down, I'm certain that they have a very clear idea in their minds as to who really did! They—"

A sudden sharp cry from the inner room interrupted Myerst. Breton and Spargo started to their feet and made for the door. But before they could reach it Elphick came out, white and shaking.

"He's gone!" he exclaimed in quavering accents. "My old friend's gone—he's dead! I was—asleep. I woke suddenly and looked at him. He——"

Spargo forced the old man into a chair and gave him some whisky; Breton passed quickly into the inner room; only to come back shaking his head.

"He's dead," he said. "He evidently died in his sleep."

"Then his secret's gone with him," remarked Myerst, calmly. "And now we shall never know if he did kill John Maitland or if he didn't. So that's done with!"

Old Elphick suddenly sat up in his chair, pushing Spargo fiercely away from his side.

"He didn't kill John Maitland!" he cried angrily, attempting to shake his fist at Myerst. "Whoever says he killed Maitland lies. He was as innocent as I am. You've tortured and tormented him to his death with that charge, as you're torturing me—among you. I tell you he'd nothing to do with John Maitland's death—nothing!"

Myerst laughed.

"Who had, then?" he said.

"Hold your tongue!" commanded Breton, turning angrily on him. He sat down by Elphick's side and laid his hand soothingly on the old man's arm.

"Guardian," he said, "why don't you tell what you know? Don't be afraid of that fellow there—he's safe enough. Tell Spargo and me what you know of the matter. Remember, nothing can hurt Cardlestone, or Chamberlayne, or whoever he is or was, now."

Elphick sat for a moment shaking his head. He allowed Spargo to give him another drink; he lifted his head and looked at the two young men with something of an appeal.

"I'm badly shaken," he said. "I've suffered much lately—I've learnt things that I didn't know. Perhaps I ought to have spoken before, but I was afraid for—for him. He was a good friend, Cardlestone, whatever else he may have been—a good friend. And—I don't know any more than what happened that night."

"Tell us what happened that night," said Breton.

"Well, that night I went round, as I often did, to play piquet with Cardlestone. That was about ten o'clock. About eleven Jane Baylis came to Cardlestone's—she'd been to my rooms to find me—wanted to see me particularly—and she'd come on there, knowing where I should be. Cardlestone would make her have a glass of wine and a biscuit; she sat down and we all talked. Then, about, I should think, a quarter to twelve, a knock came at Cardlestone's door—his outer door was open, and of course anybody outside could see lights within. Cardlestone went to the door: we heard a man's voice enquire for him by name; then the voice added that Criedir, the stamp dealer, had advised him to call on Mr. Cardlestone to show him some rare Australian stamps, and that seeing a light under his door he had knocked. Cardlestone asked him in—he came in. That was the man we saw next day at the mortuary. Upon my honour, we didn't know him, either that night or next day!"

"What happened when he came in?" asked Breton.

"Cardlestone asked him to sit down: he offered and gave him a drink. The man said Criedir had given him Cardlestone's address, and that he'd been with a friend at some rooms in Fountain Court, and as he was passing our building he'd just looked to make sure where Cardlestone lived, and as he'd noticed a light he'd made bold to knock. He and Cardlestone began to examine the stamps. Jane Baylis said good-night, and she and I left Cardlestone and the man together."

"No one had recognized him?" said Breton.

"No one! Remember, I only once or twice saw Maitland in all my life. The others certainly did not recognize him. At least, I never knew that they did—if they did."

"Tell us," said Spargo, joining in for the first time, "tell us what you and Miss Baylis did?"

"At the foot of the stairs Jane Baylis suddenly said she'd forgotten something in Cardlestone's lobby. As she was going out in to Fleet Street, and I was going down Middle Temple Lane to turn off to my own rooms we said good-night. She went back upstairs. And I went home. And upon my soul and honour that's all I know!"

Spargo suddenly leapt to his feet. He snatched at his cap—a sodden and bedraggled headgear which he had thrown down when they entered the cottage.

"That's enough!" he almost shouted. "I've got it—at last! Breton—where's the nearest telegraph office? Hawes? Straight down this valley? Then, here's for it! Look after things till I'm back, or, when the police come, join me there. I shall catch the first train to town, anyhow, after wiring."

"But—what are you after, Spargo?" exclaimed Breton. "Stop! What on earth——"

But Spargo had closed the door and was running for all he was worth down the valley. Three quarters of an hour later he startled a quiet and peaceful telegraphist by darting, breathless and dirty, into a sleepy country post office, snatching a telegraph form and scribbling down a message in shaky handwriting:—

Rathbury, New Scotland Yard, London. Arrest Jane Baylis at once for murder of John Maitland. Coming straight to town with full evidence.
Frank Spargo.

Then Spargo dropped on the office bench, and while the wondering operator set the wires ticking, strove to get his breath, utterly spent in his mad race across the heather. And when it was got he set out again—to find the station.

Some days later, Spargo, having seen Stephen Aylmore walk out of the Bow Street dock, cleared of the charge against him, and in a fair way of being cleared of the affair of twenty years before, found himself in a very quiet corner of the Court holding the hand of Jessie Aylmore, who, he discovered, was saying things to him which he scarcely comprehended. There was nobody near them and the girl spoke freely and warmly.

"But you will come—you will come today—and be properly thanked," she said. "You will—won't you?"

Spargo allowed himself to retain possession of the hand. Also he took a straight look into Jessie Aylmore's eyes.

"I don't want thanks," he said. "It was all a lot of luck. And if I come—today—it will be to see—just you!"

Jessie Aylmore looked down at the two hands.

"I think," she whispered, "I think that is what I really meant!"

Printed in Great Britain
by Amazon

43618172R00126